ROMY SOMMER

By day ....ts and .... s for my not-so-glamor..... job .. making movies. But at night I come home to my two little Princesses, and we dress up in tiaras and pink tulle … and I get to write Happy Ever Afters. Since I believe every girl is a princess, and every princess deserves a happy ending, what could be more perfect?

www.romysommer.com
@romy_s

Also by Romy Sommer

Waking up in Vegas
The Trouble with Mojitos
To Catch a Star

Not a Fairy Tale

ROMY SOMMER

Harper*Impulse* an imprint of
HarperCollins*Publishers* Ltd
77–85 Fulham Palace Road
Hammersmith, London W6 8JB

www.harpercollins.co.uk

A Paperback Original 2015

First published in Great Britain in ebook format by Harper*Impulse* 2015

A catalogue record for this book is
available from the British Library

ISBN: 9780008135577

For my mother, a pillar of strength to so many people.

Chapter One

If just one more person congratulated her on her loss, she would smack them. Nina gritted her teeth and smiled like a crazy person as she threaded her way through the crowd and along an outdoor walkway. Out on the terrace, she breathed in deeply. Not exactly fresh – no one would call LA air fresh – but the crisp February air was better than the suffocating warmth inside.

This was as close as she could get to crawling into a corner and letting the tears flow.

It's just an award. It's an honor to be nominated. There's always next year. You're in great company.

The platitudes were meaningless. Everyone in this town knew you were only as good as your next job and right now she didn't have a next job. The history books were littered with the names of has-beens who came close but never won. And who remembered them now?

But put "Oscar-*winner*" in front of your name and everyone knew who you were. Oscar-winners didn't need to screen-test for coveted roles along with every other hopeful in a town filled to bursting with the hopeful, the pretty, the thin.

The bowl of west Los Angeles sprawled beneath her feet, a carpet of lights. No longer needing to keep up appearances, she dropped her smile and rubbed her aching facial muscles.

"Drink this." Someone pressed a glass into her hand. She sniffed at the dubious liquid before raising her eyes to its donor. Or rather to the wall of chest at eye level, before she looked up higher into a pair of amused green eyes.

She would have smiled again if it didn't hurt so much.

Dominic Kelly. Even when he wasn't clowning around, Dom always made her want to smile. He had a way of looking at a woman that made her feel special and beautiful. As if he could see through the hype to the person lost inside.

She didn't care that he had that effect on all women. She *did* care that he slept with all the others yet had never made a move on her.

"It's brandy. It'll make you feel better," he said.

"I don't drink."

"You're in recovery?" He frowned, no doubt remembering an evening or two during the filming of their last movie when she'd danced the night away with a lurid cocktail in hand.

"Of course not!" She didn't blame him for the assumption, though. At least half the people at this party were probably in recovery from one addiction or another. And even though they'd partied together throughout production on the one movie they'd worked on together, she and Dominic really knew nothing about each other.

For that matter, there was no one here tonight who really knew her. They only knew the public image, the person they wanted her to be. The lie.

She lifted the glass to her lips and sipped. Fire burned down her throat and brought tears to her eyes before the alcohol settled in her belly. He was right. It did make her feel better, if for no other reason than that it made her feel like a giddy teen at the prom again. That had been a good night. She'd been a winner that night.

She sniffed, inhaling the decadent scent of her favorite meal a moment before she spotted the In-N-Out box in Dominic's hand. Her stomach flipped.

"Want to share?" He held up the burger box from the food

truck parked outside the party venue.

Her stomach flipped again, but she suppressed it. Ruthlessly. "I only just managed to fit into this dress. One bite and I might split the seams."

Dom's gaze swept over her, settling on her hips. Her very-far-from-size-zero hips. She sucked in her stomach, but he only grinned. "That's a sight I wouldn't mind seeing."

"Yeah, you and every camera in there. I don't think so. I need to sit."

She wove her way between the sofas scattered around the deck, leaving Dominic and his burger to follow in her wake. A few of the sofas were occupied by people in serious conversation and at least one by a couple making out. Despite her curiosity, Nina refrained from looking too hard to see who they were as she led Dominic toward an unoccupied area of the terrace, shielded from view by potted palm trees.

The scarlet shoes with their three-inch heels were killing her feet. She kicked them off and wiggled her toes. Bliss!

Then she sagged down on the sofa and breathed a dramatic sigh of relief as she put her bare feet up on the glass coffee table.

Dominic's eyebrows lifted as he sprawled beside her, slinging an arm across the back of the chair, but he said nothing. Though he wasn't close enough to touch, she could feel the heat emanating off him, and he smelled of the sea. Not the storm-wracked waves that made her stomach clench, but lazy holidays and suntan lotions and laughter.

She resisted the crazy urge to lean in closer to breathe him in. There were cameras everywhere at this party, and that was so not a picture she wanted to see online in the morning, either.

In the town where gossip was a billion-dollar industry, she'd worked hard to keep her image clean. Nooky in a corner of a party was definitely a no-no. Which put it up near the top of the list of things she most wanted to do.

Right behind 'Eat a burger with all the trimmings!'

She tried not to drool as Dominic tucked into his, and instead looked out at the view and sipped the fiery brandy. Down there, below the roving spotlights that illuminated this party-to-end-all-parties, were real people living real lives. She could hardly even remember what that felt like. As much as she envied their anonymity, their freedom to come and go without their every move scrutinized and torn apart, she wouldn't swap her place up here on the hill with theirs for anything.

That was her addiction: fame. Being admired, being loved, was something she'd worked very hard for. And while losing might not be fun, at least she'd never need to worry about a mortgage payment again. She was living the fairy tale, with more money than her teen self could have imagined, doing what she loved. And she was adored. She had everything she'd ever wanted.

Almost everything.

If she could just get the one role that would make people sit up and notice, which would make people see her as something more than the ditsy rom-com heroine…

Dominic stretched and propped his expensive Italian shoes on the glass table beside her bare feet. "Last year's *Vanity Fair* after-party was a complete crush, but it was much more fun." He sighed. "Or maybe I'm getting jaded. Nothing is ever as good as it was."

"I didn't see you here last year."

"You didn't know I was alive last year."

"That's not true." She'd known who he was long before they'd been introduced. She still remembered the first time she'd seen him at some party a couple of years back and asked the hostess who he was.

He was an impossible man to miss. Impressively built, a little rough and rugged in the looks department but gorgeous enough to make most women look twice. Muscled, without looking like one of those malformed bodybuilders. He looked more like a dancer. Of the stripper kind.

But it wasn't his looks that made Dominic stand out among

the crowds of beautiful people in this town. It was his attitude. Though he partied with celebrities, he wasn't one of the usual sycophantic hangers-on, basking in reflected glory. It was as if he didn't give a damn what anyone thought. There was the hint of aggression lurking beneath his surface, like a Navy seal or a nightclub bouncer. What woman could resist that bad-boy streak?

And then he'd smile that naughty, crooked smile...

He hadn't even looked her way that entire night. She'd been stopping traffic since she was 16 and he hadn't even noticed her. Admittedly, there were so many beautiful people in LA that women who turned heads in London or New York – or Cedar Falls, Iowa – barely warranted a second look here.

She rubbed her bare arms. Wordlessly, Dominic set down his burger and shrugged out of his evening jacket to wrap it around her shoulders.

"Thanks." She smiled, the first genuine smile since she'd heard the words *and the Oscar goes to...* ' followed by someone else's name.

Dom lazed back and contemplated her. "Where's your entourage tonight? Don't you usually hunt in a pack?"

She didn't need to see them to know where they were. Her stylist was taking a well-deserved rest after a hectic day. She'd left her PA, her 'plus one', back at the Governors' Ball. Her agent was inside, working the room, schmoozing all the producers and hopefully trying to get Nina a job that wasn't yet another rom-com. Her publicist, Chrissie, who'd conned her way into a VF party invite by promising a story to a sub-editor, would be getting her picture taken with as many *somebodies* as she could.

"Congratulations, by the way."

Oh no, not Dominic too. She really didn't want to have to smack him. And she didn't have much energy left to do it.

"I hear you've done very well for yourself since we worked together on *Pirate's Revenge*."

She blinked. Not what she'd expected. "What do you mean?"

Aside from a minor role playing Meryl Streep's daughter and two very long and tiring promo campaigns for her previous movies, she hadn't worked since *Pirate's Revenge*. Even this nomination was for the movie she'd filmed before her jaunt to Westerwald for *Pirate's Revenge*, yet another fairy tale re-imagined. The situation was getting dire. She'd needed the award tonight to break the dry spell.

"You landed yourself a little prime A-list steak since then."

Ah. She smiled. The one thing that was going very right in her life.

These last few months hadn't been entirely wasted. Dating fellow actor Paul de Angelo had kept her name in the spotlight and he'd introduced her to more useful contacts in the last month than her agent and manager had done combined.

They worked well together, both driven, both serious about their careers, both happy not to get too much in each other's space.

It was thanks to Paul she'd been invited to read for this year's hottest role, the lead role in a trilogy based on the bestselling novels that had been so popular people had camped outside bookstores for days to get their hands on the final installment. That Nina had read the books before they'd turned into a phenomenon had to be significant, right? It was kismet.

Strong female lead roles were hard to come by, and she didn't want to spend her entire career playing someone's daughter or the lead's romantic interest. The accessory.

No, this role was *hers*.

Except the read hadn't been the golden opportunity she'd hoped for. It had been something of a novelty playing to a lukewarm audience. A not-very-pleasant novelty.

Paul had been supportive and encouraging. "They just don't see you as tough enough for the role. You need to show them you're more than just another pretty face."

It wasn't her face they'd been worried about. The casting director's exact words had been "you're a little too *soft* for this role."

6

Or, as her agent, Dane, had said, a little less diplomatically, "Lose 20 pounds, get some muscle and some attitude, and you might stand a chance."

She turned now to Dominic. "Can we meet tomorrow?"

He arched an eyebrow. "Mr. A-Lister not ringing your bell?"

She rolled her eyes dramatically. Trust him to think everything was about sex. Not that she hadn't already imagined sex with Dominic a few dozen times. "In your dreams. I don't want to sleep with you. I have a business proposition."

"Intriguing." He rubbed his chin, as if the thought of any woman not wanting to fall straight into his bed was something he hadn't considered before.

"Lunch at Cecconi's?" she pushed.

"I have a much better idea." Dominic's grin was pure mischief. "25 Degrees at the Hollywood Roosevelt serves the city's best burgers."

Great, just what she needed. Not. But any self-respecting LA restaurant would serve salads, too, wouldn't they? "Twelve too early?"

"Twelve is fine." Dominic looked over her shoulder. "Your minder's here."

She turned to follow his gaze. Her publicist bore down on them.

"What the hell are you doing out here?" Chrissie stopped before their sofa and frowned as she looked from Dom's jacket around her shoulders to Nina's bare feet, then back to the tumbler in Nina's hand. Or at least as much of a frown as her perfect, botoxed forehead allowed. "The action is *inside*." She waved towards the party. "The cameras are there and all the people who need to be reminded you exist."

"My feet were sore." Nina wiggled her bare toes and Chrissie's frown deepened.

The excuse sounded as lame as it was. Nina was in the illusion business, after all. If she couldn't stand for half a night in tight heels without hiding the pain, then she didn't belong here. But

7

admitting to an insane urge to throw something wasn't going to go down any better.

An actor could trash a hotel room and everyone would call him a rock star, but an actress behaving badly would be labeled as difficult and would never work again. Ask Lindsay Lohan. Nina was struggling enough with the last bit as it was.

With an apologetic shrug for Dominic she slipped her shoes back on and handed him his jacket. He tossed the remains of his burger in a nearby bin and rose with her. "Yeah, this party blows. I'm gonna head over to Elton's and see if that one's more fun. Want to join me?"

Chrissie turned narrowed eyes on him. "Who are you?"

"Chrissie, this is Dominic Kelly. He was the stunt coordinator on *Pirate's Revenge*. Dom, my publicist, Chrissie."

Chrissie swept an assessing glance over Dom, her gaze lingering on the muscular chest beneath his dress shirt. A tight and not entirely pleasant smile curved her plumped lips. "You might want to hang around for the next ten minutes. There's a show you shouldn't miss."

It sounded like a warning, but Nina couldn't fathom why.

Chrissie turned to her. "Be quick. You're needed inside."

She hurried ahead and Nina followed more slowly, Dom keeping pace beside her. He sent her a questioning look and she shrugged. Chrissie clearly had something up her sleeve, but Nina had no clue what it was. The only thing she knew was that her stomach had clenched with an anxious sense of foreboding she hadn't felt in years.

Back in the central party room, her nerves steadied. She looked out across the room heaving with bodies, hundreds of beautiful people making conversation and playing to the cameras. A carnival of glitter.

Party guests came and went from the specially constructed photo booths, and on the far side of the purpose-built, glass-walled structure, a group of dancers gyrated to a rock standard

8

played by the live band.

The party hadn't yet reached that kick-off-the-shoes-in-abandon phase that happened when celebrities partied together, relaxed in the safety of their own numbers and the absence of fans and hangers-on, but it was headed that way.

No matter which way she turned she saw stars. Actors, actresses, musicians, and singers, supermodels and fashion designers, directors and powerhouse producers. People who were desperate to be loved and admired, people who'd reached the top and who would do anything to stay there. Every single one of them famous and all of them driven. She belonged here and she'd do absolutely anything to stay a part of it.

She caught the eye of an actress she'd worked with a few years ago. The other actress blew her a kiss and Nina waved back. "Bitch," she muttered under her breath.

Dominic leaned in to whisper in her ear. "I don't think that kiss was meant for you."

"You and Jordan?" she asked in disbelief. Ugh. She thought he had more class than that.

"Most adventurous eight hours of my life. Come to think of it, it was probably while the two of you were playing sisters on that TV show." His grin widened. "Though that was before she started on the botox. I don't have many standards, but I don't do botoxed women. Now don't frown at me like that. There's a camera headed this way."

She smiled as if her life depended on it. The urge to hit or throw something was back in full force.

"Would you like your picture taken?" the photographer asked, waving his camera at them.

She and Dominic did the cheek-press, smiling straight into the camera. It was practically an art in this town, but the soft rumble of Dominic's mocking laugh vibrated through her, spoiling the effect. As the photographer moved on to the next group, she stepped on his foot, not hard enough to inflict pain but hard enough to let him know she didn't enjoy being laughed at. Or reminded that, if the rumors were true, he'd bedded half this town. The entire female half, with the exception of her.

Dom only laughed louder. "Don't take it so seriously. That picture will never see the light of day. When they're sifting through the images to upload they're going to ask '*who's this nobody with Nina Alexander?*' and hit delete."

He didn't sound the least perturbed. But then what little she'd seen of him, Dominic was a man so confident in his own skin he didn't give a damn what others thought. She wished she knew how that felt. She'd spent a lifetime faking confidence.

Dom's gaze shifted to the stage. "Your new boyfriend really does like the limelight."

She looked, just in time to see Paul take the microphone from the band's lead singer. He tapped the mic and a few heads turned. The hum of voices dropped as more and more heads turned at the unexpected interruption.

"Hi everyone, are you enjoying the party?"

The crowd murmured its confused assent. They were here to mingle, to see and be seen. Speeches weren't part of the program.

"I'm Paul de Angelo." As if he needed to tell them who he was. "I apologize for interrupting the party, but please bear with me. Would Nina Alexander please join me up here?"

What?!

As Paul looked out over the assembled guests, searching for her, Nina frantically looked for the nearest exit. The anxious knot in her stomach pulled suffocatingly tight.

But there was no hope of escape. The people around her turned and looked, and the crowd's buzz started again, nearly drowning out the sudden buzz in her head. Then Chrissie was beside her, grabbing her arm and pulling her forward. "Get up there!" Chrissie hissed through impossibly white teeth.

Nina cast a desperate glance back at Dom, who suddenly seemed like an anchor in a tumultuous sea, solid and strong. Then he was swallowed up in the crowd as Chrissie propelled her forward.

On either side of her, people nodded and smiled and greeted her. It was almost like the walk winners did up onto the stage at the Dolby Theatre. Almost.

She couldn't see their faces or hear their words. The sound between her ears had become a maniacal trill and the anxious presentiment she'd felt earlier sky-rocketed all the way from a knot in her stomach to throw-up territory.

She'd only felt this way once before in her life and that hadn't ended well.

She reached the stage and Paul leaned forward, extending his hand to help her take the giant step up. Though her body had turned numb, she took his hand and he pulled. She'd dreamed of this night since she was nine, imagined the graceful glide up to the stage on Oscar night in a hundred different ways. This wasn't how she'd pictured it at all.

"What are you doing?" she whispered, but Paul only smiled as he turned back to their audience. "As you all know, Nina was up for Best Supporting Actress tonight, but didn't win."

Great, thanks for rubbing that in.

He raised his champagne glass to the winner, still cradling her golden statuette. "By the way, congratulations, Jen." The crowd laughed. "But I'm hoping I can turn the night around for Nina."

Paul set down his champagne glass and got down on one knee.

Her heart crashed to a stop. Far from numb now, her entire body burned. He wasn't really doing this? Not here, not now?

It was romantic. It was so, so stupid.

He took a black velvet box out of his pocket and held it out before him. "Will you marry me?"

An *aaah* whispered through their audience, rising in pitch to an *oooh* as he opened the box and the most enormous diamond ring Nina had ever seen caught the light.

This wasn't happening. He couldn't be doing this. Black spots clouded her vision but there was nothing to grab onto, no one to hold onto.

She liked Paul, but she didn't want to marry him. Marriage wasn't part of her big plan. Where she came from marriage was a lifelong commitment and she wasn't ready to give up the single life yet – if ever – and certainly not for someone she barely knew.

Paul was the longest relationship she'd ever had and they'd only met a few months ago.

But neither could she reject Hollywood's most eligible bachelor, the man most women in this town – in this country – would kill to be with. Not here. Not now.

If she turned him down in front of everyone she'd be branded a heartless bitch. And that wasn't going to help her win the ultimate in peer awards any time soon.

The silence stretched, the audience growing restless, starting to murmur.

She could say yes and accept another wave of fake congratulations and then tomorrow she could call it off…

Tension etched lines around Paul's pin-up blue eyes. "You really know how to make a man beg," he joked.

The crowd tittered, but there was tension in that sound, too.

Paul could take her career places she hadn't even begun to imagine. They could be Hollywood's new power couple, the new Brangelina.

On the other hand, she might spend the best years of her life as Mrs. de Angelo, always in the shadow of her more-famous husband – and then find herself out on her ass, replaced by a younger model as soon as her prime was over.

A prime spent with a man whose idea of fun in the bedroom amounted to keeping the light on.

She had to make up her mind.

Saying "yes" now didn't have to mean forever. Perhaps just until she got the "part of all parts." Who could it hurt?

She opened her mouth to speak and heard Gran's voice in her head. *Whatever you do in that place, girl, you just remember where you came from. You work hard, you hold your head high, and you don't ever compromise who you are.*

She shook her head.

"What?" Paul obviously hadn't intended the word to be magnified around the room. It bounced off the walls as people began to cough and snigger.

But their embarrassment had nothing on Nina's. This was it. This was the end of everything. Turns out she wasn't prepared to do 'absolutely anything' after all.

Marriage for the sake of her career was one of them. Even a fake engagement. It was up there with sleeping her way into a job. Gran would tan her hide if she said yes.

"No."

This time Paul did speak for the microphone. "You're such a joker."

"I don't want to marry you, Paul. I don't want to marry anyone."

He stared at her.

She cleared her throat and tried again. "It's not you, it's me. I just don't think I'm the marrying kind."

She didn't need a microphone for her words to carry. They seemed to take on a life of their own, echoing around the vast room.

The moment hung, suspended in time, as she looked into Paul's eyes and he looked into hers. Then his eyes narrowed, wiping away the disbelief, and the tsunami crashed in upon them.

"Do you know who I am?" he demanded. Then he rose, snapping the black box shut and jamming it into the pocket of his tux. He thrust the microphone back at the band's lead singer and jumped down from the stage. Fury radiated off him and the whispering crowd parted before him, people stepping back into one another in their haste to give him space.

"You said she'd say yes," Paul flung at Chrissie as he strode past.

The words sliced through Nina. *This* was the story Chrissie had promised the sub-editor? Who was she working for anyway?

The music began again, normal conversation resumed, but still

13

Nina stood frozen on the stage. She knew what every one of them would be talking about. Who.

This wasn't good.

She couldn't breathe.

She had to get out of here.

She jumped off the stage, no one to help her down now, and the hem of her couture ball gown snagged on the edge of the stage. The fabric ripped, a long, drawn-out sound, but she didn't care.

"What the hell did you just do?" It was Chrissie, face pale beneath her flawless Californian tan.

"You knew he was going to propose in front of everyone?" Nina took refuge in anger.

"Of course. We had it all planned out. This was supposed to be your big moment. And you just throw it away? How could you be so stupid?"

"You should have warned me!" Because then Nina would never have left the Governors' Ball for this after-party. She'd still be back at the Dolby Theatre and her career and her reputation would still be intact. She would never have had to make such a terrifying decision in front of everyone.

Tears burned her eyes. She blinked them away. Crying now would only make it worse. What if her make-up ran? But she was tired and over-wrought from what had already been a very long evening, and it took huge effort.

She had to get out of here.

The only exit she knew was the same one she'd entered through, the entrance onto Sunset Boulevard where she'd have to run the gauntlet of half the world's media.

Yet more cameras.

She couldn't trust herself to hold it together for the length of that walk. She couldn't trust herself to hold it together long enough to make it across the room.

"We have to get her out of here."

Thank heavens. A voice of reason. Relief swamped her as she

14

faced her agent.

It was short-lived.

"Hold up your dress. You're baring your butt to the world." Dane grimaced as he gathered up a handful of ripped silk and thrust it at her. "Couldn't you have worn a sexy thong at least?"

The unshed tears burned all the way to her throat. How long had her supportive granny pants been on display to the entire room? And was Martin Scorsese looking straight at her?

"Would it have killed you to say yes?" Dane continued through gritted teeth. He didn't even look at her. His gaze scoured the room, searching for a way out, just as she had done. "We'll say you're not well. You haven't been well all week. You didn't know what you were saying." He turned to face her at last, giving up hope of a quiet exit. "I'm very disappointed in you. What were you thinking? Paul's a powerful man in this business. He has a lot of influence, and you humiliated him in public. You can kiss Sonia goodbye now."

A scalding tear slipped over her fake lashes and down her cheek. These were her friends, her support group. How could they turn on her like this?

"Maybe the press outside won't have got wind of this yet?" Dane said hopefully.

The look Chrissie sent him answered that one quickly enough.

"I'll get her out of here. I know a back exit."

All three of them turned to look at Dominic. The relief in the faces of her agent and publicist would have been insulting if she hadn't felt the same.

Dominic grinned. "We're going to walk out of here as if we don't have a care in the world. You can manage that much, can't you sweetheart?"

Nina nodded. The tears had stopped their insistent push against her eyelids. She already felt calmer. If she wasn't still so aware of the sea of eyes all around, she would have leaned into him.

"Do it," he said, holding her gaze, daring her. His eyes sparkled.

They were an unusual color. Mesmerizing. Like dark emeralds flecked with gold. He placed his arm around her shoulder and pulled her against him.

How had he known what she was thinking? She breathed in the scent of the wild sea, simultaneously frightening and exhilarating, and gave in. She leaned into him.

"That's it. You're an actress, so act. Now just follow my lead."

His cheeky grin was back in place. She managed a weak one of her own. "You're enjoying this," she meant it to sound accusing, but the words came out more curious.

"Of course I am. You just rescued me from dying of boredom." He leaned close to whisper in her ear. "Besides, the look on your minder's face was all the reward I needed."

Of course. The note she'd caught in Chrissie's tone had been intended to warn him that he didn't stand a chance with Nina. Instead, she was leaving the party with him.

She stifled a hysterical giggle.

Dominic took her free hand and led her through the crowd, not towards the kitchens or a service entrance, as she'd hoped, but straight toward their host. She prayed he knew what he was doing.

It wasn't easy walking with one hand clasped behind her back, holding her gaping dress together, but she kept her chin up and she smiled. Not the furious, bright smile of before. She aimed more for a Mona Lisa effect now. It was about as much as she could manage.

Though people looked at them as they passed, with expressions ranging from sympathetic to curious to gleeful, no one stopped them to talk until they stood before the editor-in-chief of *Vanity Fair* himself, Graydon Carter. Satirical journalist, media mogul, social arbiter and celebrity in his own right.

Nina had never said more than two words to him in her life.

Graydon turned at their approach, smiling. "Leaving so soon, Dom?"

Dom grinned and shrugged. "You know how it is – I have a

thing for damsels in distress. Thanks for another great dinner, and we'll talk about that canoeing trip soon."

Had Dominic been invited to the dinner and viewing party earlier in the night? Those tickets were gold. You practically had to be in Graydon Carter's inner circle to be invited.

She did a rapid recalculation of this 'lowly' stunt man.

"I look forward to it." Graydon's eyes twinkled as he shook Dom's hand. "There's certainly never a dull moment with you around." He glanced down to where Nina clutched her torn gown together, then summoned over a minion with an all-access security pass around his neck. "Ms. Alexander has had a wardrobe malfunction. Please take them out the private exit." Then he turned to Nina. "Thank you."

She tried to sound as cool and amused as he did. "My pleasure. But what for?"

Graydon's grin reached ear to ear. "For providing me with the headline story for our webpage tomorrow."

She wished she hadn't asked.

The tuxedoed minion led them through the dining area, where the most privileged guests had sat for dinner, to an exit she hadn't known existed.

"Shall I call the valet to bring your car around, Mr. Kelly?" the minion asked Dom.

"No need. I'm parked right outside."

The minion frowned. Nina only just managed to stop her own frown from wrinkling her forehead. When she'd arrived there'd been a mile-long traffic jam and police everywhere. No one could have parked within walking distance of this place.

They passed two security checkpoints before they reached the exit to the back end of the Sunset Plaza parking lot and the minion left them. Nina dropped Dom's hand and breathed in the cool night air. There were no fancy black Escalades parked out here, just vans and other working vehicles.

"What now?" she asked. "Are you going to sneak me out in a

17

delivery van, or do you have a magical flying carpet stashed out here?"

Dom grinned. "As good as. How precious is that dress of yours?"

She glanced down to assess the damage and groaned. "I think it's past saving."

"Good." He kneeled down and with a quick rip tore the remaining skirt off her dress.

"What are you doing?" she asked, trying to stop him. But she was too late. What had once been a slinky, scarlet, floor-length evening gown was now the length of a cocktail dress. A very short cocktail dress, with an uneven hemline that barely covered the granny pants.

Shit. Her PA was going to have to be very inventive to explain these new modifications to the designer.

He handed the torn expanse of fabric to her, then removed his jacket. "Cover yourself with this." He helped her into the jacket, then placed his hand on her lower back to guide her between the cars.

To a motorbike.

No, not just any motorbike. A KTM offroad bike, with fiery orange paintwork and gleaming chrome. Not exactly subtle, but it was close and wouldn't get stuck in the traffic jam out front. Nina nearly wept with relief.

A quick escape was worth the loss of one couture ball gown.

"Where do you want to go?" he asked, handing her the helmet hooked over the handle- bars.

"There's only one," she pointed out.

"I wasn't expecting to leave with a passenger. You wear it. Anything happens to that pretty face, you can kiss your career goodbye. But my career…" He shrugged. "Let's just leave it at that."

The helmet was going to wreck the beautiful curls her stylist had labored over all day. But no one would see her now. They were as good as home free.

She pulled the helmet on, her fingers fumbling with the

chin-strap. Dom stepped close to help her and she caught her breath.

A light bulb popped.

She looked around.

Just when you thought things couldn't get worse…they did. Not a bulb, but a camera flash.

The pap who'd spotted them gave a shout and began to run toward them, camera held high.

Dom lifted her onto the back of his bike as if she weighed nothing, then straddled the seat between her legs and revved the bike to life. The roar nearly drowned out his voice. "Where are we going?"

"Anywhere," she shouted back. Anywhere but home. The condo was barely a few blocks from here and the press would be all over it in two minutes as soon as this story broke.

She laughed. "I'm starving. I'd kill for a burger right now."

Dom grinned back at her. "Hold on tight. I know just the place, but it's gonna be a long drive."

Chapter Two

Once he'd put enough distance between them and Sunset Plaza, and he was sure they didn't have a tail, Dom slowed the bike.

It was the perfect night for the long twisting ride along Sunset Boulevard. A clear spring evening, with a cool breeze sweeping in off the ocean and a pretty woman with her arms wrapped around him.

And to think he almost hadn't gone to Graydon's party.

There was no way he could take her to 25 Degrees now. Or any place else where she might be spotted and recognized. Not in a torn evening gown that barely covered her ass. Even with the ban on social media at the party, he'd bet the story was all over Twitter by now.

She'd turned down Paul de Angelo – the most eligible bachelor in this town and one of the few people who could be called a 'star' these days. She was either very brave or very stupid, but either way he admired her. In a town so full of fake it was almost impossible to recognize real, Nina Alexander surprised him by being real. A woman who said what she thought. There weren't a lot of actresses who knew how to do that anymore.

No wonder de Angelo had stormed out the party. He'd been in this town so long he probably didn't know how to deal with someone who didn't play the game by his rules.

At the end of Sunset, where the ocean stretched wide and the bright moon cast a silver beam across the water, Dom turned onto the Pacific Coast Highway. The salt-tanged wind whipped about them and Nina's grip tightened around his waist.

When he glanced back at her, she was smiling, looking more relaxed than she had all evening and a whole lot less like she wanted to cry. Then she rested her cheek on his shoulder and he concentrated on the road ahead.

In Malibu he cruised into the McDonalds drive-thru and pulled up at the window. Nina shifted behind him, relaxing her grip around his waist as he placed their order. Then she held the paper bag between them for the few more miles it took to reach his destination.

He parked at the side of the road, deserted at this early hour, and climbed off, stretching stiff legs. His hip ached, more than usual, and he rubbed it absently before helping her down from the bike.

Her cheeks were flushed, her eyes bright. "Where are we?"

"Point Dume, the best beach in LA. Not a great surfing beach, but I love to come here when I need space to think." The ideal place to escape the crowds and the hustle of the city.

He guided her along the trail to the steep, metal staircase which plunged down to the rocky shore. She removed her shoes, then followed him cautiously down the dark stairs. As they walked along the rocks to the sandy part of the beach, a series of barks drifted to them through the dark.

"Only the sea lions," he said, catching Nina's shudder.

Her gaze stayed on the patch of darkness the sounds had come from. "Is it safe here?"

"Safer than most public beaches after dark." There wasn't much he was afraid of, and the odd homeless drifter punting for change certainly didn't bother him.

They sat on the beach and looked out over the moonlit sea as the waves washed in, digging their toes into the soft sand. He took the packet of fries Nina refused, smiling as she bit into the burger.

21

She closed her eyes and savored the taste, all her concentration focused on the food.

"What?" she asked, looking up and catching his grin. She wiped at the sauce dribbling down her chin. "Have I sprouted another head? Or are my granny pants showing again?"

"No, though now I'm really tempted to take a peek under that jacket. It's a rare sight to see a woman enjoy her food the way you do."

She shook her head. "I'm going to pay for it tomorrow."

"It *is* tomorrow." He licked his salty fingers. "Who's Sonia? Your agent said you could kiss Sonia goodbye."

"Sonia Fairchild."

He shook his head. "I'm still not getting it."

"From the *Revelations* books."

"Books? Those are the things you have to sit down for hours on end to read, right?"

Nina's wide, dark eyes reflected the moonlight. "You don't read?"

"Unless it's the Hollywood edition of *Vanity Fair*, no. Would that be a deal-breaker?"

She bit her lip for a moment, considering him. He didn't need to be a genius to decode that look. He'd seen it often enough on other faces over the years. She was figuring him for all brawn and no brains, the stereotypical stuntman. He shrugged it off and tossed the empty fries packet into the paper bag.

"The Revelations trilogy is a fantasy series in which angels and demons come down to earth to fight the final battle between good and evil. Sonia's an ordinary girl trying to get through college when she loses her family to this new holy war. Then she discovers she has some special skills, kind of like Neo in *The Matrix*, and she goes Ninja to save the world."

"She sounds like a kick-ass chick. I might like her."

"They're casting the movies based on the books and I want to play her." Nina sucked in a breath. "That's why I wanted to meet with you."

22

He arched an eyebrow and waited for her to go on.

"Every actress from here to London wants to play Sonia. It's the role of a lifetime. Paul got me a chance to read for the part, but the producers weren't convinced. I've been stereo-typed as the ditsy romantic interest for too long. They don't see me as the intense, hard-core action type. They're looking for someone more *heroic*." She flinched at the last word.

"And you thought I could toughen you up to help you get the role? If it helps, you're already my hero. It takes guts to do what you did tonight – to stay true to yourself."

She bit her lip. "I guess there isn't any point bothering now. They'll never take a chance on me after tonight."

"You turned down a marriage proposal. It's not like you mainlined heroin in front of everyone or got so wasted they had to call the cops."

"I might as well have. Paul has a lot of influence and I hurt his feelings."

It wasn't his feelings that were hurt. Dom shook his head and stretched out on the sand. "The days of any one person controlling this business are long gone. He's not the only one with friends."

He knew a few people, too. But how much did she really want this? Because he wasn't going to put himself out for some fickle actress who wasn't prepared to do the work. His reputation was all he had going for him right now and he wasn't about to throw it away for a pretty face. Pretty faces were cheap as dirt in this town.

Character, now that was a different creature entirely.

Nina bit into the burger, taking her time over it before she spoke again. "I'm still an idiot. I could have said yes and then changed my mind later, in a less public place."

"He's the idiot. Who in their right mind proposes to a woman in front of a crowd like that?" Only someone with an ego the size of the Antarctic would be so confident of being accepted. Only someone who cared more about the spectacle than about the woman he'd proposed to would share such a private moment with a room full of strangers.

Or… "When an actor has been on the market as long as Paul de Angelo has, without even one failed marriage behind him, the rumors start."

"Paul is NOT gay."

"He doesn't need to be for the gossip to spread. You know that. You've obviously heard the rumors. But an engagement would shut them up for a little while. A very public engagement at the party hosted by the hottest celebrity magazine on the planet would shut the rumors up a whole lot longer."

She bit her lip as she digested the thought. "You think he was only dating me for his image?"

He hoped she didn't want an answer, because he couldn't answer honestly without offending her. Not that she looked particularly offended. Or heart-broken. "Why didn't you want to marry him?" he asked instead.

She shrugged and looked away, but nothing could hide the flush that stained her neck and cheeks. Not even the moonlit darkness.

"Tell me," he coaxed. "There's no one here but you and me, and the sea."

She shuddered, still not looking back at him. "I couldn't imagine spending the rest of my life with him. I'd grow bored and I'd want excitement, and quite frankly I don't see any point making a promise to spend my life with someone, knowing from the very beginning that I wouldn't keep it."

He nodded slowly. He hadn't realized they had so much in common. He grew bored quickly too and craved excitement, and he never made promises he couldn't keep.

"How would *you* propose?" she asked, licking her fingers.

The question was unexpected and not one he had an answer for. He hadn't given proposals any thought before. The opportunity had never come up. Or to be more precise, he'd never met a woman he liked enough to live with, let alone marry. He loved women, with the emphasis on the plural. But settling down with just one? She'd have to be something really special for him to give up all the others.

He shrugged. "Some place like this, I guess. Some place special, where we can be alone. Shall we take a walk?"

They dumped the paper bag in a garbage can and walked along the beach, sipping their sodas. The tide crept in, filling up the tidal pools.

Nina walked with her arms wrapped around herself, his jacket incongruously large on her, dwarfing her curves. He didn't need to see them to remember those voluptuous curves. He'd spent the handful of weeks they'd worked together admiring them.

She'd gone out of her way to tempt him with them too, not that it had taken much effort. With her throaty, sexy voice, full, red lips and big, dark eyes that could go from a dangerous glint to wide and innocent in a moment, she was temptation personified.

But contrary to popular opinion, he was able to control his impulses. Nina was different from the other women he met. Though she batted her eyelashes at him, same as every other woman, she didn't look at him like he was an object. And if he was honest with himself, it terrified him.

He was okay with being objectified. He didn't mind that most women only wanted him for his body. Their low expectations were easy to satisfy.

He wasn't sure Nina would be satisfied.

They strolled in silence and he left her alone with her thoughts as he enjoyed the stillness and the soothing tumble of the breakers on the shore.

One thing in Nina's favor: she didn't feel the incessant need to talk. With most women in Hollywood there was only one thing that made them stop talking. Admittedly, then they were usually moaning his name instead.

They reached the end of the long curve of beach and paused.

"You know, I've never been to the beach in LA," Nina said. She wrapped her arms around her chest, hugging herself as if she was cold. But she wasn't cold. She looked almost haunted.

"You should make more effort. We have some great beaches. Some excellent surfing, too."

She shuddered. "No thanks. I don't like the sea."

And there was *his* deal-breaker. He loved the sea and spent every spare moment at the beach. He lived within a stone's throw of the ocean just so it would be the first thing he saw every morning.

They meandered back the way they'd come, Dom splashing through the shallows, Nina keeping as far away from the lapping edge as she could. He watched her out the corner of his eye.

In public she always appeared so confident, so sparky, but here, alone in the dark with no one to primp and pose for, she seemed a different person, vulnerable, lost. It tugged at him.

As he'd told Graydon, he was a sucker for a damsel in distress.

He paused to look out across the restless ocean.

He'd heard of the *Revelations* project somewhere, and that it was in pre-production. He didn't know much, but he'd heard enough to know that it was very different from any movie Nina had done before. It wasn't surprising she was a long shot for the role, but if she wanted it enough, he had no doubt she could do it. He'd watched her perform opposite his friend Christian in *Pirate's Revenge* and he knew she was worth more than the roles she usually played.

He could help her. Unconsciously he rubbed the constant ache in his hip again. Why was he even considering it? He wasn't in any shape to conduct an actress boot camp.

He could find someone else to train her… He discarded the idea as quickly it came. Perhaps it was the arrogance of professional pride, but the thought of her spending all her time the next few weeks working with someone other than him made his stomach revolt.

"What are you thinking?" she whispered beside him. She'd ventured into the shallows, tentatively letting the waves bury her bare feet in the sand.

Though she didn't like the sea, she'd faced its challenge. He liked that in a woman.

Nina was just as obsessed with how she looked and what people thought as every other actress he knew, and she probably lived on a diet of grated carrots and lettuce leaves most of the time, but she had potential. She didn't seem like the kind of woman who'd have a hissy fit if she broke a nail working out.

"Why me?" he asked. "Why not book yourself into a boot camp or hire a personal trainer?"

She shook her head. "Anyone can do that. I need to be better. To win this role I'm going to need to do a lot more than just run on a treadmill or do Pilates classes. I don't only need to get physically fit, I also need to get into Sonia's headspace. I need someone to push me, to challenge me. I need to be able to walk and talk like her. Now when I walk into a room, people see the girl next door, maybe a little sassy, a little outspoken, a bit of a klutz, but no one would think of me as a badass. I want to be able to walk into the casting director's office and have her think Lara Croft just walked in."

He raised an eyebrow. "And you think I'm going to be able to teach you all that?"

She grinned, expression cheeky. "You're the most badass person I know."

"I'm not badass. I live in the suburbs and drink green tea."

"What can I say? I don't get out much." She cast him a sideways glance, all but batting those too-long fake lashes of hers. "Besides, you wouldn't really want me to go hang out in some biker bar to learn to be badass, would you?"

He frowned. Not that he believed she would, but even the mere thought of Nina in a bar full of drunken men was enough to make his fists clench. "It takes most people a lifetime to become badass. How much time do you have?"

"Six weeks. But I'm an actress. With the right training, I can fake it."

He looked at her, saying nothing, and she hurried on, "There are so many things I haven't yet done in my life that Sonia would know how to do. That's all I'm asking, is for you to help me do a few of those things."

"Things like?"

"Load and fire a gun, be able to hold my own in a stage fight, take a fall." She grinned. "Ride on a motorcycle and walk on a beach at night."

"There are stunt schools that teach those sorts of things."

She shook her head. "And have a whole bunch of people watch as I make a fool of myself? No thanks! I trust you."

He ignored the obvious flattery. "A stunt school would be more all-rounded. You need trainers who can do vehicular stunts and pyrotechnics and weapons training. I'm a martial artist with a specialty in falls." And he wasn't even good at those these days. He flinched at the memory of his last fall, from a Paris hotel balcony to a snow-covered lawn. Without the luxury of airbags or protective clothing. It had been one jolt too many for his already- damaged body.

"But you have the connections," she persisted. She made her eyes big and round. "Please?"

He did have the connections. And he could do this. The risk was minimal. But whether he should was another matter entirely.

Mistaking his hesitance for reluctance, her face clouded over. "I'll pay you well."

He shook his head. "It's not about money."

"You already have plans for the next few weeks?"

He looked away. "I haven't got any work booked in." And he'd love an excuse to postpone the surgery. "Why do you want this role so much? Tell me about this script and what you need to learn and I'll consider working with you."

The radiance in her face was enough to take his breath away. He'd be the first to admit his ego needed stroking a little now and then, too, and when a woman looked at him like that it made him feel like a hero. He needed that feeling more than ever these days, now that he'd been forced to face his own mortality.

They strolled back the way they'd come, and as they walked, she talked about the role. Here in the quiet of the beach, with no one else around, her voice washed over him, slow and sensual and mesmerizing. But was that a soft, Southern accent creeping in? He'd been sure she was from somewhere in the Midwest.

He shook his head. Perhaps he'd imagined it.

What was certainly not his imagination was the passion she felt for this script. More than simple admiration for the role, it was as if she wanted to *be* Sonia.

"This story really means something to you." He sat down on a sandy spot high up the beach and patted the ground beside him.

Nina sat beside him, pulling her knees to her chest, and looked up at the sky, not answering him for a long moment. "I read the books at a very hard time in my life. Sonia's story helped me through it. They took me very far away from what I was going through."

He watched her face, the moonlight turning her expression stark.

She sucked in her lower lip. "I've always been the odd one out in my family. For the Alexanders, duty and service to others have always been more important than personal happiness. I'm not like that. Playing Sonia is the closest I'll ever get to saving the world single-handed."

That was a hell of a lot of pressure to put on oneself. What kind of superhero family did she come from? Probably cops or military. But he didn't ask. He didn't want to know. He never asked women about their families. Because when you asked those kinds of questions you jumped straight into 'complications' territory.

He stretched out on his side, cushioning his head with his arms, and a moment later she lay beside him, not close enough to touch, but close enough that he could feel the rise and fall of her breathing.

29

Their gazes held and desire sizzled through him. He'd wanted her from the first time he'd seen her, and the temptation now to take what he wanted was almost more than he could stand. So why didn't he? It wouldn't take much to close the distance between them, to lose himself in those full, pink lips.

He rolled away to lie on his back and look up at the clear, night sky.

He had very few scruples when it came to women. As long as it was consensual and legal, she was fair game.

But somehow with Nina he couldn't bring himself to make a move. Perhaps because she deserved so much better than him. She deserved better than Paul de Angelo, too.

She most definitely deserved better than casual sex or a one-night stand, which was all he was looking for.

She was so quiet he wondered if she dozed. He wouldn't be surprised after the day she must have had. The preparations for Oscar night were almost as grueling as the event itself. Not unlike the rush of working on a film set: exciting, challenging, invigorating, and exhausting all in one.

But when he turned his head to look at her, she was awake, watching him through half-lidded eyes. With a small smile she crept closer and laid her head on his chest. He let her.

For a long time they lay together in silence. He draped his arm over her and she snuggled into him. She had to be cold in what was left of her fancy dress.

She shifted against him, resting her chin on his chest to look up at him. "Aside from the adrenalin rush, what's the best part of your job?"

He had to pause a moment to think about it. The adrenalin rush and the challenge of daring to do the impossible were the reasons he got out of bed every day. "The anonymity. I love the fact that I get to do this fun job, but at the end of the day I can go for a jog along the beach, or drink in a bar without someone sticking a camera phone in my face."

He could tell by the look on her face that it was exactly the opposite of why she did what she did. She shrugged. "Will you help me?"

"We can talk about it in the morning."

"As you reminded me earlier, it *is* the morning."

"Then we can talk about it when we've both had some sleep." He wasn't going to make any rash promises tonight. Not with the smell of her perfume clouding his judgment and the softness of her hair tickling his chin.

Besides, she was in a heightened emotional state and who knew if she'd still feel the same tomorrow? Who knew if she'd even remember to say "thank you" to him for rescuing her tomorrow?

Not that it mattered. He didn't go around rescuing damsels for the glory. He was just a sucker for a woman with tears in her eyes and tonight she'd had that look written all over her.

Tonight she needed a friend, someone at her side, not because of who she was and what she could do for them, but just to be there for her. He could do that.

And tomorrow…

Tomorrow had a way of taking care of itself.

Nina said nothing. Her lids hung heavy and she laid her cheek against his chest again.

He watched a satellite orbit slowly across the sky and when it disappeared from sight, he stirred, moving his aching limbs. "I should take you home before it gets light and the rest of the world wakes up."

"I don't want to go home. Can't I just stay here?" She murmured.

"If you don't mind getting some very curious stares from the early-morning beach walkers."

She sighed. "You're right. I'm damned if I stay and damned if I go, so home it will have to be." She rolled away from him and sat up, reaching for her shoes. "Is my make-up smudged? If it is, we'll need to find a restroom somewhere so I can try to fix it up. If I have to get past the inevitable cameras, at least I don't want

31

to look as if I've fallen to pieces."

"There is another option. You could come home with me."

She eyed him coolly for a long moment before she answered. "Thanks, but no thanks. I really appreciate everything you've done for me tonight, but I'm not *that* grateful."

"That wasn't a proposition. I have a guest room you can use."

"You don't want me?" She pouted, her big eyes rounding in a typical actress way, as if her entire being depended on being wanted and adored every moment of the day.

He laughed, hoping she was just messing with him. "You've had an upsetting and emotional night and I won't take advantage of that. I don't have many morals when it comes to pretty women, but I don't prey on them in their moments of weakness." Preying on their easiness tended to be way less complicated. "When I make love to a woman, it's not because she's grateful, or confused, or out of some misguided need for comfort. When you come to me, it'll be because you want *me*." He stood and dusted himself off. "And just for the record, of course I find you desirable. I am a man, after all."

There was that smile again, the one that turned her luminescent and could make the strongest of men feel like a million bucks. The smile that was pure old-school Hollywood glamour.

They climbed back to the road. She straddled the bike behind him again, her body pressed up against his, her arms wrapped around his waist, and he smiled too.

The drive all the way back to Venice Beach suddenly didn't seem so far.

Nina wasn't sure how she'd imagined Dominic's house, but this wasn't it. Not the stereotypical penthouse apartment of a bachelor, all chrome and glass, but a craftsman cottage in a quiet walk street in Venice, bright-colored amid a lush garden oasis just visible now in the light tinge of dawn.

She was too tired to notice much more as she followed Dom

through the house to the guest bedroom.

He hovered in the door and she turned to face him. "Thank you. For everything."

The crooked grin curved his mouth, and it wasn't gratitude that had her hoping he would lean in so she could feel that grin against her lips.

"For what it's worth…" his voice was a purr that started at the top of her spine and whispered all the way down. "I'm glad you turned down Paul de Angelo."

He pulled the door shut behind him and she found herself staring at it for a long moment, her pulse racing and her mouth dry.

Removing her make-up was a mission, with nothing more than soap and water at hand, but she managed to get rid of the worst before she shucked off the remains of her destroyed evening dress and crawled between sheets smelling of lemony fabric softener.

It was only as she closed her eyes to let sleep claim her that she remembered what Dominic had said. Not "*if* you come to me," but *when*.

Even if she'd wanted to, she couldn't stop herself from smiling as she drifted into sleep.

Chapter Three

The angle of the light was all wrong. Nina forced open eyelids that seemed stuck together. Her mind was awake, but her body resisted. She snuggled deeper into the warm, soft duvet with its alien scent and peered out.

Her emotions were less easy to appease than her body. As the memories of the night came crashing back, so did the disappointment, excitement, humiliation, and turmoil. But her most overwhelming sensation was relief.

She'd done the right thing.

She was so not going to be one of those celebrities who racked up marriages and divorces faster than they racked up air miles.

What had Paul been thinking? They hadn't even met each other's families yet. How would her family feel hearing the news of her engagement from whichever reporter first managed to track them down for a comment?

She could imagine what Gran would have to say, and none of it would be printable.

Even so, she'd probably committed career suicide last night. But she couldn't lie in bed all day and pretend it hadn't happened. She'd have to get out there and face the music.

She stretched in the luxurious warmth of the bed and lifted herself up on her elbows. A large room, all in white but somehow not clinical. Golden sunlight slanted through the gap in the gauzy white curtains, across the white hardwood floor and onto the four-poster where she had slept. On one wall hung a dozen pictures in matching dark-wood frames. She climbed out of bed and moved to take a closer look.

Miniature movie posters; the kind they gave away free at movie theatres on opening nights. It was a moment before she registered they were probably all movies Dominic had worked on. Not all Christian Taylor movies, though she'd assumed they always worked as a team.

On the antique bench at the foot of the bed lay a pile of neatly folded clothes with a note. *Hope something fits.* She lifted the clothes gingerly. A pair of ladies' sweatpants, jeans, a couple of t-shirts, and a hoodie. She didn't want to think too closely who they might once have belonged to. She didn't want to think too closely about what their owners had worn to go home in either. But at least they would be more comfortable than a way-too-revealing, torn evening gown.

She showered and dressed in the grey sweatpants, a plain-white t-shirt, and the hoodie. The fact that the jeans were at least two sizes too small didn't help her mood.

When she emerged from the bedroom, the house was eerily quiet. She tiptoed down the passage and into the open-plan living area, careful not to disturb her host if he still slept.

The living rooms were warm and homely, with scatter cushions and vases, an unexpected window of stained glass in the dining area, and a wall of framed family photos Nina didn't look at too closely. This was nothing like the carefully styled "I'm a sensitive man" look Paul's decorator had created, with native American art on the walls but not a personal picture in sight.

Dom's house had a haphazard warmth and feminine touches that suggested the action man with a reputation for going through women quicker than most men went through underwear had at least one home-making woman in his life.

Nina clenched her jaw and headed for the kitchen. It took her a couple of impatient minutes to figure out how to work the state-of-the-art coffee machine in the corner of the kitchen, then she set to ransacking the cupboards for something to eat.

Dom had a surprisingly well-stocked refrigerator for a bachelor. Fruit, vegetables, pro-biotic yogurt and freshly squeezed organic juice. After last night's decadence, she should stick to All-Bran and water, but instead, she grabbed a banana muffin and a tub of yogurt, then sat at the kitchen counter with her espresso. The house didn't have much of a view, but the back yard was certainly pretty, enticing her to enjoy its delights. A wooden patio set stood on the small redwood deck, with a wall of lush greenery beyond. A grapevine grew across the trellis that shaded the deck, and a wind chime hummed a melody as it stirred in the breeze.

She rose to head to the sliding doors and caught sight of the wall clock. She only just managed to stifle a groan. Mid-afternoon already. Everyone she knew had to be worried sick and wondering where she was by now. At the very least her PA, Wendy, would have expected her to report in a few hours ago.

Now, where the hell was her cell phone? Nina clapped a hand over her mouth, suppressing another groan. She'd left her purse at the coat check. At the one-of-a-kind, once-off party venue, which was no doubt already being dismantled.

She could only hope some journo wasn't going through her cell phone photos right now. Was there anything incriminating on there? Aside from a couple of no make-up selfies, she hoped not.

Using the landline in Dom's kitchen (who even still had one in this day and age?) she called the only number she could remember off the top of her head. She hoped Dom wouldn't object to the long-distance call.

"Hello?" Jessie's voice sounded tentative down the line.

"Hi, Jess."

Her sister screeched so loud, Nina had to hold the phone away from her ear. "Where the hell have you been? I've been calling and calling, and finally some intern from *Vanity Fair* answered your phone. She didn't believe it was yours either. She was convinced an A-list celebrity would own something fancier."

Nina rolled her eyes. "I left it at the after-party."

"That good, was it? Did the party cheer you up, then? You sounded so down after the awards ceremony."

So her sister hadn't heard the biggest news of the night yet. "The Governor's Ball was really wonderful. How did your appointment go this morning? Did it take – are you pregnant?"

Jess's hesitation was all the answer she needed. Nina's heart sank. How many IVFs had her sister already tried and failed?

Jess cleared her throat. "Give me all the details. How was the VF party? Who was there? Drop some names. Was it really as glamorous as it looks?"

Allowing herself to be diverted, Nina sipped a mouthful of espresso and launched into a description of the after-party as best she could. But her stomach pulled tighter as she talked. She had to get this over with. Jessie couldn't hear from some other source. She steeled herself. "Paul proposed."

"Shut up! Why didn't you tell me you guys were that serious? "

"Because we weren't. I didn't see it coming." She stumbled for words. "I didn't know what to do. He asked me in front of everyone. And I mean *everyone*. I said 'no'."

"Are you mad?" Her sister screeched again, and Nina held the phone away from her ear. Not Jessie too.

"I don't want to marry him. I mean he's nice and everything, but he's not...I can't see myself with him for the rest of my life." She couldn't see herself with *anyone* for the rest of her life. She had little enough privacy as it was. But if she was going to spend her life with someone, it would be someone who set her alight, not someone who'd eventually wear her down.

As the words of her favorite country song went, she was "better in a black dress" than in a white veil.

"You mean he's not your One." Jessie sighed. For someone who was constantly telling Nina how out of touch she was with reality, her sister was such a hopeless romantic.

"By saying no I think I've undone any good the nomination did for my career."

"So what do you do next?"

Good question. Nina bit her lip. "I have a plan, but it's not going to be easy and I'm a little scared."

"You'll be fine." Jessie used her professional voice, the reassuring tone she used on her patients. "I know you. You'll do whatever it takes and you'll be great. Things always work out for you."

If only she had the same faith in herself that Jessie did. But Jessie was the strong one, not her. Her sister was the glass-half-full kind. Nina, on the other hand, had yet to see any evidence for Jessie's belief that everything happened for a reason. Sometimes shitty things just happened.

"Thanks, Jess. I'll call you tomorrow, okay?"

Her next call took two other phone calls just to track down the right number. "Are you mad?" her PA, Wendy, demanded. "How could you turn down *Paul de Angelo*?"

This was going to be a very long day.

Nina set Wendy to track down her purse, gave her a list of things she needed and Dominic's address, then hung up.

The last call was the one she'd been dreading most. Dane was still as cold to her as he'd been the night before, but at least he took her call. "Paul's been busy this morning," he said. "The press are not painting a flattering picture of you. There's a lot of speculation that you've been two-timing him. You're not going to be able to get a Hallmark movie after this."

Well there was the upside. No more rom-coms. Maybe she could start to prove herself as a serious actress now, with roles worthy of the Alexander name.

"I'm sending Chrissie over to you. You're going to need her help more than mine to get you out of this." Dane hung up.

Great. So Paul had started the media machine moving while

she slept. Well, there was nothing she could do about it stuck in Venice Beach, so all she could do was wait.

There was still no sign of Dominic. Either he was a very sound sleeper, or he'd gone out. Either way, she was hardly going to go upstairs to find out.

She pushed open the glass sliding door and stepped onto the deck. Beyond the wall of green she discovered another little yard, a paved suntrap patio edged with raised beds of bright-colored spring flowers. She stretched out on the sun lounger in the little garden. The golden late-afternoon sun warmed her and, unable to fight exhaustion any longer, her eyes drifted closed.

She woke with a start when a shadow fell over her. Wiping her mouth and praying she hadn't drooled in her sleep, she sat bolt upright. It wasn't Dominic.

A petite blonde woman stood over her, hands on her hips as she stared down at Nina. She wore her wavy, sun-streaked hair in a high ponytail. The woman pushed her sunglasses up onto her head to reveal a pair of curious, assessing gray eyes.

"Hi," she said, sounding neither cool nor friendly. "Is Dom around?"

"I don't know." Nina scrambled up. "I haven't seen him for a while."

The blonde moved out of the sun and Nina noticed that she wasn't as young as she'd first appeared. Tiny lines fanned out from her eyes. But she still had the figure of a teenager, and long, shapely legs that made Nina feel the rush of inadequacy that seemed to be her default setting here in LA.

"He probably went for a run on the beach with Sandy." The woman's mouth pursed in disapproval. "I'm going to pack away his laundry." Casting another assessing glance over Nina, the other woman headed back indoors.

Nina followed, equally curious.

Either Dom had an unusually sexy housekeeper, or he inspired serious devotion in his girlfriends. In which case it was no wonder he seemed so disinterested in her. She was less than useless at doing laundry.

And who was Sandy – another girlfriend?

For the nearly four weeks they'd worked together in Westerwald, Nina had been cursed with the hotel suite across the hall from Dominic's. She'd witnessed the procession of visitors he'd had. Hotel staff, women from the film crew, girls he picked up in nightclubs, dressed in skirts so short they could have caught hypothermia in the winter weather. Even her own make-up stylist had once slipped out of his hotel room at some ungodly hour, lipstick smudged and straightening her clothes.

Nina had been amazed they all seemed happy to move on with a smile, and never had a bad word for him afterwards.

She couldn't fathom why. She'd suffered from the most irrational envy since the day they met. Most likely because she saw so little of his attention.

Last night he'd said he desired her. So why did he chase every other woman yet ignore her? What was it about her that Dom found so easy to resist, even when she'd been single and available? Was it because she wasn't as anorexically thin as everyone else in LA?

There were shopping bags of fresh groceries in the kitchen. How the blonde was going to find place in Dom's already well-stocked kitchen to pack them away, Nina had no idea.

She found the other woman folding freshly ironed sheets into the linen cupboard in the passage. The woman turned and smiled. "Those fit you well," she commented, eyeing Nina's borrowed clothes.

Oh, heavens above – were they hers?

Nina felt the beginning of a hot flush creep up her neck. She didn't usually blush – she was a good enough actress to cover when anyone fazed her – but this petite blonde with her cool, gray eyes was seriously unnerving.

The other woman laughed. "Relax! I don't bite. Would you like a cup of coffee while we wait for Dom and Sandy to get back?"

Nina pulled herself together. She'd been nominated for an Oscar, after all. She could play cool every bit as convincingly as anyone else. She smiled and tossed back her hair. "Thank you. That would be lovely. I could do with another espresso."

Hopefully the caffeine would banish the grogginess of her afternoon nap.

The blonde began banging open doors in the kitchen. "Damn," she said. "Kathy must have been here already. I can't find any space in this kitchen."

Nina resisted the urge to raise her eyebrows. Did Dominic have a harem thing going on? Or was there some sort of competition between the women in his life to keep him fed?

The blonde made cappuccinos for them both and, without asking, added a large dollop of cream and sugar to Nina's cup.

Nina hesitated a moment before deciding that rejecting the cup held out to her would be rude, so she took it and perched on one of the high stools at the kitchen counter to take a tentative sip. The other woman moved to sit across from her.

"You're Nina Alexander, right?" the blonde asked.

"I am. And you are?"

"Juliet." Juliet offered her hand across the table and Nina shook it primly.

"You turned down Paul de Angelo to come home with Dom?" The blonde asked conversationally.

Nina choked on a mouthful of cream. "Good news travels fast."

"Your very public rejection of Paul made the morning news. You know, I always thought he was gay."

Luckily this time there was nothing left in her mouth to choke on. "He's not," she managed. Vanilla, but not gay.

"Oh good. And now he's single, too. I don't suppose you could introduce me?" The gray eyes sparkled. "No, I suppose not after last night. So what was wrong with him that you didn't want him?"

Sheesh, this woman sure knew how to go straight for the jugular.

41

"There's nothing wrong with Paul. He's a real gentleman. The word 'suave' was practically invented for him. He's polite and attentive, very focused on his career, and doesn't live wildly like so many other big movie actors."

He always got the best table in any restaurant, and he knew everybody who was anybody in this town. The perfect boyfriend, as long as you didn't expect fireworks in the bedroom. And until he'd ruined it all by proposing.

Juliet wrinkled her nose. "He sounds terribly dull."

Nina bit back a smile. That too. Paul was surprisingly boring for a star. All the way down to his predictable Prius. She shrugged. "He'll make a wonderful husband to the right woman." It just wouldn't be her.

Juliet winked. "Dom is never dull, but you probably know that already." She dipped her spoon into her mug and stirred thoughtfully. "I'm guessing he rode to your rescue last night?"

Nina nodded. "He saved me from complete humiliation."

"That's our Dom. He has a Knight in Shining Armor complex. He's always getting into scrapes over women. Ask him to tell you the story about the time he...."

A bell pealed and Juliet jumped to her feet. "Who on earth would ring the gate bell? Everyone Dom knows would walk straight in."

Nina cursed under her breath. She'd have loved to hear Juliet's story. "It'll be my PA."

While Juliet headed off to let the newcomer in, Nina poured the rest of the creamy cappuccino down the kitchen sink. Much as she loved the taste of real cream in her coffee, she really didn't need yet another spread in OK! magazine pointing out the cellulite on her thighs.

When Juliet returned it wasn't only Wendy who followed her into the kitchen, but Chrissie, too.

"Your entourage has arrived," Juliet announced.

Chrissie frowned at her. Either the botox was wearing off or her publicist was seriously unhappy today. "Why haven't you taken any of my calls?" she demanded, sliding into the seat Juliet had vacated across from Nina. The confrontation seat, Nina was discovering.

"I'm sorry. I left my phone at the party," Nina explained. Chrissie terrified her, but she was good at what she did and Nina was even more terrified of losing her. Especially now that she needed all the good PR that money could buy.

"I have it. I checked. Everything's still in there." Wendy handed over Nina's purse, cell phone and a large Louis Vuitton hold-all. "And I brought the things you asked for."

Nina sent her a grateful smile.

Chrissie looked a little mollified. "I'll have an espresso. Black, one sugar," she instructed Juliet before turning her back on the blonde. Juliet stuck a tongue out behind her back and Nina had to bite her tongue to stop herself laughing.

Wendy wasn't as restrained. Her giggle earned a quelling glare from Chrissie.

"I have a Plan," Chrissie announced. "I think we should work with the story Paul's putting out there, but turn it around. We're going to say you've met someone else and fallen head over heels in love. You didn't plan to, but it just happened."

Not quite the plan she'd had in mind. Nina shook her head. "Remember the fallout when Kristen Stewart was caught cheating on Robert Pattinson? I don't think that would work in my favor."

Chrissie smiled. "It's risky, but here's the cincher." She paused for dramatic effect. "He's going to be a completely ordinary man. Not a star. Just a Regular Joe. It'll be like the reverse of George Clooney dating the waitress. People already see you as down to earth, so we'll play on that and win you sympathy."

"Who's the lucky guy – anyone I know?"

"Dane has some out-of-work actors on his books. I'm sure one of them will jump at the role for the right amount."

This was what she'd come to – having to pay someone to pretend to be her boyfriend? Sheesh! And people thought the life of an actress was all glamour.

"How is an actor a regular guy?" Juliet asked from the coffee machine. Chrissie ignored her.

"I have a better plan," Nina said. "I don't need a new boyfriend, just a new job. This is the perfect opportunity to reinvent myself as an actress with a little edge. I'm done with rom-coms. I still want to go after the role of Sonia, and I've asked Dominic to train me."

"Who's Dominic?" Chrissie asked.

"The man whose hospitality you're enjoying." Juliet plonked an espresso cup in front of her so hard she splashed coffee on the counter. She'd added cream to Chrissie's cup, too.

"Oh, the stunt man."

"Stunt *coordinator*. What would be in it for Dom?"

Chrissie finally looked at her. The two blondes eyed each other.

"Who are you?" Chrissie asked, looking down her nose at Juliet.

Juliet crossed her arms over her chest. "Consider me Dom's manager."

Though Juliet had to be at least a head shorter than Chrissie, Nina thought they were pretty evenly matched in the formidability stakes.

"*If* we go with this idea, we'd pay him, of course." Chrissie said. "With a bonus thrown in if Nina gets the role." She glanced around the open-plan living area, which was probably half the size of Nina's bedroom. "He could get a bigger place, perhaps something up in the hills."

Juliet shook her head. "Not everyone wants to live in the hills, and not everything is about money."

Nina shuddered. As much as she agreed with the last sentiment, not everyone wanted to live by the sea either.

"He's a stunt man and getting on in years. His career won't last forever," Chrissie said.

Nina flinched at her publicist's callous tone. Besides, Dominic wasn't any ordinary stunt man. He was bright and energetic and magnetic, and he clearly had friends in high places. He didn't want Nina, or her fame or money, or he'd have made a move on her a

44

long time ago. The way most men did.

"So what *does* Dom want?" she found herself asking.

Juliet's cool, gray eyes met hers, and Nina had the oddest sensation that this formidable blonde knew exactly how much that question had been burning inside her, and that she wasn't only asking how to get Dom to agree to train her.

Juliet smiled as her gaze flicked past them. "Ask him yourself."

"Ask me what?"

As one, the four women turned to the kitchen door where Dom stood, holding a panting, creamy-colored Labrador on a leash. He wore trainers, baggy board shorts that hung low on his hips, and a sleeveless shirt that clung to his chest with sweat. Though Nina didn't notice them in that order.

Another blush began to burn her skin.

Dom stepped in through the open door. "What are you doing here, Jules?"

"I brought you some groceries."

"Kathy's already been." He scowled at her. "I've told you I don't need anyone to do my shopping."

"Of course you do." Ignoring his glowering expression, Juliet moved to give him a quick peck on the cheek. She had to stand on tiptoe to reach. "And how else are you going to have clean sheets for your guests?" She fired a quick, mischievous glance in Nina's direction.

"I have a housekeeper."

Juliet dropped to her knees to scratch the dog's ears. It tried to lick Juliet's face and she laughed, pushing the dog's head away. "Down, Sandy. Sit!"

So this was Sandy! Nina's chest suddenly felt lighter and she wanted to laugh. Not quite the harem she'd imagined, nor did Dominic appear to appreciate Juliet's attentions.

Nevertheless, he didn't send the blonde away, nor did he bat an eyelid when, quite at home in his kitchen, Juliet filled the dog's water bowl and set it down for Sandy.

Nina cleared her throat. "We were talking about what sort of payment to offer you to train me up for the role of Sonia."

"I haven't agreed to that yet."

"I still think my idea is better," Chrissie muttered.

Nina shook her head and kept her attention focused on Dom. Not that he wouldn't have had her attention anyway. His presence filled the small, sunny kitchen. "Please?" she asked, making her eyes big and begging.

One corner of his mouth quirked up in a near-smile and her heart dropped. She knew what was coming. He gave her that look every time he was about to turn away from her, usually in some other woman's direction. It was that night in the Landmark Café bar in Westerwald all over again. She'd practically thrown herself at him, and he'd left with a thin, pouty brunette instead. "We need to talk about that. Just you and me."

She didn't need his pointed glance at Chrissie to know what he meant.

"I'll wait for you in the car," Wendy said, taking the hint.

Chrissie was less easy to move. Between them, Nina and Wendy had to each take an elbow to propel her towards the door. "I really appreciate that you came all the way here, and I'll call you later," Nina said.

"Who puts cream in an espresso anyway?" Chrissie huffed, finally accepting Wendy's lead. Nina shut the kitchen door behind them and faced the room. Juliet hadn't moved.

Dom poured himself a glass of water from the fridge dispenser. "Feel free to leave any time, Sis," he said.

His sister! It took all Nina's effort not to grin.

"Yeah, yeah, I get it. You want to be alone." Juliet wrinkled her nose. "You might want to have a shower first, though!" She shoved his shoulder playfully. "I'll be happy to keep Nina company while you change."

He glanced at Nina and she shrugged.

"Go ahead. I need to change too, anyway," she said.

He scowled at Juliet again. "Any embarrassing stories and you're out."

She stuck out her tongue at him and Dom rolled his eyes. "If you'll excuse me?" he asked Nina.

She nodded, unable to speak. The image of Dom in the shower had grown roots in her brain. Damn this blush. Was it ever going to go away?

When she looked back at Juliet, the other woman had a wicked glint in her eyes. "So you and he haven't yet…?"

The blush burned even hotter. How the hell could his sister tell whether she and Dom had slept together or not?

"Why not?" his sister demanded. "Most women can't resist our Dom. Are you really that picky when it comes to men?" Her eyes narrowed with speculation. "Or is it not men you're interested in?"

Nina stiffened her back and stared right back at Juliet. "What happens between me and your brother is none of your damn business. If you want to know why he and I haven't had sex, then you ask *him*." She would love to know, too.

Juliet grinned, and her cheeky look very closely matched her brother's. "You can't blame a girl for being a little protective of her baby brother."

Nina collected her bags off the counter and headed to the guest bedroom. Any relief she might have felt at Juliet being his sister rather than his lover had evaporated in a moment. She could only thank the heavens her own sister wasn't as meddling.

"You still here?"

Only Jules remained in the kitchen when Dom returned, freshly showered and dressed. She looked up from the magazine she was flicking through. "Now that's better. You're more likely to seduce a famous actress dressed like that."

"I don't want to seduce her. She's a potential client. And I really don't need dating advice from you, thank you very much."

Not that he hadn't already learned everything he needed to

47

know about women from his sisters. Like just how much drama they could be.

Jules frowned. "You can't seriously be considering her request? You have surgery scheduled. It's not as if you need her money, and she sure as hell doesn't need you. That uppity publicist has a Plan B to set her up with some poor schmuck who doesn't mind running around at the beck and call of a celebrity, so let them get on with it."

He rummaged in the refrigerator and didn't make eye contact. Why had the thought of Nina with someone else, even if it was nothing more than a set-up, made him lose his appetite? "I can reschedule the surgery."

"Please think about this carefully, Dom. You can't afford to leap first then look."

When had he ever done anything so rash? "Risk assessment is what I do for a living. So trust me to know and understand the risks."

"And healing broken bodies is what I do for a living, so you should trust *me*. You know what the doctor said. You need to stop pushing yourself or you're going to damage your body beyond repair. Fix the damage that's already been done before you can barely walk! And until then, you need to stop running."

"The moment they start cutting through muscle and putting metal body parts inside me, my career is over. What am I going to do with the rest of my life?"

There it was, that specter that had hung over him for months now. His job was who he was. It was the reason he got up every morning. Without it, he'd be lost.

He was still a few years shy of forty; too old to re-train, too young to retire.

He'd be the first to admit that agreeing to prepare Nina for this role was a convenient way to buy himself more time to figure out what he was going to do with the rest of his life.

He shook his head. "My hip, my pain. I can manage it."

"But you don't have to live with the pain. A hip replacement is nothing to be ashamed of, and you'll still have a full range of movement afterwards. Without pain."

"Will you please keep your voice down?" He glanced past Juliet to the closed door of the guest bedroom. "Have you ever heard of a stunt man with a hip replacement? It'll take months before I'm back to normal. Months of sitting around, unable to work. And if word gets out that I'm no longer fit, no one will hire me."

"You always knew this job was going to have a limited lifespan. What did you think you were going to do when you got older?"

He hadn't. He'd lived every day as it came and not spared a thought for the future. "I'm still young," he said. "I've got a lot of good years ahead of me. When I can't cope anymore, *then* I'll reconsider the surgery."

"Please don't wait too long. The better shape you're in when you have the surgery, the quicker you'll recover."

He rolled his eyes. "Is the lecture over yet, Sis?"

She sighed. "I don't want to see you any more damaged than you are already."

They'd been having this same argument for more years than he could remember. "I know you want what's best for me, but I'm not a kid anymore. You need to butt out and let me make my own decisions. And you can tell the others that, too."

"So your decision is to turn yourself into a glorified fitness trainer for a few weeks? Why? Forget training her. Just get her out your system and move on, the way you usually do."

He shook his head. "It's not like that. She's not like that."

Juliet shrugged. "If this is really only about training her, then you need to be realistic, Dom. She might have passed the cream test, but she's still a spoiled celebrity. She's never going to see this through. As soon as the going gets tough, she'll be gone. Is she worth damaging your body further?"

"How about I let you know?" He loaded fresh strawberries, yogurt, and a generous handful of granola into the blender and switched it on, its roar drowning out any chance of further conversation. Finally taking the hint, Jules closed her magazine and hopped down from her stool. "I'll see you on the flip side."

The kitchen door had barely closed behind her when Nina emerged from the guest bedroom. Not a coincidence, he was sure.

The sweatpants were gone, replaced by tailored trousers and a white frilly blouse that dipped dangerously low between her breasts. He swallowed and forced his gaze higher. She'd done her hair and make-up too. She was back to being Nina the Movie Star again, not the vulnerable woman he'd walked on the beach in the dark with last night.

She slung her bag over her shoulder. "Thank you for helping me out last night. I really appreciate it."

At least she hadn't forgotten to thank him.

She shifted awkwardly, as if there was something more she wanted to say, and cleared her throat. "About what I asked you last night…I don't want you to feel pressurized. You can say no."

Had she overheard his conversation with Jules? He was man enough that he didn't want a beautiful woman to see him as weak or feel pity for him. He kept his expression neutral and nodded.

"But will you consider it? If you change your mind, here's my private number." She held out a piece of paper with a phone number scrawled on it and he took it silently.

"Goodbye then," she said and headed for the door.

"Meet me at 25 Degrees at 12 tomorrow."

She paused mid-stride.

"It's a day later than we intended, but it's as good a place to start as any. No promises yet. I need to see what you're capable of before I agree to anything," he said.

The smile she threw him was almost enough to knock him off his feet. A man could definitely get used to being looked at like that.

"And wear comfortable clothes; clothes you don't mind getting dirty in."

Then she was gone, leaving nothing but the soft scent of her perfume in the air.

Chapter Four

Dom choked on his draft beer as he caught sight of Nina at last. She couldn't have shouted 'celebrity who doesn't want to be recognized' any louder. The oversized designer sunglasses and headscarf were enough to make anyone look twice, especially here in Tinseltown.

She hovered in the door of the restaurant, nervously scanning the room before she spotted him in one of the back booths and made a beeline for him.

She slid into the seat across from him, her back to the rest of the restaurant, and undid the headscarf. Her long, sleek dark hair tumbled loose.

"Hi." The coquettish smile she sent him was enough to make up for the 15 minutes she'd kept him waiting.

The waitress who brought their menus was clearly well trained. She pretended not to recognize Nina.

"I'll have the Number One burger with extra fries," he said, handing her back the menu.

Nina's face took on a pinched look for a moment, then she placed her order. "I'll have a Pellegrino and the chopped vegetable salad."

The waitress met Dom's eye. He grinned. He agreed. He'd had such high hopes Nina wasn't going to be just like every other image-obsessed actress. She'd even passed the cream test.

This was a test his sisters had devised years ago. They deliberately offered a woman a beverage she usually didn't drink – in a town like LA where every woman was on a diet, cream and sugar were the obvious choices. If the woman caused a fuss, she was written off as high-maintenance. If she accepted the cup and was polite enough to sip, his sisters considered her a keeper.

It was a good test. He'd even used it a few times himself. No one even semi-famous had passed the test before Nina.

"Those aren't exactly the kind of comfortable clothes I had in mind," he commented, eyeing the pretty blouse and short skirt she wore.

She shrugged. "What if someone sees me here and takes pictures? Wendy has my bag in the car with a change of clothes."

"You've left your PA waiting outside?" he asked.

"Of course not! She's running an errand for me and she'll be back soon."

Their food arrived quickly. As he dug into the burger, Nina averted her gaze, but she couldn't disguise the hungry look she cast his fries.

"Go on," he said with a quick grin. "You know you want to. Besides, you're going to need to start bulking up. I'm going to make you work off those calories very quickly."

Her grin as she leaned forward to steal a single fry off his plate was less movie star and more the Nina he remembered. And her satisfied sigh as she savored the fry was the most sensual thing he'd seen in years.

"Aren't you…?"

Nina smiled and nodded at the two young women who approached their table.

"Could we have our picture taken with you?" the bolder of the women asked.

Dom took the phone handed to him and snapped a few pictures of them posing with Nina, attempting to look as cozy as best friends. By the time the women finally removed themselves, his burger was cold. And Nina had stopped casting lustful glances at his fries. She turned back to him with a half smile. "And that is why I don't leave home in sweatpants. So when do we start my training?"

"As soon as we've eaten and I'm sure you're not going to pass out from lack of sustenance I'm going to put you through some paces to test your fitness and agility."

"I have a personal trainer and I work out every day in the gym at my complex. And I used to be a cheerleader in school." Her smile oozed confidence, but she sounded defensive.

"Sweetheart, that has to have been at least ten years ago. No offence, but I need to know what I'm working with *now*. And just because you push weights with some gym bunny in an expensive health club does not make you fit."

He scanned her body, or at least what was visible above the tabletop. She was in good shape and clearly worked out, but she didn't have the build of an athlete. For what he'd require from her, she needed core body strength, not legs that would look good blown up on a movie theatre screen.

"I won't be as easy on you as your trainer," Dom warned. "I'll expect a hundred per cent commitment from you. I'm going to make you work and I don't want to hear any complaints."

She smiled, full of genuine confidence now. "I won't complain."

Several hours later she wished she hadn't said she wouldn't complain. Dominic had taken her on his motorbike to a training facility up in the hills, and he'd put her through a commando obstacle course. He'd made her run, crawl through dark tunnels, climb ropes and a series of increasingly steeper and higher barriers, swing across a ravine and jump from a height into a bed of mats.

Her legs and arms ached, she'd scratched her shins, and she wanted to cry from the way her breath tore through her throat. The sun baked down. She was over-hot and dripping with sweat. And there was still one more obstacle to go.

Dom kept pace beside her as she ran as hard as she could up the slope. She didn't want to imagine how she looked: red-faced, panting, with her hair matted to her face and her t-shirt plastered to her skin. They crested the low hill and Nina baulked at the sight below her.

"You know how to swim?" Dom asked. He had no right to look so clean and able to breath. He hadn't even broken a sweat.

She nodded. "Swimming pools, yes. But that…"

"That" was an oversized pond. No, it was too wide and too deep to be called a pond, too stagnant to be called a river. And the smell…

Memories she didn't want hurled themselves at her. She swallowed the gag reflex.

"Showers and cold drinks are on the other side," Dom said. "I'll meet you at the clubhouse." He pointed to the wooden building on the far side.

And then he was gone, jogging away from her with a backward wave and a grin she would have loved to wipe off his face.

She looked back at the water obstacle that lay before her. Fear gripped her stomach and again the gag reflex choked her. After several hours of torment, she no longer felt like sassy, confident Nina Alexander. She felt like the scared, plump kid she'd been in that other life so long ago.

Not just scared. Fear squeezed her chest. She sagged to the ground and eyed the water.

She didn't need to shoot in water for the movie. Well, there was one scene in the third book… she swallowed. But that's what stunt doubles were paid for.

She could call Dom back – tell him she couldn't do this. And she could call this whole stupid thing off and go back to playing the rom-com princess.

She could, but she wouldn't. She hauled herself up onto shaking legs. Then, drawing in a deep breath and closing her eyes, she jumped.

The water wasn't as deep as she'd expected. It only reached to chest height. And at least it was cool, unlike that choking, merciless water she remembered. She began to wade. Water weeds caught at her, wrapping around her legs. Panic set in as she struggled against them. But they only gripped tighter.

She couldn't breathe.

Survival rule #1: don't panic. Her father had told her this years ago when she'd climbed too high up a tree and gotten stuck on a branch that had cracked beneath her weight. He'd talked her down, slowly, calmly.

She stopped fighting. Tears burned against her eyelids as the old memory choked her even more than the weeds. Survival rule, my ass. Fat lot of good it had done him.

She tried to move again, but the tangled weeds still held her tight. Trapped.

The tears threatened to spill over. Who was she kidding? She couldn't do this.

She looked for Dom, but he was far away, circling the dam, not looking her way. She tried to shout for him, but the tears clogged her throat and all she managed was a whimper.

The black spots were back, dancing before her eyes.

I can do this. She breathed deeply to calm the surge of fear and panic. *I won't cry. He mustn't see me cry.*

When she no longer saw black spots before her eyes, she held her breath and dived down to yank the strangling weeds off her legs. It took three dives to finally free herself, then she pushed up to the surface and began to swim, slowly, careful to keep close to the surface to avoid the tangling weeds that still seemed to reach out to her with their greasy tentacles.

Her already aching muscles protested with every stroke, but she pushed forward, keeping her gaze locked on the distant building that slowly, slowly grew nearer.

Just another few feet, another stroke… on the far bank she dragged herself out and lay panting in the dry, prickly grass. The relief was so great she wanted to cry. She'd done it. She'd actually crossed it and it hadn't killed her.

She wasn't that weak, frightened little girl anymore.

Dom's shadow fell over her. He held out an outstretched arm to pull her up and she took it gratefully. She didn't know if she could have stood on her own. Her legs shook so much from the unaccustomed strain, and just a little bit of terror.

"How did I do?" she asked as they headed towards the clubhouse and she finally found her voice again.

"In six weeks I want to see you do it in half the time," he said.

"Does that mean I'm trainable?"

He nodded, and this time she did cry, a few hot tears leaking down her dirt-stained face. Whether they were tears of joy or fear, she had no idea. She had to do this again in a few weeks? What had she signed up for?

She was so thirsty that she downed the tall glass of water Dom handed her in a minute flat. His eyes crinkled as he watched her. When she was done, she wiped her mouth with the back of her sleeve. Though the movement probably added even more grime to her face.

"What the hell are you doing?" she asked as he took out his cell phone and snapped a picture.

He grinned. "I want to remember this moment. This might well be the first time I've seen an A-list actress covered in dirt and mud she actually earned."

"If that picture ever appears on the net, my people will hunt you down and kill you." But she said it with a laugh. He was right. The only time she'd ever been this dirty, the dirt had been painted onto her by a make-up artiste. It had taken nearly as long to paint on as it had just taken her to do the obstacle course.

And the only time she'd felt this liberated, this powerful… actually, she couldn't even remember ever feeling this high. She'd done it. She'd faced one of her oldest fears.

"Anything else to drink?" Dom asked, raising his hand to summon the grizzled older man behind the serving hatch.

Nina nodded. "I'm going to live dangerously. You can make my next one a beer. But I need that shower first." Though she doubted one shower would be enough to get the mud out of her hair.

The shower only had cold water and no shampoo, but at least she was a little more presentable when she returned to the bar area. Dom's eyes glinted as she slid onto the chair across from him. Was that admiration in his gaze?

Great! If only she'd known the way to attract his attention was to submit to torture, humiliation, and terror she wouldn't have wasted all that effort trying to flirt with him during the filming of *Pirate's Revenge*.

The beer not only slaked her thirst, it eased a little of the stiffness already setting into her muscles. "So what's next?" she asked.

"Next I take you home." His mouth curved upwards in that suggestive half-smile that made her stomach flip.

She straddled the bike behind Dom as he revved the engine. She had to shout her address into his ear over its roar. Then she hung on tight as he headed back toward town. It was already growing dark when they wove through the streets of West Hollywood and into the tree-lined avenue where she lived.

"This is where you live?" Dom helped her off the bike and looked up at the unassuming mid-century stucco building. "I'd have thought after four seasons on a successful TV show, you'd have gone for something fancier."

"It's not all about money," she said, with a small smile. "I bought this place the first time the show was renewed and it still suits me fine. I don't need anything bigger and it's easy to lock the door and leave if I go away on a shoot."

And the heavy security ensured at least a modicum of privacy.

Her muscles had already begun to seize up and she needed Dom's help to remove the helmet, too. Her arms ached too much to hold up. "Besides, I won't be on top forever, and when the day comes when I'm no longer relevant, I don't want to have blown everything I ever earned on a lifestyle I don't need."

No matter how great the temptation, she'd never over-reach herself and risk being homeless again.

Dominic looked impressed. Wasn't that just typical? She finally got the man's attention and she was too tired to capitalize on it. She stood awkwardly beside the bike and glanced around. Looking the way she did right now, she didn't want to hang around on a public sidewalk any longer than necessary. "Do you want to come inside?"

"Sure."

He followed her inside, through the security gates with their keypad access, past the guard, and across the cool, quiet lobby to the elevator. They rode up in silence. She let him into her unit, a tight knot forming in her stomach as he looked around without a word.

"Stylish," he said. But it didn't sound like a compliment. "How long did you say you've lived here?"

"Six years." Compared to his homely bungalow, her apartment looked unlived in, even clinical. But it was her safe place, her refuge from the constant bombardment that followed wherever she went these days. Very few people were ever admitted past the door.

"You take minimal to a whole new level." Dom followed her into the open-plan kitchen and leaned against a granite-topped counter as she opened the fridge.

She shrugged. "I don't like to get attached to material things." Or to people.

She pulled a bottle of beer out the fridge; one she hadn't even remembered was there. "I also don't have much to offer you. Will this do?"

He nodded, took a bottle from her and popped the lid. She watched as he drank, swallowing hard against the tug of desire that shot through her. God! It was like watching beer porn.

Now that she had him here, she didn't quite know what to do with him. She was too tired, too achy, and too dirty to make any attempt at seduction. Thank heavens there was no one else to see her and judge her in this sorry state. Dom seeing her like this was bad enough.

"So, when do I start my training?" she asked.

His eyes glittered. "You already have. But I'm wondering if you even need me at all. We just need a video of you doing what you did this afternoon and we can send it in as your audition tape."

"Nice try, but I'm not letting you off the hook that easily."

He smiled, moving closer, to stand right in front of her so she was forced to look up at him. "I won't let you off the hook that easily, either. I'm going to make you work. First, we're going to need to build your core strength and improve your endurance. I want to teach you some basic tumbling and martial arts, and I have friends who can teach you the other skills you need: firearms training and driving."

"I drive," she said defensively. Though not often since she'd become famous. The day after she'd stopped for gas and been mobbed at the gas station she'd offered the super- organized production assistant on her current movie a job. Wendy had driven her car ever since.

"A stick shift?" Dom asked.

Slowly she shook her head. She hoped he couldn't read her thoughts because he did not want to know what image had just popped into her head at the thought of handling a stick shift. Sheesh! But she'd turned into a raging mess of hormones in his presence.

"You're also going to meet some of the friends I work with. If you want to get inside the head of some badass people, that's as good a place to start as any."

"Will there be any more like you?" she looked up at him through her long eyelashes and smiled. It was hard to do coy when you felt like you needed a very long soak in a bath to decontaminate, but she hadn't been nominated for an Academy Award for nothing. Even if it had only been for Best Supporting Actress, and even if she hadn't won.

That naughty smile ticked up the corner of his mouth. "Any more like me in what way?"

She met his gaze head on. "Sexy, single…"

He held her gaze for a long moment, saying nothing. Then his gaze dipped to her lips. "Are you flirting with me, Ms. Alexander?"

"Is it working?"

His smile deepened, into the one he used to soften his brush-off. "I need a day to get a few things sorted and to speak to the rest of my crew. Meet me on the Venice Beach pier at six-thirty on Thursday morning." He leaned in and brushed a kiss against her temple. Her lungs forgot to breathe. "Thanks for the beer."

He let himself out the apartment and she was still standing in the kitchen, leaning against the counter to keep herself up. She was pretty sure the boneless feeling in her legs had nothing at all to do with the excruciating workout of the afternoon.

But her emotions weren't nearly so boneless. She pushed herself away from the counter and headed for the bathroom.

Yet again, she'd practically thrown herself at him, and he'd walked away. What was it about her that a man with *his* reputation with women could keep walking away?

She was more than half an hour late. Dom paced the pier, drawing curious stares from the early-morning fishermen. He hadn't brought his mobile. Should he head home to fetch it? Perhaps she'd decided to bail already and he was wasting his time here.

He was on the verge of giving up waiting when he spotted her, a curvaceous figure in leggings, a running jacket with the hood pulled up and big sunglasses jogging towards him down the pier, scanning the area as she ran.

He set his hands on his hips. "You're late. I thought you'd already changed your mind."

She shook her head. "I'm so sorry. There were reporters camped outside my building, so we had a hell of a time getting out, then the driver had to lose them before we could come here."

He led her down to the beach and they headed north, jogging along the soft sand.

"I could go running with an ordinary trainer," she pointed out.

"This is just the warm-up. You'll be running every morning to build your stamina."

She cast him a coy look. "Is that how you keep up your stamina?" She wasn't talking about his exercise regimen.

He ignored the question. Of course, she knew his reputation. He made no apologies for who he was and what he did. But he didn't feel like discussing his sex drive with Nina, of all people.

The beach was not yet busy, though the sun was up over the horizon. In spite of the easy pace he set, Nina was panting for breath by the time they'd reached his usual halfway mark.

"This is so much easier on a treadmill," she wheezed, bending over, her hands on her knees. "And my calves are still sore from yesterday."

"It'll get easier."

"Please tell me I get coffee when this is over?"

"You get coffee when this is over."

He let her have a rest before they turned back. She collapsed on the beach, her hoodie falling back and her ponytail swinging free. But not before she'd first checked their surrounds, that no one was watching her.

Dom resisted the urge to roll his eyes. Vain much?

She removed her sunglasses and he realized the fake eyelashes were gone. Why she needed them, he had no idea. She had the longest, glossiest natural lashes he'd seen.

"It's really pretty here," she said, looking out over the breakers toward the horizon.

"So maybe you can be converted to liking the sea?"

She shivered. "It's still way too scary."

He'd seen enough people caught in riptides, or surfers submerged by waves, to know the sea could scare the faint-hearted. But knowledge was the only way to combat fear. Staying calm and knowing how to reduce the risks were more important in any crisis than brute strength.

Every stunt he did was planned to within an inch of its life, and rehearsed and rehearsed to eliminate as much of the unknown as possible. There was still an element of danger – he wouldn't do it otherwise – but Nina needed to learn that preparation eased the greatest fears.

"Did you have a bad experience with the sea?" he asked.

She rose and dusted the beach sand off the seat of her pants. "Let's head back. I could really use that coffee now."

He took pity on her and they ran back along the pedestrian paths rather than on the soft sand.

He took her back to his house and they ate breakfast on the deck, Sandy running mad circles around them and Hana, his housekeeper, serving them fresh coffee.

"You need some feeding up," Hana observed, and Nina laughed.

"You and my Gran are the only people on the planet who tell me that. Everyone else wants me to live on a diet of celery sticks."

Hana shook her head and piled more bacon on Nina's plate before heading back inside.

Nina trimmed the fat off the bacon and snapped her fingers for Sandy. As the dog nuzzled against her hand, eating up the fatty bits, Nina laughed and scratched between her ears.

"You like animals?" he asked, surprised. Her pristine, white apartment was so clearly not home to any pets.

"I had a dog just like Sandy when I was a teenager." She rubbed her face against the dog's fur so he couldn't see her face, but he heard the catch in her voice. "I still miss her."

"You should get another," he suggested.

"And who would look after it when I'm away on a shoot? I

even managed to kill a cactus once."

"You have a PA," he reminded her.

She shook her head. "Wendy goes wherever I go."

"She didn't come with you to Westerwald." He would have remembered.

"I gave her some time off. Her sister was having a baby." That was definitely a catch in her voice. She downed the last of her coffee and stood up. "I'm ready. Where are we headed next?"

They walked the short distance to the dojo where he often worked out. On the soft matting he tested her basic tumbling skills, showing her how to fall and roll safely. She wasn't half bad and she still had some of that flexibility she must have learned cheerleading. She managed the shoulder rolls from kneeling easily enough, but break falls and dive rolls from standing required more effort. And a great deal of touching and close proximity.

When he'd fantasized about having his hands all over her, he hadn't imagined he'd be showing her how to hold her head or correcting her posture.

He held out a hand to help her up from the mat. She came up with too much impetus and had to grab hold of him to steady herself. He caught her arms.

They stood chest to chest, both breathing heavily, though it wasn't from exertion.

He should step away. He should let her go. Instead, his arm snaked around her waist and Nina looked up at him, her pupils so large and dark that it was like looking into a deep well. She ran her tongue over her lips and every part of his body sprang to attention.

"You can let me go now."

Slowly and reluctantly he let her go and stepped away. Barely half a day in her presence and he was already finding it difficult to remember all the very good reasons why he hadn't taken her to bed long before now.

Number one being that he was only a step away from being

a man whore and she was … Nina. Smart and sexy and spunky, and definitely in a class of her own.

He had nothing to offer a woman like her, and he had better remember that.

They had lunch at a tiny Italian bistro frequented by the trendy advertising set.

"I can't go in there," Nina whispered urgently. "I'm not dressed to be seen."

"And you won't be," Dom assured her.

The owner himself took their orders. Nina was careful to keep her back to the room, hiding behind a leafy pot plant.

"Your usual?" Antonio asked.

Dom nodded.

"What's that?" Nina asked.

Antonio lowered his voice. "Salmon pesto pasta. Special family recipe, but it's not on the menu. My wife makes it only for Dominic."

"Make that two," Nina said, with a smile that won her another fan.

Antonio headed back to the kitchen and Nina cast a furtive glance around the restaurant. "What if someone recognizes us?" she whispered.

"Would that be so bad?"

"With the rumors Paul's been spreading about me, someone might assume you and I are having an affair."

Again, would that be so bad? Clearly it was, because her brow furrowed with anxiety.

He shrugged. "No one's paying us the least attention. Look – a room full of people too busy texting to pay any attention to us."

After lunch, which Nina devoured ravenously, he took her to the firing range at a police training facility. Two days of almost constant physical exertion and she was looking forward to the rest. Except that the target range wasn't the walk in the park she'd expected it to be.

Though Dom let her sit while she learned the theory of firearm safety, actually learning to load and fire a gun was another matter. The intense concentration required to fire at the life-size paper targets was exhausting, her ear drums were left ringing in spite of the ear protection, and her wrist and arm ached from the revolver's recoil.

"You have good hand/eye coordination," the instructor said. He was an ex-SWAT officer and a hard taskmaster, not given to praise, so she glowed at the compliment. "But you still hold the gun like a girl. Next time we'll work on improving your grip. I want you handling these weapons with confidence before we move you onto rapid fire and combat shooting."

It was late afternoon when Dom rode her home on his bike. She wrapped her arms around him, pressed herself against the solid heat of him between her legs. Forget the adrenalin rush of the bike ride, it had nothing on the rush of hormones flooding her.

This time, when he turned into her street, he pulled up to the curb half a block from her condo.

"Oh hell," she moaned. "I was sure they'd have left by now."

The street had been overrun. There were more cars than she'd ever seen in the quiet street, and the huddle of reporters guarding the tall gates at the entrance to her building had swelled to double the size.

She still wore the same running gear she'd left in this morning, creased, sweaty, and dirt-stained now, and she hadn't had a chance to touch up her make-up. "They can't see me like this," she groaned, immensely grateful for the bike helmet concealing her identity.

"They can't see you looking like a kick-ass action woman? Isn't that the whole point of this exercise?"

If only she looked kick-ass. At best, she probably looked like a love-starved teen with the hots for her teacher. "The training's for the benefit of the film's producers and director, but not how the reporters will spin it. They'll make it look like I'm falling to pieces over Paul." Or worse, like she'd been cheating on him. "What the hell are they doing here, anyway? All I did was turn down a frigging marriage proposal, not end world hunger."

Unless someone had spotted them together and blabbed? All those cell phones in the Italian restaurant, Antonio, Dom's friend at the firing range...

Dom looked back at her. "We have two choices: we either go through them, or we go someplace else."

She wasn't usually such a coward, but after the couple of days she'd had, she wasn't up to facing down reporters. She'd have to call Wendy to sneak her back into her apartment again. And then repeat all over again in the morning. She pulled at the neck of her t-shirt but it did nothing to ease the suffocating feeling. Even her refuge wasn't safe these days. The idea of a big house in a gated community grew more appealing every day.

"Someplace else," she decided. She gave him another address and he turned the bike around.

Chrissie's suite was on the fourth floor of a glass and steel office building not too far away. The lobby was mercifully empty, but the security guard gave them a curious look as he buzzed them through. Nina almost wept with relief to find her publicist still at her desk.

"There's a mob of reporters outside my building," she said without preamble as she strode into Chrissie's corner office.

Chrissie broke into a smile. "I know. Isn't it wonderful? You're back as front page news and I'm a genius!"

Foreboding whispered down Nina's spine. "What have you done now?"

Chrissie held up her mobile phone. Nina stepped closer to look at the picture that filled the screen. She and Dominic in the booth at 25 Degrees. It had been taken at the exact moment she'd leaned across to steal the fries off his plate. Dominic's face was part-obscured, but hers was clear as daylight. The mix of hunger and mischief in her flushed face was unmistakable. On the plus side, she definitely did not look like a girl pining for her ex.

66

She looked like a girl in lust.

As long as no one realized it was food that had put that look on her face, rather than a man. Though the man hadn't hurt.

"I had my photographer follow you," Chrissie said, beaming. "You were so clever to choose that restaurant. There's nothing more All-American than a burger diner. We're going to turn you back into America's sweetheart, everyone's favorite girl next door. And now everyone will be wondering who this paragon is who's stolen your heart from Paul."

She still didn't get it. Nina didn't want to be the girl next door anymore. And she was pretty sure Dom didn't want to be anyone's paragon.

Dom reached over her shoulder and removed the phone from Chrissie's hand. "Are there any other pictures?" he asked. His voice sounded tight.

"That's the only one I've put up on Instagram so far. I'm drip-feeding them to keep the press intrigued."

Nina had never seen Dom angry before. His lips pressed hard together and the skin around his mouth turned white with tension. His eyes glinted in a way that made her shiver. "I agreed to train Nina. I didn't sign up to have my name and face dragged into the tabloids."

Chrissie's eyes widened.

"You upload any more pictures, or so much as whisper my name, and you'll regret it. Get it?"

Chrissie nodded.

Without another word, Dom shoved the phone back at her, turned on his heel and strode from the room.

"Shit." Chrissie laid a dramatic hand over her heart. "He can be scary. Does he really mean it?"

Nina nodded.

"I don't get it. Who wouldn't want to be linked to you?"

Nina didn't get it either. She shrugged. Perhaps he thought it would interfere with his love life. "Dominic likes his anonymity."

67

"He was the one who gave me the idea. The way he made it look as if you'd left the Vanity Fair party together…" Chrissie sighed. "It was all so perfect. He's exactly the 'ordinary man' we were looking for."

Nina shook her head slowly. Dom was anything but ordinary. "I thought you didn't approve of him when you first met him?"

Chrissie shrugged. "Not when you still had a shot at Paul de Angelo. I mean *hello*? Paul's an international superstar and your stunt man is a nobody. But since Paul isn't an option any more, I have to admit the stunt man is a very nice piece of eye candy."

Nina swallowed a smile. Better than nice. And it didn't hurt that he had brains, too. And a sense of humor. And that crooked smile. "From now on, please run your plans by me first. Until then, can you make the press go away?"

She found Dom outside in the hall, leaning up against the wall. The pinched looked around his mouth had disappeared.

"I'm sorry I lost my temper," he said.

"That was you losing your temper? You should see me in a rage sometime."

He grinned and the knot inside her chest loosened. "I have. Remember that scene we shot on the pirate ship where you threw the dagger at Christian?"

She laughed. "You're right. You've already seen me at my worst, haven't you?"

Like after the commando course. He even had the picture to prove it. Now if *that* image ever found its way onto Instagram…

Dom nodded towards the door she'd just come through. "Will she back off now?"

Nina nodded.

"Good. Because I can't train you with a media circus watching our every move. If this keeps up, it's seriously going to affect your training." His eyes brightened. "But I have a plan, and we're *not* going to run it by your publicist. Will you trust me?"

She hoped he didn't notice her pause. She nodded and forced a smile. "Is there any question?"

Chapter Five

They met at Dom's house. Dom and Nina, Wendy, and another of Dom's sisters.

"Are there any other sisters I need to know about?" she whispered to Dom, once Kathy had given her the third degree.

"Laura and Moira," he answered.

He had *four* sisters?

"Any brothers?" With any luck he'd have an equally hot brother – one who didn't have an aversion to her.

He shook his head and handed her the tray of teas and coffees. She carried it to the dining room and set it down on what little space of the dining table Kathy had left clear of make-up and wigs.

"This one looks the most like Nina's hair," Kathy said, lifting up a long, sleek, dark-haired wig. "I'll need to trim it to the right length, though."

Yeah, it looked like her hair…after three hours of taming in a hair salon.

"I won't pass for Nina," Wendy said. "I'm too tall." And too skinny. Nina bit back her bitter laugh. One of the best things about hangers-on was that they never said those kind of things where she could hear. People on the street, on the other hand, seemed to think she was deaf. *"She's a lot bigger than I thought she'd be"* was a common refrain, right after *"She's a lot shorter than I thought she'd be."*

"You won't have to stand in for Nina," Kathy said. "Dom has a friend about the right build."

A short while later, the friend let herself in the back door. "This is Vicki," Dom said, giving the newcomer an affectionate hug. "She's a stunt woman and part of my team."

Nina's eyes narrowed.

Vicki was fair to Nina's dark, but they resembled one another closely enough. Except that where Nina had a tendency to plump, Vicki had a tendency to muscle. Not the butch kind of muscle, either, but the athletic, *I always look good in a bikini* kind.

While Kathy prepped the wig, Dom told them his plan. "In the dark, Vicki will easily be mistaken for Nina. Wendy, you'll need to get her into Nina's apartment. You pack a couple of suitcases for her, then she's going to walk out the front entrance, get into your car in full view of the reporters, and you're going to drive her to the airport. Make sure she's followed and that everyone sees her go inside. At the airport, Vicki will lose the wig, change clothes, and head back here."

Nina shook her head. "That's a great plan, but the moment I go home again everyone will know it was just a ruse."

"You're not going home. That's what the suitcases are for."

She set her hands on her hips. "Since you seem to have all the answers, where exactly will I be living the next few weeks?"

She really didn't want to book into a hotel. There was never any privacy in a hotel, and sooner rather than later someone would tip off the press.

"Here."

Four mouths gaped open.

"Are you sure about that?" Kathy asked, recovering first.

Dom sipped his green tea. "Why not? No one will think to look for her here."

"Because you haven't lived with anyone in over a decade."

"How hard can it be? It's only for a few weeks."

70

She would be with Dominic 24/7. The thought sank in and her heart sank with it. She needed her space. She needed to be able to escape from people and Dom's house was, quite frankly, a train station with people coming and going.

But even worse was the thought that she'd be with *Dominic* 24/7. To think there'd been a time when she'd wished she could find a man who wasn't always trying to get into her pants. Now she'd found one, the idea of being around him without respite for her self-esteem, or her libido, gave her chills.

Her confidence really didn't need any more knocks.

"Wendy can find me an apartment nearby."

Dom shook his head. "It'll be too risky. There's certain to be someone who'll recognize you coming or going, and then we'll have the press back on our heels again."

She didn't point out that someone could notice her coming and going from Dom's house, too. Or were women coming and going such an everyday thing that his neighbors no longer even noticed?

Her jaw clenched. "You aren't worried I'm going to cramp your style?"

Dom's mouth curved in that crooked grin that set her stomach fluttering. "I can survive a few weeks without bringing someone home, if that's what you're worried about. Besides, we're going to be working most of the time. There won't be time for anything else."

Kathy sat Nina and Vicki side by side as she worked on Vicki's make-up. Nina was fidgeting in her seat by the time Kathy applied the finishing touches, though this hadn't taken even half as long as her daily make-up routine for her role in *Pirate's Revenge*.

"Wow, that's brilliant," Wendy said. "As long as no one gets too close, they'll believe it's Nina they're seeing."

"Kathy's a professional make-up artiste and a damn good one," Dom said, from the living room, where he was now playing a game on the Wii. "She works on TV commercials."

"Handy for you," Kathy threw back, with an impish grin that matched her brother's.

71

"How often do you guys do this?" Wendy asked.

Kathy winked. "More often than you can imagine."

After Wendy and Vicki left, Kathy packed up her make-up kit. She glanced over her shoulder at Dom, still engrossed in his game in the living room, and dropped her smile. "Make sure he doesn't overdo it these next few weeks. If he hurts himself training you, I'm going to hold you responsible," she said in a low, urgent voice.

She let herself out the back door and Nina stared after her. She thought her own sister was over-protective, but Dominic's sisters took it to a whole other level. One only had to look at the man to know he could take care of himself.

With nothing to do but wait, she headed to the guest room and ran a hot bath full of bubbles. Maybe along with soaking away the day's muscle strain, she could soak away the tension the Kelly sisters seemed to inspire in her.

Dom tossed the Wii controller on the sofa and ran a frustrated hand through his hair. What was Nina doing in there? He'd heard the bath water running, but surely she couldn't *still* be in the bath?

For the thousandth time he pictured her lying there, nothing but bubbles to cover her nakedness. His body stirred.

What if she'd fallen asleep in the bath? Perhaps he should go check on her. Halfway down the hall he heard the soft click of a door and caught himself.

This was stupid. If she was going to stay with him for several weeks, he'd have to get used to having a hot, naked woman on the other side of the door. And he'd have to get used to keeping his hands to himself.

He opened the glass patio doors and whistled for Sandy. He would take a run. Though it was already growing dark, a run was sure to dispel some of the testosterone coursing through him.

Client. Actress. High maintenance. Nina. As he pounded the pavement, Sandy lolloping alongside him, he repeated the mantra over and over in his head. All the reasons he needed to keep his hands off her.

Only she hadn't seemed so high maintenance when she'd lain her head on his chest that night on the beach. Or when she'd endured the obstacle course without a word of complaint. The course was designed for elite police training, not for pampered movie stars, but she hadn't pouted or complained or given up. He'd expected her to beg for a rest at least once. But she hadn't, and that, more than anything, had finally convinced him to train her.

Whoever Nina was, she wasn't the sunny, easy-going personality she projected to the world. Nor was she the vulnerable, haunted woman he'd glimpsed on the beach at Point Dume. The Nina who'd done the obstacle course yesterday was driven, stubborn, determined. She was a woman who didn't take "no" for an answer, and who never gave up.

He admired her.

But no matter how low maintenance she was, no matter how different from the actresses he'd met before, Nina wasn't an easy-come, easy-go kind of girl either, and for Dom there was no other kind worth contemplating. He'd developed a super-sensitive radar where women were concerned, and he could tell at thirty paces if she was the kind of woman who'd expect him to still be there when she woke up in the morning.

No matter what she'd told de Angelo at the *Vanity Fair* party, Nina was one of those women.

Dom ran harder, further, and faster than he usually did these days, until the pain in his hip was too much to bear. He had to slow to a walk for the return trip.

He might as well not have bothered for the good it did. When he walked in the door, she was on the sofa with her legs curled beneath her as she read a book. She wore a pair of yoga pants that molded to her hips and a loose-fitting t-shirt, her hair twisted up into a messy knot on her head.

"You're blonde!"

And she wore glasses. He hadn't known she wore glasses. It was

73

just about the sexiest thing he'd ever seen, and that was before she looked up at him and smiled, a flirty smile that brought out the laughter in her dark eyes.

He was hard all over again. Back to square one.

At least the change in focus made the pain in his hip more bearable.

"Do you prefer blondes?" she asked, batting her long eyelashes. "I thought I might be a little less recognizable like this."

He shrugged. He preferred her as a brunette, but he wasn't about to admit to any preference where she was concerned.

Disappointment at his lack of reaction flashed through her eyes, then she returned her attention to her book and he busied himself in the kitchen, throwing spaghetti into a big pot on the stove and stirring up a sauce. After a while, Nina laid her book aside and came to stand beside the kitchen counter. "Do you need any help?"

He shook his head.

"I should have guessed you can cook."

He shrugged. "If you've ever tasted my mother's cooking, you'll know why I taught myself to cook."

She laughed, then looked away. "Vicki brought my stuff."

He nodded.

"I invited her to stay but she had other plans."

He nodded again. If she'd asked Vicki to stay, perhaps that meant Nina wanted to be alone with him about as much as he wanted to be alone with her.

She toyed with the salt cellar on the counter and wouldn't make eye contact. He'd seen his sisters do the same thing enough times to know what it meant.

"Spit it out," he said. "Whatever it is you want to ask."

She caught her lower lip between her teeth again, something he noticed she did when she was nervous. And when she wasn't wearing her buoyant movie-star persona. "Were you and she...?"

"I don't kiss and tell," he said firmly, and reached for a bottle of wine from the rack above his head. He made no apologies for

74

the women he'd known, and he had nothing to hide, but he felt a sudden and urgent need for alcohol.

He passed the bottle to Nina. "There's an opener in the drawer behind you and glasses in the cabinet."

She poured the wine and handed him a glass.

"You not having any?" he asked. She shook her head, biting her lip again. God, she had to stop doing that. It turned her lips plump and pink, making her look as if she'd just been thoroughly kissed. If only.

Nina helped to set the table, opening and closing cabinets to find where everything belonged. He had to grit his teeth against the intrusion and remind himself that this was going to be her home too for the next few weeks, and he had no one to blame for the invasion into his space but himself and his big mouth.

Still, it made better sense to have her close and away from public scrutiny if they were going to get results.

When the food was done, he served it into bowls and they moved to sit at the dining table. He hadn't sat at the dining table in years. Dinner was usually on a tray in front of the television. The only company he ever had who stayed for meals were family.

They ate in silence and he noticed as her eyes began to droop. When they were done, and she rose to help clear away, he took the bowls out of her hands. "Go sleep. You've earned it. I'll see you at six-thirty in the morning."

At seven o'clock he ceased his pacing and knocked on her bedroom door. There was no response, so he pushed the door open. The room was still in darkness, the curtains pulled shut. He strode across the room and threw them open. The morning light drew a whimper from the bed. Nina lay with her face buried in the pillows. She pulled the sheet over her head to block out the sunlight.

"You're late," he said. "Get up."

"Just another ten minutes," she begged. Her voice was huskier than usual, going straight from his ears to his groin.

"You've already had ten minutes. Three times."

"I think my alarm clock might be faulty. It keeps switching off."

"It's called the snooze button." He hoped she was decent under the sheet. If she wasn't, she was about to have a very rude awakening. He pulled the sheet off her and breathed a sigh of relief. Or disappointment.

Beneath the sheet she wore a pair of boyish boxers and a gray t-shirt with the words *In Your Dreams* emblazoned across her chest.

Yeah, she had been.

"You're such a drill sergeant," she complained, trying to pull the sheet back over her head.

He held tight on to it. "That's Sergeant Dominic to you. Now get up. I want you out of bed and ready for a run in ten minutes."

"I won't even be able to get my make-up done in ten minutes!"

"The later we leave, the more populated the beach will be, the more chance there is you'll be seen."

Ten minutes later she was dressed. Sans make-up. He grinned. Her buttons were way too easy to push.

They jogged the short way down the narrow walk street between houses to the beach, Sandy running excited circles around them.

Today he pushed Nina further than they'd run the day before. "By the end of your second week you should be able to run the entire distance from Venice Beach pier to the Santa Monica pier and back again."

"You're trying to kill me," she said, panting for breath.

"Nonsense. I usually do that distance every day." At least he had until he'd done his hip in.

The shooting pain was almost as much as he could bear. He'd need a pain pill to face the return journey, but he'd wait until Nina was distracted before he swallowed the one stashed in the pocket of his shirt.

She looked up at him through her long lashes, all innocence. "Yes, but you've never had to run with puppies the size of these." She cupped her breasts and fluttered her lashes. Innocent? Yeah

76

right.

And naturally, with an invitation like that, he couldn't resist looking, even though he knew exactly what he would see. Nina's breasts were gorgeous, full and round and perky. Were they natural? God, he would give anything for a feel.

He swallowed his grin. "Want to bet? When you can outrun a speeding car wearing heels, a wig and fake boobs, *then* you can complain."

Again, they ate breakfast in the dappled sunshine of his deck before heading to the dojo, where he started her on some basic martial arts moves. Beyond the doors of their training room, out on the main floor, a class of six-year-olds were being put through the same moves.

Unlike the six-year-olds, Nina was a quick learner, with good posture and even better balance.

"You should have done martial arts rather than cheerleading," he commented. "You could have gone far."

Her mouth quirked. "I did go far. All the way with the school's star football player, in the back of his father's Beamer." She sighed dramatically, laying a hand over her heart. "He was my first."

He took revenge by tripping her off her feet and pinning her to the ground.

"I didn't see that coming," she cried. "That's not fair!"

Neither was the fact that he couldn't do worse to the footballer, whoever and wherever he was. It was stupid, it was irrational, but the thought of anyone laying a hand on Nina made him want to do bodily harm.

He lifted himself off her before his body could betray itself anymore. "Just for future reference, your heart is on the other side," he said, turning away.

Lunch was nothing more than a couple of ready-made sandwiches grabbed on the way to the race track, where yet another friend of his awaited them, a former race-car driver turned stunt driver. She was certainly getting her money's worth, being trained by some of the best in the business.

While Evan taught Nina how to shift gears and work the car's clutch, Dom sat on the sidelines and scrolled through the gossip websites. The reporters had taken the bait. There were pictures of 'Nina' at the airport and a 'source close to her' had revealed she was on her way to a romantic tryst with the new love of her life in the Bahamas. At least Chrissie had come through for them and bought them some time.

By the time the sun dipped toward the horizon, Nina had managed several circuits of the race track without stalling Evan's car. They pulled up in front of where Dom waited in the pit lane.

"Thank you for your time," Nina said, kissing Evan on the cheek. Her face was flushed and her eyes bright. If that was how she looked after taking a few corners at moderate speed, he couldn't imagine how she'd handle the adrenalin rush of being shot off an air ram.

It was after dark when Dom finally rode her home on his bike. They parked in the garage beside his shiny, new, fire-engine-red Jeep Wrangler and Dom unlocked the door and let them into the yard. Light spilled from the house and the glass sliding door on the patio stood wide. Visitors? Nina sighed. She didn't feel up to facing any of Dominic's sisters.

But it wasn't one of Dom's sisters this time. A teenaged boy sprawled on the sofa, his attention focused on the large flat-screen TV, the Wii controller in his hands.

He bore a striking resemblance to Dom, with the same light-brown hair cut short, the same green eyes. The kid was leaner and wirier than Dom, but the resemblance was so strong that she froze at sight of him. It hadn't even occurred to her Dom might have a child. Or children.

It was one thing for him to play the devil-may-care bachelor, travelling the world, partying until all hours, a different woman every week, but if he had kids…

She shook her head. Dom didn't seem like the kind of man

who shirked his responsibilities.

"Hiya, kid," Dom greeted him, swinging his gym bag onto an armchair. "You and your mom fighting again?"

The kid grunted a reply, his attention still riveted on the game.

"I need a shower," Nina said. She had to cross the teen's path. Only when she obscured the screen did he notice she was even there. He looked up and his eyes widened. "Hey, aren't you…?"

"Yes, she is. Now get your shoes off my sofa and greet my guest." Dom bumped the kid's feet to the floor. "This is my nephew, Eric. Eric, this is Nina."

Eric's eyes were still wide. "Good going, Dom! I thought you only dated waitresses."

"Nina and I are not dating, and whatever gave you the idea I only date waitresses?"

"Mom. She told Aunt Juliet the other day you're never going to settle down if you keep dating waitresses and barmaids."

"And your mother thinks you never listen to her."

"I don't listen when she's talking about boring stuff. Why does she think you only date waitresses?"

Dom looked over at Nina. "Weren't you going to have a shower?"

"It can wait. I want to hear the answer to that question, too."

He rolled his eyes. "I don't only date waitresses. I only date women who aren't looking to settle down. I like women who don't expect anything more of me than I'm willing to give. The fact that most of the women I meet who fit that description work those kinds of jobs is purely coincidental."

Grown-up translation: he only did casual sex.

"Feel free to tell your mother that too," he said to Eric.

"Shouldn't you be getting married at your age?" Eric asked.

Dom sent him a quelling glare. "Now I *know* that's your mother speaking."

"It's a good question. What's wrong with getting married *at your age*?" Nina teased.

"Aren't you the one who told a room full of people that you

aren't the marrying kind?"

"Yeah, but I'm nearly ten years younger than you." She grinned, stepping out of his reach.

Dom rolled his eyes and headed for the kitchen. "If you're staying for dinner, kid, you should let your mom know where you are."

Nina headed for the shower. She'd turned it into a joke, but it wasn't just an age thing. She had no plans for marriage and babies. *If* she married, some day in the distant future, it would be part of her career strategy, not because she was 'settling' for anything. And whoever she married would need to bring a great deal more to the table than even Paul had.

Her sister Jess was the settling kind, the one who'd married her college sweetheart and lived in domestic bliss, desperate for a baby to go with the picket fence.

Nina was too focused on her career to even have time for a relationship. Paul had been the first guy she'd dated in years who hadn't complained when he came second to her career. Because she'd come second to his, too. It had been a happy arrangement until he'd spoiled it with that stupid proposal.

And until yesterday she hadn't even contemplated living with a guy.

She showered and changed into a shift dress and sandals, dusted her face with make-up, pulled on a light cardigan against the evening air, and returned to the living room. The only concession she didn't make to vanity was that she opted for her glasses instead of contacts.

"It's a lovely evening," she said, heading for the kitchen cabinets where Dom kept the crockery.

The swift look of appreciation in Dom's gaze went a little way to soothing the knot inside her that had grown every time he'd touched her then just as quickly pulled away, as if she'd somehow stung him.

She tossed her hair over her shoulder. "Shall we eat outside?"

80

He nodded and she moved to set the table on the deck for dinner. They ate out on the patio, in the soft yellow light of the oil lamps hanging from the grapevine trellis. Their citronella smell filled the air. The sound of distant breakers on the beach and the mellow music of the wind chime filled their silences.

"So what did you fight with your mom about this time?" Dom asked his nephew when they were done.

The boy shrugged. "She thinks she knows everything."

"Your mom's a pain in the ass, but she usually knows what she's talking about."

Eric shrugged again. "But she's not a guy. She doesn't understand guy stuff."

"Want to try me?" Dom asked.

Eric was quiet for a long moment. He glanced Nina's way and she looked away, pretending to listen to the night sounds, pretending not to hear. Just like she did in public when strangers called her name.

"There's this girl…" Eric told his story in halting sentences. Nina stole a glance at Dom and their eyes met. He grinned, eyes crinkling, and winked.

While Eric poured out his heart to his uncle, Nina cleared away their dishes and fetched a beer for Dom and a soda for Eric. When she returned to her seat, she risked another glance down the table. Dom had schooled his expression, listening seriously to his nephew.

"Your mom might be right," he said. "But I'm going to give you a little man-to-man advice. Girls don't want you to talk about feelings and shit. They want you to listen to them talk. So next time a girl asks what you're feeling, ask her how *she's* feeling."

Nina rolled her eyes.

"You don't agree?" Dom asked.

She turned to Eric. "I don't think you should be asking your uncle for dating advice. He might be great at getting a woman into bed, but he's not so great at keeping her there. If you're serious about this girl, you need to talk to her. You need to tell her you

81

what you feel for her."

"Give the kid a break. He's only sixteen. He's hardly looking for a life partner right now."

Eric nodded fervently. "Exactly."

"And neither's she." Nina shrugged. "But what do I know? I just remember what it was like being a 16-year-old girl."

"Did you have a serious boyfriend at 16?"

"Not exactly." That had been her *annus horribilis*, the year she preferred to forget. She'd had bigger worries on her mind than who she'd be going to the movies with on a Friday night. "The only thing a girl of any age wants is a boy she can be herself with. No pressure. No expectations. So start by being her friend first."

Eric nodded slowly. "I can do that, I guess."

"Why don't you bring her round here sometime? We can go to the skate park and you can hang with your cool uncle." Dom suggested.

Eric didn't look convinced and Nina laughed. "Yeah, because what every kid wants is to hang out with *old* people like us."

Eric's expression brightened. "Would you be there?"

She shook her head. His girlfriend didn't need to see Eric starstruck over a famous movie actress. Nina knew exactly how that would feel. Not unlike how she'd felt walking down the red carpet at the *Vanity Fair* party a few yards behind Scarlett Johansson. "I'm lying low. I probably shouldn't be seen in such a public place just yet." She caught Dom's eye. "Though I've always wanted to learn to skateboard."

"Didn't you once skateboard in an episode of your TV show?" Eric asked.

"That was my stunt double."

"The unsung heroes of the movies," Dom said.

"Yeah, your lot make my lot look so good." She grinned back. "But I did my own roller blading, if that'll make you think better of me."

After Eric left, Nina moved to pack the dishwasher while Dom took out the trash. Then he came to stand beside her, arms crossed over his chest as he leaned against the counter.

"Eric's mother, Moira, is my eldest sister. She's very bossy, but she hasn't had it easy. She married her college sweetheart, then a few years ago he left her for his dental hygienist. He's moved back east and started a new family, and Eric misses having a man to talk to."

Nina closed the dishwasher door. "You seem to be doing a pretty good job."

He uncrossed his arms and stepped closer, crowding her in against the dishwasher. His mouth curved in that crooked grin. "That's not what you thought earlier. And I'm good at getting women into bed, am I?"

"So rumor has it." She batted her long eyelashes, which was hard to do with glasses on. That was the one distinct disadvantage of having eyelashes other women would kill for. "Are you flirting with me, Mr. Kelly? Because if you are, I should probably warn you that I'll expect you to follow through."

He held her gaze. Now that it was clear that he wanted no-strings, and she wanted no-strings, commitment-free, completely-not-settling-down fun, would Dom make a move?

Her body thrummed with anticipation.

No such luck.

He stepped back.

"Following through would be a very bad idea. Sleep well. We leave for our run at six- thirty sharp tomorrow morning."

He turned and headed upstairs to his room, and she was left in need of yet another shower. A cold one this time.

Chapter Six

Dom hadn't been kidding when he said there'd be no time for play.

Every morning started with a run on the beach, and every morning she woke swearing, desperate for another ten minutes of sleep. On the plus side, he hauled her out of bed so early they practically had the beach to themselves. The few surfers who were there before them seemed to know Dom and, beyond a waved greeting, left them alone.

For Nina, it was bliss to hang out in a public place without having to pose for pictures or sign autographs. Not that she got to hang out much. Every day Dom pushed her further, and though she was sure her legs wouldn't make the distance, every day she felt stronger and fitter. By the end of her first week she was able to run the full distance from pier to pier without feeling as if she wanted to die.

Back again was a different matter.

By the time they returned home each day, she was wide awake, fully focused – and ravenous. Wendy was usually there before them, and as they ate breakfast she ran through all Nina's business: the invitations, phone calls, scripts, and errands.

After breakfast, Dom and Nina spent several hours at the dojo, where they worked on her tumbling and martial arts skills, and on strengthening her core muscles. This was her favorite part of the day, just the two of them together, laughing, joking, teasing.

The afternoons weren't so easy. Some days, they practiced shooting clay pigeons at an outdoor range in the hills. Some days she had driving lessons with Evan. Not just driving – by the end of her first week he had her doing hand-brake turns and controlled skids. And one afternoon Dom took her trampolining. She could barely walk after that one.

She needn't have worried about being alone with Dom. They were hardly ever alone. He had so many visitors drop by in the evenings, she began to wonder if he'd planned it. His nephew and niece, his sisters, his friends, even his neighbors stopped by one evening to share a bottle of wine. Nina refused to feel guilty for hiding out in her room and pretending to sleep. Exhaustion wasn't merely a convenient excuse to avoid being sociable. Every night she was so tired that she dragged her aching body to bed at least two hours earlier than her usual bedtime.

But just because she didn't have time or energy didn't mean she didn't think about sex. A lot.

Every time Dom touched her, she thought about sex. And he touched her a lot. Massaging her calves when she got a cramp, a hand on her arm or her shoulder or her waist as he corrected her stance or showed her how to do a move, his hand against her lower back as he guided her through a door...

It was so long since someone had touched her in any way that wasn't intended as foreplay. It drove her so crazy, it might as well have been foreplay.

But while her temperature seemed to spike so often she was sure she had to be running in a state of constant fever, Dom appeared completely unaffected. It was impossible to miss that he was a tactile person. So how was it possible that he, the legendary seducer of anything in a skirt, didn't feel as desperately tempted as she did to take this further?

As much as she thought about it, she made no move to take it further either, though. Her fragile self-esteem couldn't take any more rejection from him.

"I haven't heard from you since forever," Jess complained. "Why don't you call me anymore?"

Nina shifted the phone to her other ear. "I'm sorry, Sis. Dom's been working me so hard I barely get a moment to sit."

"How *is* the hottie?"

"Still hot. Have the reporters stopped calling?"

"Yes, thank heavens! They all want to know where in the Caribbean you are. You won't believe some of the things I've been offered in return for a tip-off. They tell me you're with your new lover. Is there anything I should know?"

"Nothing at all."

"You and Dominic haven't...?"

"Definitely not! How's Gran?"

"She's good. She asked me to tell you that you did the right thing. She saw one of Paul's movies the other day, the one where he plays that crooked cop, and she decided he's far too intense for someone delicate like you."

Nina laughed. She'd never felt more delicate than she did right now. Even her bruises had bruises.

"So how's the training going?" Jess asked. "Or more to the point, how are you coping living in someone else's space?"

"I've lost at least five pounds." Not the answer her sister was looking for, she knew.

"Any idea yet if this ploy of yours is working?"

"Nothing." But then she'd been too preoccupied this week to beat Dane's door down for updates. "What's new on your side?"

"We've decided to try for one more IVF." Her sister dropped the bombshell as if she were discussing going out to buy milk and bread. Maybe, after nearly five years of trying, that's what it had become.

"Can you afford it?" Nina's heart contracted as she spoke. It was a stupid question. Of course Jess couldn't afford it, but she'd do it anyway. Her sister wanted this baby so much she'd bankrupt herself for the chance. "Just tell me how much and I'll cover the costs."

"You don't have to."

"Don't be silly. Of course I want to help."

And money was by far the easiest way to help. She still wasn't entirely sure if her sister's comments over Christmas dinner had been serious or not. "You could have one for me," she'd said. "It's not like your lifestyle would have to change. We'd raise the baby."

Nina prayed it was Jess's sick idea of a joke. She loved her sister and wanted her to be happy, but there was no way she was putting her body through pregnancy for anyone. Bloating, stretch marks, scars… she had enough trouble keeping herself in peak shape without *that*. Not to mention half a year off work… There was no way she'd be able to play a role as physical as Sonia with a baby growing inside her.

"Thank you." Jessica gulped down an uncharacteristic sob on the other end of the line. "So what do you have planned for the weekend?"

For the first time in forever, Nina didn't have any plans. No parties, no red-carpet events, no 'show your face to the producers' visits to fancy restaurants.

"I'm hoping I get to catch up on some sleep this weekend."

Dom, entering the kitchen where she sat perched on a stool at the counter, shook his head. "We work," he mouthed.

Her heart gave a tiny skip.

"Dom's telling me he's going to make me work all weekend." She sighed dramatically. "He's such a slave driver."

"Then why do you sound so happy?" her sister asked.

"I'm hanging up now," Nina warned. "Give my love to Lucas and to Gran."

"Who's Lucas?" Dom asked, stretching out on the sofa in the living room.

Nina moved to sit beside him. "My brother-in-law." She eyed the big bowl of buttery popcorn between them on the sofa. She couldn't remember when last she'd eaten popcorn. Quite possibly not since she was 16 and she'd decided to make herself over as the new, slimline, popular Nina. "What's on TV tonight?"

"You're not going to bed yet?" There was a glint in his eye.

"It's Friday night. I'm going big." And for once there were no visitors. No one she needed to keep up appearances for, and no reason to hide in the guest bedroom.

Dom offered her the bowl. She shook her head. But it wasn't the most convincing shake. Surely she could risk one tiny handful? But that was the thing with popcorn – once started it was impossible to stop.

"I thought you were going big?" he asked, the glint turning into that full-blown, mischievous grin.

No one here but Dominic to see if she snuck the smallest handful of popcorn. She pressed her lips shut, but that couldn't stop the smell of warm, buttery popcorn from teasing her nostrils. Her mouth watered.

"Was that your sister on the phone? Tell me about your family." He reached into the popcorn at the same moment she did and she snatched her hand back as if she'd been bitten.

She shrugged, sitting on her hands to stop them straying again. "There's not much to tell. Typical nuclear family: mom, dad, two kids. End of story."

"Sounds very normal. So what makes them such superheroes?"

She shrugged, hoping it appeared offhand and not as tense as she suddenly felt. "They're all first responders of some kind. Cops or nurses or firemen. Jess is a trauma counselor for FEMA and her husband works for FEMA, too. My mother's a nurse. These days she works with the Red Cross, travelling all over the world from one disaster to the next."

"And your father?"

"He died when I was 16. Then we moved in with my Gran. She was a nurse in Korea. That's where she met my grandfather."

They were all heroes, saving the world in their own ways. All except Nina, who was the only one who'd 'chased her own self-serving ambitions' as her mother had so delicately put it the last time they'd been in the same room together.

She was the anti-Sonia.

Dom nodded, seeing way more than she wanted him to see. She tried not to squirm under his gaze.

"Does your sister have children yet?"

Ouch. She shook her head.

"Is she older or younger?"

"Older, by just 18 months."

He grimaced. "Two years between me and Juliet."

"I can't imagine how your mother stayed sane with five children. And something tells me you were just as much work as the other four put together."

He laughed. "Yes, but I had five mothers. Juliet may only have been a toddler when I was born, but she picked it up from the others soon enough."

"I noticed." Though his housekeeper, Hana, came in three days a week, his sisters still babied him. They dropped in unannounced with fresh groceries. Sometimes it was just a note on the kitchen counter. One day there was a calendar page with a date the following week circled in red and the word *arthroplasty*.

"What's an arthroplasty?" she'd asked.

Dom screwed up the page. "Nothing."

Nina stretched now beside him on the couch, her arm brushing against his as she crossed them over her chest. Anything to keep them away from that bowl of temptation. As she turned her head, she caught the flare of interest in Dom's eyes, a moment before he suppressed it. Hmm…maybe not so unaffected after all?

She couldn't give in to one temptation, but the other… "My neck is sore. Will you massage it for me?" she asked.

He nodded and sat up straighter on the couch, moving the bowl of popcorn aside. She allowed herself a momentary victory grin as she moved to sit before him on the floor and pulled off her shirt.

His intake of breath was audible. Definitely not as unaffected as he made it seem.

She sat before him wearing nothing but a pair of leggings and her lacy black bra, praying no one would choose this moment to drop by. Her eyes fluttered closed as Dom kneaded and massaged her neck and shoulders. His fingers were warm and supple, strong enough to work out the kinks in her muscles, gentle enough that the usual fantasy began to spin itself through her head. She closed her eyes and let it play against her eyelids.

She knew what he was. She knew he'd had more women than she cared to think about. If scuttlebutt on set was true, sometimes he'd had more than one at a time, too.

But she'd also heard enough from her make-up stylist to know that sex with Dom would be good. Better than good. It could be life-altering.

And considering she and Paul had been nothing more than okay together… she couldn't quite suppress a needy moan at the thought of just how good that orgasm could be.

Dom jerked his hands off her and she blinked her eyes open.

"It's late," he said. "You should get to bed. We have another early start tomorrow."

Fine. If that's what he wanted. But she didn't put her shirt back on when she rose.

As she got ready for bed and set her alarm clock she heard Gran's voice. *Do something that scares you every day.*

Gran had encouraged Nina to chase her dreams, to become an actress when everyone else said it was a long shot and a bad idea, and she should stay in college and get a real job.

Nina pulled the bed covers over her head and lay still in the dark, listening for the soft sounds of movement from the floor above, where Dom was also getting ready for bed.

No matter how well he pretended to be unaffected by the chemistry sizzling between them, he wasn't that good an actor. The same tension that bubbled beneath her skin affected him too, she was sure of it.

Tomorrow she would do something very scary and she'd make a move. If he shot her down again, then so be it. She'd swallow the rejection and put him out of her mind – somehow – and get on with her life. But if he didn't… she smiled into the pillow. If he didn't shoot her down, it could be life-altering.

On Saturday morning, Nina only hit the snooze button once before Dom strode into the room and stripped the bed covers off her. "I want you ready to hit the beach in ten minutes."

"Go away," she grumbled. "It's Saturday."

"You don't get weekends off, and you're late again," he barked, suppressing a grin.

She lifted her head off the pillows and craned her neck to look at the illuminated face of the alarm clock. He didn't need to look to know what numbers stood there.

Nina gasped. "Half past eight? How did it get so late? I am *so* sorry." She swung her legs out of the bed. "Okay, I'll be ready in ten minutes."

"You have five."

"What happened to the ten minutes you told me I had?!"

"You wasted five of them arguing with me." He ducked out the door before she could throw anything at him, and headed back to the kitchen to make them fruit smoothies, allowing himself a grin only when her bedroom door closed between them.

He swallowed as Nina entered the kitchen. She stood with hands on her hips, looking like an angry pixie. "I checked my cell phone. It's not even six yet!"

He unpeeled his tongue from the roof of his mouth and held out a tall smoothie glass to her. "Good, then you have time for this before our run."

She didn't move to take it, so he set it down on the counter.

"You should thank me. I finally fixed that problem with your alarm clock."

"By changing the time?"

He danced out of her reach as she took a swipe at him. "You need to move quicker in a fight. And don't give away your next move with your eyes," he advised.

Nina stuck out her tongue at him, then turned her back to lean over the counter as she sipped the smoothie. He had to swallow again.

"Cut-off denim shorts aren't exactly good running gear," he managed. Or good for going unnoticed. She'd be causing traffic accidents going out in public dressed like that.

She threw a cheeky smile over her shoulder. "I'll survive."

Yes, but would he? Her shorts were so short he didn't need to exercise any imagination to see the soft, pale flesh of her butt peeking out beneath the denim.

And she wore her glasses again. He'd always had a thing for women in glasses. It was part of the school-marm fantasies he'd enjoyed ever since Ms. Mitchell taught him tenth- grade science. Just as well physics had been his favorite subject or he'd have learned nothing that year.

Noticing how his gaze stroked down her long, bare legs, Nina wiggled her ass. He bit back a groan. She was too damn sexy for her own good, and his corresponding hard-on was hugely inconvenient.

It hadn't taken her long to figure out how to press *his* buttons.

With all the typical arrogance of a celebrity used to getting her own way, Nina clearly didn't take 'no' for an answer. By now, any other woman would have realized this wasn't going to happen.

She really should find herself a nice man who wasn't going to sleep with her and walk away. One who would take care of her and be there for her.

Which certainly wasn't him. He already had four needy sisters. He didn't need another needy woman in his life.

But that challenge she'd issued still boiled his blood every time he thought of it. *I'll expect you to follow through.*

He'd been told he was a natural flirt. And following through on a little fun flirtation and taking it all the way wasn't usually a problem for him. Nor was he used to being noble around a woman. He didn't know how much longer he could keep his natural inclinations reined in.

He'd been such a good boy all week. For someone not used to denying himself when it came to the opposite sex, this was killing him. He wanted to flirt outrageously with her. He wanted to 'follow through' on the flirtation even more. He wanted to explore her sensitive spots and have her scream for him with a desire bordering on madness.

What was the worst that could happen if he gave in to the urge to scratch this itch? Aside from losing a lucrative paycheck and never seeing her again?

They headed down to the beach for their morning run. It was still too early in spring for any but the most dedicated surfers to be on the beach, and none of them noticed or cared that a celebrity was among them. Catching the perfect wave was a far higher priority. He watched the black figures head out into the surf with envy.

Nina didn't complain when he set a faster pace than the previous days, and her breathing seemed less ragged than it had earlier in the week, though when they finally stopped for a rest she dropped on the sand as if she couldn't stand for another moment. He wasn't sure how much of that was real and how much was simply the usual actress drama.

She stretched out her long legs and arched her back, so he couldn't help but notice the swell of her ample, firm breasts. His palms ached with the effort not to touch.

He turned away, whistling to Sandy, and they headed down to the water's edge.

One thing he was pretty sure of now was that Nina was deliberately trying to seduce him. It was a novel feeling to be chased – he was usually the one doing the chasing.

And as he'd told her that first night, he was a man, and like most men he tended not to be able to think rationally when a sexy woman threw herself at him.

Right now his brain had ceased to think altogether and his body was taking over. It was asking questions like *'Why not?'* and *'What harm could it do?'*

Sure, unlike the other women he dated, he wouldn't be able to say "thank you" and walk away afterwards. At least, not for another five weeks. But how hard could it be to stay interested in one woman for a few weeks?

It would be like an all-you-can-eat-buffet, and then she'd be out of his life as soon as her training was over. After that, if she got the role in *Revelations,* she would be out of town for months on end for filming. Enough time for them both to move on.

As far as his body was concerned, this didn't have to be complicated. And as usual, his head was having a very hard time keeping his body from calling the shots.

Nina propped herself up on her elbows and watched Dom and Sandy frolic in the surf. She had to admit the sea looked calm and unintimidating today. It washed in and out the beach in a hypnotic rhythm.

She couldn't remember when last she'd felt this relaxed. In spite of the constant physical exertion of the last few days and the constant fizz and sizzle of sexual tension in her veins, she felt as if she were on vacation, as if she'd left the stress of her tanking career behind in her pristine, white apartment. It would still be there when she got back, but for this brief lull it felt good to have fun and find the joy in life again.

And a week of living with someone hadn't been as excruciating as she'd expected, either. Dom let her have her space when she needed it and didn't object if she didn't want to talk. With him she didn't feel as if she needed to be "on" all the time. He'd already seen her at her worst, so she could simply be herself, or as much of herself as she could ever risk being with another person.

She closed her eyes and breathed in deeply, the salty, sultry tang of the sea that reminded her of the scent of Dom's skin, and imagined trailing her tongue across his skin, licking, tasting...

Her eyes flew open.

He was running up the beach toward her, shirt now off, and when he sat, raining droplets on her, he sat close enough that she could feel the energy and vitality radiating off him. Sandy flopped down between them, panting hard, and she reached out to pet the dog.

"What are we doing today?" she asked, trying to stifle the raging lust buzzing through her. And failing.

"How do you feel about horses?"

"I enjoyed the *Flicka* books as a kid. Does that count?"

He flashed his crooked grin. "At least it means you don't yet have any bad habits we need to break. We'll be visiting friends of mine who have a horse ranch near the Santa Monica mountains."

He leaned on his side, resting on his elbow, his attention focused on her. The space between them shrank until nothing existed but the rise and fall of their breaths. He was all long, lean strength and muscle, and so utterly gorgeous. She watched one large droplet trail down over smooth, solid pecs before she yanked her eyes away, up over his freckled shoulders to his face.

But that was even worse. Because her gaze snagged on his. That emerald gaze pinned her, looked right into her.

She wanted madly, desperately, to lean into him, to kiss him.

Be brave. Do it.

He hadn't moved away, either.

This was her moment.

But she wasn't ready. She was still too scared. What if he discovered that she wasn't as perfect as her on-screen image? What if he saw right through the careful grooming to the girl underneath and was disappointed? What if he rejected her again?

With an effort, she dragged herself out of his enchantment and pushed herself up off the sand. Whistling to Sandy, she raced off down the beach with the wind at her heels.

When she glanced back, Dom had risen too, to give chase. She sped up, not wanting to be caught, not wanting him to look in her eyes and see her desire and her fear and her insecurities.

She didn't have a hope in hell of outrunning him. Dom caught her up and grabbed her around the waist, swinging her off her feet.

She shrieked, fighting against him, but what chance did she have against a *jiu jitsu* expert with more than twice her strength?

One thing at least she'd learned these last few days. She shifted her weight, catching him unawares and throwing him off-balance, and they collapsed in a heap on the wet sand, rolling together until he had her pinned beneath him. She looked up at him, eyes wide, breathless with laughter.

This last week he'd touched her a thousand times, but that had been nothing on the searing sizzle between them now. Today her bare legs and skimpy t-shirt were no barrier to the prime male body pressed against hers.

Neither spoke. Neither moved.

Then Sandy was on top of them, licking their faces, all exuberant excitement. Dom rolled off her and stood, extending a hand to help her up. Swallowing bitter disappointment, she took his hand. But when he pulled her to her feet, he caught her around her waist and didn't let go.

"Why are you running from me?" he demanded.

"I'm not running."

He looked down into her face and slowly shook his head. "Bullshit."

She could play the flirt, cock her head, and say something about how much fun it was to be chased. She could make a joke, or lie, or brush him off, or push him away.

She did none of these. The way he looked at her, he could already read her fear and insecurity. She tried to avert her gaze, but couldn't. He held her captive. "I could ask the same of you.

You've been running away from me all week. Don't you want me?"

His hands slid down from her waist, over her hips, to rest on her butt. With a gentle tug, he pulled her against him. "I want you."

The hardening at his groin was unmistakable.

"What's changed then?"

He shrugged. "I still think it's a bad idea. I'm your trainer. And I'm a cad." He lowered his head, traced his tongue along the edge of her mouth. "But you are a very hard woman to resist."

She pressed her lips against his as triumph soared through her. No more fear, only want and need. He kissed her back, both fierce and gentle at the same time, and there was no way he could deny now what he felt. Her hands settled on his ribs, splaying wide over the t-shirt that pulled tight over his abs.

A low hum vibrated through them, growing more insistent. Dom swore and pulled away. Through her daze, she registered that the hum was his cell phone. He ignored it.

"Answer it," she said.

"It can take a message."

But the moment was gone. The heat in her body fled in an instant as icy sensation slid down her spine, reminding her where they were. She pulled away, out of his embrace, and he let her.

With a frown, he pulled the still-ringing phone from his back pocket and answered it. The voice on the other end carried loud enough for Nina to hear. "Hi, handsome."

"Hi, Olivia."

Nina looked away.

"You free today? You want to come around?"

Great. A booty call.

"I can't. I'm working."

"Pity. Tonight, then?"

"I don't think I'm going to be able to make it. Another time, perhaps." He cut off the call.

Cold, crazy jealousy rose up from Nina's stomach. She forced it back. "I don't want to be a cock blocker. If you want to meet your girlfriend, go ahead." She said it lightly, careful not to look at him.

"She's not my girlfriend." He put the phone back in his pocket. "I like Olivia. She's uncomplicated."

The kind of woman who wouldn't ask him for anything more than he was willing to give. Nina swallowed the bile in her mouth and stepped away.

"But I don't want to see her. I'm here with you now."

If only. He might be here with her, but it was only because she was paying him for his time. Just like everyone else she'd met since she became famous. She couldn't trust anyone's attention any more. They all wanted something from her – money, a brush with fame, or an entry into her golden lifestyle.

Everyone loved the playful Nina. No one cared to know the real Nina, the person behind the carefully constructed image, the one with doubts and insecurities and an overwhelming fear of losing everything again.

Her chest ached. It was better this way. By keeping her real self walled up tight inside, she couldn't be hurt. She couldn't be exposed.

Which was why Dom should be such a safe option. He wanted complications even less than she did. He didn't want to be seen with her, didn't want ten minutes of fame for being the guy who banged Nina Alexander. He only wanted her for her body.

Simple, right?

Except it wasn't that simple anymore. She wanted to be more than another notch on his bedpost. A girl had to have a little self-respect, after all.

So what was she thinking throwing herself at Dom?

Her body might be screaming "*Take me!*", and he would willingly oblige, but how would her head feel about it when her pheromones finally crashed back down to normal?

Better to call it quits now, before he had the chance to see every non-airbrushed inch of her. He'd certainly had enough experience with women to be able to draw comparisons.

She plastered on her brightest smile, a smile that owed more than a little to the ditsy waitress she'd played on TV for four years running. "We should get moving. They'll be expecting us at the horse ranch."

They jogged back towards his house, not talking, not making eye contact. After a quick shower and a change, they headed out once again. Not on Dom's bike this time, but in the Jeep. She was relieved not to have to endure the intimacy of a bike ride, but the blaring music on the Jeep's sound system did nothing to fill the awkward silence between them.

Chapter Seven

Horse riding had to be the most excruciating thing she'd ever done. She bounced up and down, clinging to the saddle, feeling like a dead weight, while her butt and thighs grew increasingly raw. It didn't help that Dom's horse-master friend Ross had a pre-teen daughter who could do tricks in the saddle, while Nina could barely manage to stay on.

By the time she'd mastered the basics of how to sit right, how to hold the reins, and how to move in rhythm with the horse, it was already past midday.

Dismounting after the ride was something else entirely though. Her legs were mushy as jello and Dom had to catch her around her waist as she slid to the ground.

"Thanks," she said, hanging on to him, her hands lingering on the hard muscle of his upper arms a moment longer than necessary. But she kept her head down, letting her ball cap obscure her face so he couldn't see her eyes.

They followed Ross onto the shaded verandah of the ranch house. Nina had never been more pleased to see a cold beer in her life.

"Not bad for a newbie," Ross's wife, Gianna, said as she waved them to sit for lunch.

She was a delicate thing, slender as a pixie, and exactly the kind of woman who made Nina feel lumpy and three sizes too large. But when she smiled, full of warmth and welcome, Nina found it hard to hate her.

They ate lunch together, Nina sitting quietly and picking at her salad as she listened to the good-natured banter around her. Dominic was the same person with them as he was on set, or with his family, or alone with her. There was no difference between public Dom and private Dom.

He was lively, teasing, confident, a magnetic physical presence. People gravitated to him, like moths to a bright flame. And she was just another moth, scalding her wings as she circled him.

Heaven help her, but she felt like a giddy kid with stars in her eyes. And if she ever met Olivia, she might want to scratch her eyes out.

"So what role is Dom training you up for?" Gianna asked, leaning back in her chair and stretching with the elegance and agility of a cat.

"Sonia in *Revelations*."

Gianna's eyes widened. "I didn't think they'd cast the role yet."

"They haven't. But I want it more than anything."

Gianna's smile lit up her face. "You and me both. Those books were incredible, and Sonia has got to be the most kick-ass character ever."

"Exactly!"

"I really hope you get it. You can put in a good word and get Dom in there as the stunt coordinator, then our crew can all work on it too." Gianna's eyes shone as she turned to Dom. "You haven't committed to any other projects yet, have you?"

He shook his head. "I told you. I'm taking a break from work for a while."

It took Nina a moment to decipher the looks on his friends' faces. An odd mix of disbelief and protective concern. She didn't for a moment believe he was taking a break so he could train her. There was something else going on here.

101

But Dom's expression had shut down entirely and she couldn't fathom what it was.

"You always work together as a team?" she asked Ross, hoping to ease the sudden tension in the air.

Ross nodded, his frown lifting as he focused back on her. "Everything we do involves a high level of trust. Stunt people often put their lives in one another's hands, so we're very careful who we work with. We build networks with people we trust, people we know will have our backs and who won't take unnecessary risks. Our team is as close as our family, sometimes even closer."

Nina heard an echo in his words. In the *Revelations* books Sonia built herself a team just like that; a team of warriors who put their lives in one another's hands, closer than family.

She blinked away a sudden sting in her eyes. It had been a very long time since she'd trusted anyone. She'd seen people turn savage for survival, and even when survival wasn't at stake, people turned savage. She couldn't even trust the people on her payroll to have her back.

And it had been even longer still since she'd felt part of a family.

"What do you have planned for the rest of the afternoon?" Gianna asked, placing fresh beers in front of the men, and re-filling her and Nina's glasses with sweet home-made lemonade.

"Rest?" Nina asked hopefully.

The others laughed.

"What did you have in mind?" Dom asked.

A grin passed between the two of them that Nina didn't like at all. Gianna's mouth kicked up into a smile. "I'd like to see how Nina swings."

Nina choked, and the others around the table dissolved into shouts of laughter. Heat flooded her cheeks.

"Not that kind of swinging," Dom said. "Gianna's a trapeze artist, and she gives lessons. You interested?"

Was she interested? She'd wanted to learn how to swing on the trapeze since the first time her parents had taken her to the circus.

But… "I'm a little heavy."

More laughter. She screwed up her eyes and tried not to let the wave of hurt and insecurity wash over her.

"You are NOT heavy," Gianna said, passing a critical eye over her. "I've had Dom up there swinging with me, and he's no lightweight, I can assure you. It's all about core strength and rhythm. Come on, give it a try."

A beach run. Horse-riding. Now acrobatics. "You're trying to kill me." She looked at Dom through narrowed eyes, but he only shrugged.

"There are demons trying to kill Sonia and she doesn't stop to rest. You want the role, you'll do this."

He was right. She'd said she didn't only want to be in good shape, she wanted to get into Sonia's headspace. In the books Sonia had to face one unremitting challenge after another, without the same chance to rest and recover that Nina got every night. She should do this.

It was the assured look in Dom's eyes that decided her. He wouldn't encourage her to do this if he didn't think she could, would he?

"Okay, I'll give it a try."

Gianna took her inside to change into snug yoga pants and a leotard, and Nina tied her hair back.

"Perfect!" Gianna said, giving her the once-over.

Nina wasn't so sure. She didn't have even a dab of lipstick on. And her wide hips and heavy breasts looked even bigger than usual when she stood beside the elfin acrobat.

Gianna led her out to the far side of the house and Nina gasped. A real-live outdoor trapeze stood in the yard, complete with ladders, rigging and thick, cushiony mattresses.

"You're not afraid of heights?" Gianna asked.

Nina shook her head.

Before Gianna allowed her anywhere near the trapeze, she first had to do warm-up and stretching exercises. Then Ross attached her to a safety line, which only made her pulse race faster, and she climbed behind Gianna to the narrow platform at least 20 feet above ground.

"You not coming?" she called down to Dom.

He waved back. "I'll be over here in the shade enjoying another beer. Don't worry. You're in good hands. Gianna's an excellent teacher."

Bastard.

From the smiling look Gianna shot her, she supposed she must have said it out loud.

"I wouldn't allow Dom up here anyway," she said to Nina. "No alcohol before you swing."

"I had a beer," Nina pointed out.

Gianna smiled. "You didn't finish it. You don't drink much, do you?"

Nina shook her head and carried on climbing.

She wasn't afraid of heights, but the platform was really narrow. She looked down and her heart leapt into her throat. "There's no safety net."

"There's no need for a net. This is a *petit volant* rig. It's not as high as a big rig trapeze, so the mattresses are more than enough. But you won't fall."

Nina wished she felt the same confidence.

Gianna's 12-year-old daughter shimmied up the ladder on the opposite side of the rig, agile as a monkey. Nina watched her in awe.

I can do this. She breathed in deeply. "What do I do?" she asked, earning a beaming smile from her instructor.

"Watch first, then we'll let you have a turn." Gianna undid the swing that was tied beside them, grabbed hold with her bare hands and leapt out over the void. On the far side, her daughter did the same. They established a rhythm, swinging backward and forward and Nina tried hard to concentrate on the instructions Gianna gave as she swung to and fro. But it was difficult. Both mother and daughter flew through the air with such grace and confidence, it was like watching poetry in motion.

Nina didn't have a hope of looking anything like them.

"Keep your legs together," Gianna called. "Long on the way down, short on the way up."

When she returned to the platform, she showed Nina how to hold the bar. "Stick your chest out, look ahead, bend your knees a little, count to three and off you go."

The butterfly effect in Nina's stomach made her want to throw up. But she counted to three and jumped.

She swung, focusing on keeping her legs together, on not looking down. A few swings to and fro and she began to feel the rhythm. *She was flying!*

The gentle pressure of the belt around her waist, with Ross at the other end of the safety line, gave her confidence to swing higher and further, as Gianna called encouragement from the sidelines.

She was five years old again and flying high, laughing and shouting for her father to push the swing higher and higher.

She let go her trepidation and her heart soared free.

At last her trajectory slowed and Gianna caught the bar, enabling Nina to get her feet back on the platform. She laughed with the exhilaration and the endorphin thrill, and Gianna laughed with her.

"So what do you think?" her instructor asked.

"That was incredible!"

"That's what we call the flying trapeze. Next we'll do what's known as the swinging trapeze. Instead of leaping off the platform and letting gravity do the rest, this time you're going to jump and grab the bar, and get it swinging from a standstill. Just like taking off on a playground swing."

A playground swing on steroids.

Again, Gianna and her daughter demonstrated what she needed to do, and again Nina did it. It was remarkably easy once she let go of her fear.

105

She really could do this. Up here, defying gravity, she didn't feel heavy. She felt light as air, and graceful, too.

Sooner than she expected, Gianna had her hanging upside down from the bar, holding on with nothing but her knees.

Out of the corner of her eye she noticed Dom. No longer sitting beneath the trees, but standing with his arm shielding his eyes from the sun's glare as he squinted up to watch her, a distinct furrow creasing his forehead.

She swung out and on the far platform Gianna's daughter pushed off a beat later. She matched the rhythmic to and fro set by the young girl. Her heart in her throat, she watched as the girl let go the swing, reaching out both hands towards her. She caught the extended hands in the grip Gianna had shown her, and laughed with triumph as they swung together.

"Very good," Gianna called. "Now at the apex of your swing, when you're right above the centre of the mattress, you let her go and she'll show you how to do a bullet drop."

Nina did as she was told and watched as the young girl did a graceful drop into the mats below. As she hit the ground, she rolled, just as Dom had been teaching Nina to do all week.

"That's enough for your first day," Gianna said, helping her back onto the platform. Nina was just a little relieved. Though the adrenalin still flowed through her, making her feel more alive than she ever had, her arms had begun to protest and her core muscles, muscles she'd hardly known existed a week ago, were also feeling the strain. And she was sure her hands and the backs of her knees were going to blister.

Gianna explained the simple dismount, then demonstrated how to do it, dropping effortlessly into the waiting mats below.

Nina stood alone on the high platform and looked down. The drop no longer seemed so high, and she was almost reluctant to fall back down to earth, to lose this sensation of freedom and weightlessness.

But she did as she'd been told. She swung out from the platform and let go in mid-air, crossing her arms over her chest and falling backwards. For a moment, she was truly free, the wind sweeping past her, then the mats rose up to meet her, too quickly. She bounced a couple of times before coming to rest, not quite the graceful landing the others had achieved. Next time.

She lay still for a moment, eyes closed as she tried to hang onto that feeling of euphoria, until the mattress dipped beside her with the weight of someone moving towards her.

She opened her eyes, expecting Gianna. Dom grinned as he stood over her.

"Well? Am I still a bastard for making you do this?"

His eyes lit up with irrepressible laughter as he smiled his crooked grin and she wanted nothing more than to seal this momentous feeling with a deep, passionate, all-or-nothing kiss. He must have seen it in her eyes because even though he held out his hand to help her up, he stepped away, putting space between them. She ignored his hand and pushed herself up off the mats.

"Yes, you're still a bastard."

Gianna beamed at her pupil as she approached. "You're a natural! And you'll make a great Sonia. The producers would have to be idiots not to give you a chance."

Nina was used to compliments. Everyone told movie stars they were good at everything. The golf instructor who'd taught her to swing a golf club a few movies back had told her she was a natural. She'd known he was lying.

But flying on the trapeze did feel as natural as breathing.

All the way back to the house, the two women kept up an excited chatter. Only once they'd changed into normal street clothes and rejoined the men did their conversation slow.

Nina's high hadn't abated much. She still felt as if she were flying. Someone should patent acrobatics as a cure for all forms of depression, because it was impossible not to feel excited to be alive with this zing in her veins.

Ross and Gianna walked them to the Jeep. As they reached the parked car, Dom tossed her the keys. "I've been drinking. You'll need to drive."

Out on the roads among other drivers? In a stick-shift? She climbed into the driver's seat and slid the key into the ignition. She could do this. She could do anything.

She'd flown. She could drive. And tonight, when she got him home, she was going to kiss Dom, whether he liked it or not. And hopefully a whole lot more than kiss. Her body hummed at the thought.

"Will we see you tonight?" Ross asked, closing her door.

"What's happening tonight?"

Gianna answered. "Every Saturday night whoever on our team is around and not working, we get together for drinks at an Irish pub in Santa Monica. There's live music and good beer."

"And excellent single Irish malt," Ross chimed in.

"Sounds like fun." Just what the doctor ordered. A chance to dress up and get wild and get laid.

"You're supposed to be out of town. What if someone recognizes you?" Dom asked.

Gianna eyed him. "It's unlike you to say 'no' to a night out. What gives?"

Dom looked at Nina. "You're not tired? I thought you might want to have a quiet night at home." He sounded hopeful and she smothered a grin. Then she caught the glance between Ross and Gianna – as if they were adding two and two and coming up with eight. Dom must have caught the look too, because he scowled.

"How can I feel tired when I feel so *alive*?" she said. "I'd love to go."

Dom shrugged. "I guess we'll see you later, then."

'What gives?' was that Dom did not feel much like sharing Nina with anyone this evening. Who would have thought the life and soul of every party would prefer to stay home on a Saturday night? But it wasn't as much the place as the person he wanted to stay in for.

And he suspected Nina on this adrenalin high would be trouble.

He gritted his teeth as he paced the living room waiting for her to appear. When she did, he *really* did not want to take her out. He'd been right about trouble.

Her newly blonde hair was tumbled messily into a knot on her head, one of those casual dos that had probably taken more than half an hour to get right. She'd done her eyes all big and smoky. And the dress...

"Jeans might draw less attention," he suggested. His mouth felt almost too dry to form the words.

"I don't feel like jeans tonight." With a slight swagger to her hips, she crossed the room. God, she smelled even better than she looked.

"Vicki certainly didn't pack that dress for you." He eyed the sheer black fabric that clung to her hips and thighs. It was a wrap-around dress that dipped between her breasts, emphasizing every single enchanting curve. And it barely reached mid-thigh.

Vicki was more a jeans and tee girl.

"No, she didn't. Wendy insisted, though. She said you never know when a girl is going to need her Little Black Dress."

Thank you, Wendy. He swallowed and held out his arm to her. "Shall we go?"

"It'll have to be the Jeep," she warned. "My hair won't stand up to helmet head."

"We won't need either," he said. "The pub's not that far, so I usually walk it." The walk home, with the fresh breeze blowing in off the sea, was usually a great way to sober up after any over-indulgence.

"Are you ready?" she asked.

Was he ever! Though not for going out and sharing her with a pub full of horny men, and there were more than enough of those in his circle of friends. One drink. Just one drink and he was bringing her home so they could pick up where they'd left

109

off when his damned cell phone rang.

The Irish-themed pub was Dom's regular hang-out spot, less than a mile from his home and a couple of blocks from the beach. When they reached the boardwalk, she paused. "I can't walk all the way in these shoes."

She slid out of her high heels to carry them in her hand. He'd never met an actress willing to walk barefoot to a party before. In public. But then, if there was one thing he'd learned in this past week, Nina was no ordinary actress. She was no ordinary woman. She was one in a million.

She deserved a man who was one in a million, too, and that certainly wasn't him, no matter what his body had thought on the beach this morning.

It was a perfect evening, neither too hot nor too cold, the air clear. Twilight had fallen, and gaudy lights spilled from the store fronts onto the crowded pavement. The air hung heavy with the scent of fast foods, and loud music thumped, different beats blaring from each store they passed. Voices and laughter rose over the music, as if the whole world was ready to party tonight.

This was nothing like their relaxed morning runs along the beach, when most of the world still slept, but instead of enjoying the raucous carnival atmosphere, Nina set a brisk pace as if in a hurry to get where they were going. He soon understood why.

"Hey, aren't you…?" someone called through the crowd.

And then "Nina! Over here!"

She carried on walking as if she hadn't heard, and when he looked back over his shoulder, she hissed at him "Don't look. Don't make eye contact!"

Then someone tried to grab her arm. Dom swung around, gripping the hand until it let go Nina's arm.

"Ouch!" a woman yelped.

"Don't, Dom!" Nina begged, her voice low and urgent. He let go.

"I am so sorry," Nina said, smiling at her assailant. "We were in a bit of a hurry."

110

How could she smile at a complete stranger who'd just grabbed her? Dom waited impatiently as she signed autographs for the woman and her friend and made small talk.

"Why didn't you just tell her to piss off?" he asked as they hurried on at last.

"And have her tell the press that I'm rude and my bodyguard attacked her?" She shook her head. "Most people respect boundaries, but some people forget what's appropriate. They think because they've seen you on the TV screens in their own homes that they know you, that you belong to them."

He'd seen Christian mobbed many times, but somehow that had been different. Most of the time, Christian loved the attention, and when he didn't want it he just gave fans The Look and they backed away. But Christian had been a trained fighter. Nina was a woman, and not a particularly fierce one at that. Maybe a tougher public image and an ability to fight back would come in useful in her personal life as well as her professional life.

Though if he were honest, he'd never resented the intrusion of Christian's fans because he hadn't minded sharing Christian's attention. He very much resented having to share Nina's.

The rest of their walk he scanned the crowded boardwalk for trouble. They were stopped twice more and each time Nina smiled and chatted, putting in more effort than a Starbucks' server, but he didn't miss the tension in her shoulders, or the way her smile seemed forced.

He'd never felt so helpless, and a mile had never seemed so far.

He only relaxed his vigilance as they reached the pub and he held the door open for her, waited as she stepped back into her impossibly high heels. The added height did more than help her look him in the eyes. In the space of a heartbeat the woman before him changed. Gone was the amiable, easygoing woman who'd chatted with her fans. She straightened her shoulders, wriggled her hips, and set a flirty smile in place. This was the Trouble look he'd been afraid of.

Then they stepped into another world of low, timber-beamed ceilings and dark, hardwood floors. Part of the bar's charm was that it reminded him of the British pubs he'd visited during film shoots abroad. The other part of its charm was that it was as unpretentious as anything in LA could be. The tables were scarred, the music was of the sing-along variety, and the waitresses actually smiled.

He'd barely stepped through the door behind Nina when one of said waitresses stopped in his path. "You made it," she said, pressing herself against him.

"Hi, Olivia." Though he aimed to kiss her cheek, she turned her head so her lips met his.

"Shall I get your usual?" she purred.

He nodded and disentangled her arm from his waist. They had an on-again, off-again sex-only relationship that lasted only as long as one of them wasn't with anyone else, and it had always seemed a pretty good arrangement. But tonight he wasn't interested. There was only one woman he could even think of making love to right now, to the point where the thought consumed him – and that was the woman studiously avoiding all eye contact.

They'd barely made it a few steps further into the room before another of the waitresses sidled up to him.

"I'll have a beer," Nina said, forestalling her.

With a curt nod for Nina and a wink for him, the waitress turned away and headed to the bar.

"Is there any woman in here you *haven't* slept with?" Nina muttered, still not meeting his gaze.

Only you. "In my defense, there aren't that many women in here," he answered.

He led her across the room towards the corner where a rowdy group was already gathered. A shout of welcome went up.

"You're late," Evan said, raising his voice over the noise.

"Hi, everyone." Dom pulled Nina forward. "This is Nina Alexander. Nina, this is everyone."

Someone whistled. Someone else clapped him on the back.

112

And Jacob, the youngest member of their crew, practically shoved Vicki out the way to clear a space for Nina at his side. "You're even prettier off the movie screen," he said, smiling at her. "What are you doing with this lug?"

"I've hired him to train me for a role," she replied, smiling back at Jacob as she slid into the space he'd made for her.

Disappointment pierced Dom's chest. So she still saw him as the hired hand?

Then she looked up at him, through her long eyelashes, and there was challenge in her gaze, as if she were saying *anything you can do, I can do better.*

"I bet you're a smooth, rich Merlot kind of girl," Jacob said, holding up a hand to wave to the bartender.

Nina glanced at the Budweiser Olivia had just handed to Dom. The other waitress seemed to have forgotten her order. "Actually, I'd rather have one of those. But make mine a light."

Dom smiled. He could see how she'd earned her down-to-earth reputation. His smile didn't last long. Jacob slid a little closer to Nina, brushing her arm with his. "I didn't realize you were from the South. You don't speak with a Southern accent in any of your movies." He leaned in. "I love a woman with a Southern accent."

Dom's fists clenched, but he reined in the white-hot anger that suddenly coursed through him. If she hadn't wanted his protection from complete strangers on the boardwalk, then he doubted she'd want to be at the center of a bar brawl.

Jacob continued blithely. "I grew up in Alabama. Where are you from?"

"Louisiana."

Dom frowned. Her IMDB biography said she was from Iowa. Though it hadn't been the most detailed bio, little more than the names of her parents and the high school she'd graduated from. He would have remembered if there'd been more.

Nina took the bottle the bartender placed on the bar counter beside her. Ignoring the ice-frosted pint glass next to it, she raised the bottle to her mouth and swigged. Then she licked her lips and set the bottle back down. Both the barman and Jacob swallowed. Dom was pretty sure he did, too.

He downed a gulp of his own beer, but the alcohol didn't help.

Nor did the next one that Olivia handed him half an hour later. He didn't bother to check if Nina wanted another. He didn't need to, with Jacob dancing attendance on her.

Jacob was nearly ten years younger than him, closer to Nina in age, and with pretty-boy features all the girls loved. He was also rapidly gaining a reputation like Dom's. Usually that fact didn't irk Dom. Tonight it did. If she didn't deserve a bore like Paul de Angelo, Nina certainly didn't deserve a heartless womanizer like Jacob.

Or himself.

He probably should have rescued her from Jacob's clutches, but there was no way he could do it without looking like a tom cat in heat.

Which would play straight into her hands. He knew what game she was playing. He'd helped enough women play it over the years, though he'd usually been the patsy the woman flirted with in order to gain the attention of the man she really wanted.

Jealousy. Until now he hadn't known what an ugly, twisted emotion it was.

Vicki slipped into the spot beside him and placed her arm through his. "So how are things going with you and Nina?"

"As you can see, she hasn't given up yet. She's tougher than she looks. In fact, if the bottom ever falls out of the acting thing, she'd probably make a pretty good stunt woman."

"I don't mean the training, I mean you and her. Have you had a lovers' tiff already?"

Dom's back stiffened. "There's nothing between us."

"Then why do you look like you want to punch something, and why does she keep shooting you little glances while she flirts with every other man in here?"

He shrugged, though he knew the answer very well. Nina was punishing him. And it was working.

Vicki's eyes narrowed as she looked from Dom to Nina. "She reminds me of me… do you remember when I spent that whole night flirting with you to force Ben to make a move on me?" Vicki clapped a hand over her mouth. "Oh my…! You haven't slept with her yet!"

He scowled. Forget that it was exactly what he'd wanted to do before fate, in the form of a phone call, had intervened. "That would be a spectacularly bad idea."

"Why? She's obviously into you."

"And I'm me, which means I'll nail any woman in the immediate vicinity, right?" He hadn't meant to sound so bitter.

"That's not what I meant." Vicki sighed. "I meant that it's clear you're into her too. You're both available, you're both adults, so what's stopping you?"

"I'm her trainer. It wouldn't be right." On at least a couple of levels. He drained his beer bottle. "She deserves a man who'll treat her right." A man who wasn't damaged goods both emotionally and physically, but since he'd done such a good job hiding the extent of his injury from his team he wasn't about to reveal it now.

Vicki chuckled. "If I remember correctly, you're pretty good at treating a woman right."

He shook his head. "Nina isn't the kind of girl who'll have spontaneous sex in the dark corner of a club or on the back seat of a car." Which was what most women wanted from him.

"Wanna bet?" Vicki smiled. "She's just had a very public break-up. What she needs now is a gorgeous sex object who can make her feel like a desirable woman again. And if there's one thing you're good at, that's it."

Yeah, that was him: the sex object.

Vicki leaned in close to whisper in his ear, and Dom didn't miss the quick sidelong glance Nina sent them. "Besides, you're not 20 anymore. You might want to try regular sex in a bed sometime." She slid her arm out of his. "I'd better get back to my husband before the famous movie actress claws my eyes out with her bare hands."

With a laugh she moved away and he frowned after her.

Vicki was right. He was getting old.

He had to admit, as much fun as he'd had in his life, the novelty was wearing thin. Most women tended to have their fun with him, then they moved on as soon as they found Mr. Right. Like Vicki and Ben. From the day he'd introduced them, neither had even looked at anyone else.

One day Olivia would meet someone too and stop calling. That was always the way it worked. They were grateful to him for being there when they needed him, but as soon as they no longer needed him...

Nina would be just the same. And her attention span wouldn't last as long as Olivia's had. Like every other actress he'd known, Nina wanted him only because he hadn't dropped at her feet. But as soon as that changed, she'd lose interest and be gone.

He rubbed his face.

He knew the score. Because he was just the same. But just once it would be nice to find a woman for whom he was the end result rather than a means to an end. For whom he was more than just a plaything.

A week ago he'd told Nina in no uncertain terms he only wanted women who weren't looking to settle down, women who wanted nothing from him but uncomplicated sex. And here he was contemplating something very, very different.

And with completely the wrong woman. There was no way a successful A-list actress would even consider a washed-up stunt man like himself. A man like him would never fit in with her ambitions.

Across the circle Jacob now had his arm around Nina's waist. She didn't push him away and Dom scowled at his empty beer bottle. He had no one to blame but himself. He'd known the mood she was in. He'd been there himself often enough. How many times had he stood at this same bar, revved-up on the high of a stunt gone well and picked up a convenient woman to help him burn off that excess adrenalin?

And after a week of pushing her away, he could hardly blame her for turning to someone else to burn it off. But it didn't mean he had to like it. And it didn't mean he had to stand here and watch.

He needed something a whole lot stronger than beer tonight.

Chapter Eight

Nina resisted the urge to stamp her foot in frustration as Dom turned and walked away to the bar.

What more did she have to do? She'd thrown herself at him over and over again, she'd dressed to kill, and now she'd spent an hour flirting with his friends in the vain hope he'd stride on over and take her away from here. Preferably to his bed.

What did it take to bring out the Neanderthal in a man these days?

Jacob's hand slid from her waist to her butt. She should push him away. He was good looking, and she had no doubt he knew how to please a woman, how to ease this buzz in her blood, but she didn't want him. Any more than he wanted her.

Jacob liked the idea of her, the idea of scoring with a famous actress, but she could have been any one of a dozen nameless actresses and it would have made no difference to him. And he *would* be disappointed if he learned that beneath the larger-than-life image she was just an ordinary girl with ordinary weaknesses.

But Dom was different. He'd seen her first thing in the morning and without make-up. He'd even seen her sweat. And still the undeniable sensual tension sizzled between them.

Right now she couldn't take that unrequited sizzle another moment longer. She needed a moment alone, a moment to regroup. She pulled out of Jacob's grasp, "Please excuse me."

The restrooms were behind the bar, down a long, dark passage that smelled of stale beer and detergent. She locked herself inside the tiny cubicle and stared at her reflection in the streaked mirror.

A stranger stared back.

A wild-eyed stranger with platinum-blonde hair.

She couldn't splash her face without messing up her make-up, so she let the cold water run over her wrists and rubbed wet fingertips over the back of her neck.

It didn't help. She still felt feverish and excited. Alcohol zinged in her veins along with the residual adrenalin high.

Who was she kidding? This wasn't entirely alcohol or adrenalin. This was Dominic Kelly, the man who'd been bringing out wild urges in her and making her want to do bad, bad things from the day they'd met.

But what if he rejected her again? Stardom was no guarantee against rejection. If anything, it made rejection worse, because who could she turn to without the risk of her feelings being splashed out there for the whole world to see, as if the public had the right to her mortification?

She met the wild-eyed gaze in the mirror again. She'd faced water obstacles, fired guns, learned to skid a car, and flown on a trapeze. So why the hell was she hiding out in the restroom, afraid?

She should be out there going after what she wanted. The same way she'd done with her career, with every activity Dom had set her these last ten days. All or nothing.

To hell with Olivia and every other woman he'd ever been with. To hell with a bar full of strangers. To hell with the possibility of rejection. She was going to go out there and she was going to take what she wanted. And if she had to, she'd do it in front of everyone. She would kiss Dominic Kelly until he couldn't say "no" any more.

Swinging open the door, she charged out into the dimly lit corridor, colliding with an obstacle she was sure hadn't been

119

there before.

Dom grabbed her arm to steady her.

"You were gone a long time," he said.

"You came looking for me?" She made her eyes big and round. It was a look most men couldn't resist.

Dom's expression didn't change at all. "It's time I took you home."

Home to *his* bed, or to the big, cold, empty bed in the guest room?

"Did you know that Jacob is a parkour *traceur*?" She was proud of that word. Even prouder that she managed it without slurring.

And that was definitely a reaction. Dom's eyes narrowed. *Yes!*

She reached up on tiptoe, pulled his face down to her, and pressed her lips to his.

Taken by surprise, he didn't respond for a heart-achingly tenuous moment. Then he wrapped his arms around her waist and lifted her clear off her feet, deepening the kiss as he did so. She clung to him, her hands sliding to the back of his neck and she opened her mouth to him, sighing her pleasure.

He tasted of whiskey, dangerous and foreign, and oh-so wickedly sinful. She drank him in, his kiss, the feel of his hands on her, one curved beneath her butt, holding her up, the other on her thigh, sliding beneath her skirt that had ridden high. He backed her against the cold, hard wall.

She moaned, writhing into his touch, grinding against him, wanting so much more, needing so much more than even this overpowering, intoxicating kiss could satisfy.

His free hand stroked the sensitized skin of her inner thigh, moving higher, to the edge of her panties, rubbing over her clit through the sheer fabric.

She moaned again, desperate, pleading, and his hand stilled.

He broke the kiss and pulled his hand away.

"Don't stop!"

He dropped his head to her shoulder. "That's the alcohol talking.

120

You've had more than you're used to."

She shook her head. "I'm not drunk, just fuzzy. It's nice to be fuzzy. Please? I've wanted this for longer than you can know." She wasn't above begging.

"Not here." He drew in a ragged breath. "I don't want our first time to be like this, hurried, in a place where anyone can find us and interrupt. I want to take my time and enjoy you."

First time. Meaning there would be more?

Her already frenetically beating heart sped up. "Then take me home."

Slowly he eased her back down to her feet, righted her dress, then he held her face between his hands. The skin of his hands was deliciously rough against her cheeks.

"Are you sure about this? Because I'm not such a gentleman that I'll be able to hold back once we start. I am *very* good at following through."

She moistened her lips and his grip on her tightened, sending another rush of dizzying lust through her. Her mouth quirked, just the teensiest bit. "Then prove it."

He pulled her down the passage to the main room of the bar. Very reluctantly, she let go his hand before they entered the room, terrified that if she let go he would change his mind and she would lose this moment and her courage.

The live band was only just setting up on the low stage. Dom dropped a few bills on the table where the others sat, grabbed her bag and his jacket, and with the most hurried of farewells he hustled her out of the bar.

Caught up as she still was in the spell of his kiss, she managed to catch the look of approval on Vicki's face, the bewildered look on Jacob's. Olivia's disappointment.

She couldn't help gloating a little.

Then they were outside on the sidewalk and the sea breeze whispered around them. He pulled her against him, wrapping an arm around her shoulder and holding her tight as he bent in for a quick, rough kiss.

When he let her go, he handed her his leather jacket against the cooler night air, and pulled his cell phone from the back pocket of his jeans. "I need to call us a cab. I don't want to risk walking you home again."

She shook her head. "As much as I hate the intrusion, I'm not going to stop living my life the way I want out of fear of a few fans. I want to walk on the beach with you." The way they had that first night. "Please?" This time when she rounded her eyes, Dom caved.

Avoiding the bright lights of the boardwalk, they headed straight to the cover of the beach's darkness, walking hand-in-hand along the sand, just another couple out on a Saturday night.

When they arrived at Dom's yard gate, her ardor hadn't cooled any, and clearly neither had his. He pulled her up the stairs to the deck, through the glass door and into the living room.

Then he crushed her against him and claimed her lips in a mind-blowing kiss that stole her breath and made the world tilt on its axis. She bunched her hands in his t-shirt, pulling him close and holding tight. There was no way he would back out of this now.

He'd promised her he would follow through and if there was one thing she knew about Dominic Kelly, it was that he was a man of his word.

When he broke their kiss it was only to pull his t-shirt over his head. She sighed greedily at the sight of him, ran her hands over his shoulders, his chest, his arms, glorying at last in the freedom to touch him, to explore the tiny nicks and scars that were the marks of his profession. His nipples were hard and dark against his skin, and she licked at them, reveling in the shudder that passed through his body.

His hands slid down her back, to rest on her butt, exactly where Jacob's had been not so long ago, but this time she had no thought of brushing them away.

She trailed her tongue down over his skin, over his abs and

down towards his stomach, and he stiffened.

"Slow down," he said. His voice sounded rough and unsteady. "I want to get you upstairs, to my bed."

She took the hand he held out and followed him up the stairs to the master suite, to the one part of the house she had never yet seen.

Light filtered through from the master bathroom, casting a mellow glow over the enormous room, understatedly decorated in beach-house whites and blues.

Sandy lay on a large cushion in a corner of the room. She lifted her head off her paws as they entered, tail wagging furiously.

"Out, girl," Dom said softly, holding the door open. "You'll have to sleep downstairs tonight." With a woebegone expression, the dog trotted down the stairs and Dom shut the door, turning to face Nina.

He didn't switch on the lights. Instead, he left her standing in the middle of the floor of the vast room as he crossed to the glass doors and opened the shutters. Moonlight spilled into the room. Beyond the doors lay a wrap-around balcony and beyond that, over the rooftops of his neighbors, lay the Pacific.

He turned and looked at her, and the moonlight illuminated his face and the gorgeous contours of his body. No crooked grin now, just a slow, heated smile that set her blood boiling.

"Undress for me," he ordered, burning eyes watching her from across the room.

There was a reason she always insisted on body doubles for sex scenes. She wasn't comfortable being seen naked. But the alcohol seemed to have blurred the edges of her usual fears, because instead of trepidation, his command made her feel powerful beyond measure.

She unwrapped the ties at her waist, opening the wrap-around dress to reveal first one breast, then the other. Then she dropped the dress to the floor. No granny pants tonight. No bra tonight, either. Beneath the dress she wore nothing but the sexiest, tiniest black-lace thong she owned. She really owed Wendy for packing her bags with such foresight.

Dom wetted his lips. "And your hair?" he prompted.

She slid her hands into her hair, undoing the careful work of a few hours ago, shaking out her tresses so that they fell loose about her shoulders.

Dom's breath hitched, but still he didn't move.

"Your shoes..."

She stepped out of the shoes. Far from feeling the loss of height, power surged through her. He did nothing but look for a long moment, and the look in his eyes made her feel like a goddess. Now she understood what all the fuss was about. The gift that Dom gave every woman he slept with.

She held her chin high and basked in the glory of being desired.

"Come here."

She crossed the room to stand before him. Dom placed a hand on her hip and pulled her close. His other hand stroked over her bare breast, the roughness of his palm stinging her skin to life beneath his touch.

"Do you know how beautiful you are?"

She managed to nod.

"And can you feel what you do to me?" He placed her hand over the bulge in his jeans. She shuddered. That made at least three times she'd felt the size of him. But now this was real. This was truly going to happen.

She rubbed her hand over the bulge and he moaned, stilling her fingers. "You first, sweetheart. I want to see you come first."

She shivered. Her orgasm had always been elusive. But if Dom couldn't get her there, with the way her body felt right now, on the verge of combustion, then no man could.

He backed her up against the bed, laid her down on her back. Then he knelt over her and kissed her. The tension inside her melted, his kiss wiping away all thought and all fear.

His hand was on her breast again, pinching, kneading, circling.

A spasm of desire shot through her, straight to her core, and she pressed herself up against him. His hand slid lower, over her stomach and down to the lace between her legs, as his mouth replaced his hand on her breast. He sucked, drawing her nipple into his warm, wet mouth, and she arched into him.

His palm pressed down on her clit, through the lace. She pushed against it, the rough scratch of the fabric adding to the pleasure building between her thighs, starting to coil outwards like the first lazy smoke from a fire.

She parted her legs, opening herself up to him. Hooking a finger beneath the lace edge, he lifted the fabric clear away and cool air rushed in, caressing her tender, inflamed skin. He brushed his thumb over her clit, stroking, teasing, and she moaned, louder now, more needy, more desperate.

Her head rolled back and she closed her eyes, her entire attention focused on that insanely slow, gentle brush of his thumb over the bundle of nerves so primed for him that she could see nothing else, hear nothing else.

With a gentle nip at her breast, he removed his mouth and slid down her body. His tongue grazed over her clit and she cried out.

No worries that she wouldn't reach orgasm tonight. With just that slow, sensual slide of his tongue she was already on the edge.

He licked and teased and sucked, and she writhed against him, her body riding the growing wave that built, built, built, then crashed over her, engulfing her. Then her body spasmed, incredible waves rolling through her as she lost herself to the sensations.

His tongue stilled. He placed one gentle kiss on her still-throbbing clit before he pulled away.

Through the daze of her afterglow she felt the bed dip and rise as he moved away. She raised her head, swallowing as she watched him strip off his jeans.

His erection stood long and thick, the engorged head pressing against the waistband of his boxer briefs. Then he stripped off those too and knelt again beside her on the bed. She licked her lips and reached out to touch. She'd never seen an erection so tall before. Her hand slid down over the smooth skin, admiring the way he flexed in her hand, the way the veins stood out against his darkening skin.

He tore open a foil packet and she held out her hand for the condom. "Let me," she said. Her voice sounded like a stranger's, thick with need. He dropped the condom in her palm and tossed away the wrapper as she rolled it on. Every nerve in her body was once again alight. As she stroked down the latexed length of him, he peeled off her panties, laying her completely bare before him.

He slid a hand along her calf, lifting her leg. With a grin, she wrapped her legs around his hips, pulling him close, skin against skin, her stomach pressing against his so she could feel his every breath as if it were her own.

He smiled as he bent down over her, holding his weight off her with the strength of his arms. Up close, he was even more beautiful, all solid, hard muscle. So beautiful that the tears pricked against her eyelids again. She blinked them away.

The pulsing head of his erection pressed against her opening for one maddening moment, but she was having none of that. He'd taken his time. He'd made her come first. Now she needed him inside her. No more delays. She'd already waited two years too long for this. Her hips surged upwards, forcing him in, and he grunted his pleasure as her already orgasm-wet body encased him.

She gasped as he pushed, burying himself deep. He stilled inside her.

"Are you okay?" he asked, stroking back the hair from her face.

She nodded, unable to speak. His erection twitched inside her, and every nerve in her body responded. He needed no further invitation and began to move inside her, faster and faster. She held his gaze, wanting to see that look in his eyes as he came, but she had no chance. Already her own orgasm, another orgasm, rolled over her, tumbling her in its rough embrace. She clung to Dom for support, her fingers raking his back as he rode her to

126

the edge of the storm, and then she was lost, sightless, senseless, lost in the pleasure.

Then he came too, his body shuddering, his voice hoarse, as he surged inside her one last time before collapsing beside her.

He pulled her to face him, holding her close against his chest, their breaths heaving. For a long, long time they lay together, his fading erection still inside her, the pulses gradually diminishing. She never wanted to let him go, buried her head in his shoulder and breathed him in, that scent of sea and sex and man.

She never wanted to let him go.

But she couldn't hold on forever.

He slipped out of her and rolled away to dispose of the condom, and she wanted so much to cry, to release the sudden flood of emotions that rushed into the space in the bed where Dom had lain a moment ago.

She wanted to hold on forever.

Turning away, she buried her face in his pillows, breathing in that soft lemony scent, dragging her tumbled emotions together. Making love to Dominic had been more intimate, more wonderful, and more scary than any other man she'd ever been with. Not that she had much experience to compare it to, but this wasn't supposed to be how casual sex felt, she was sure.

Casual was what it had felt like with Paul after months and months of dating. Casual was how she wanted it. These kinds of emotions were not allowed in her personal life. Only in that space between "action" and "cut" did she ever feel safe enough to let the emotions out. This wasn't safe.

As Dom climbed back onto the bed, she slid away, out the other side of the bed.

"Where are you going?" he asked.

"To my own room." She was careful not to look at him. "I need to wash my make-up off."

"You can wash here, in my bathroom."

"I need more than just soap and water."

"Then don't take too long."

She faced him then, needing to see if the look on his face matched the tenderness and eagerness in his voice. It did. A lump welled up in her throat. "You want me to stay?"

"Yes. I want you to stay." His eyes were too dark for her to read, but his soft voice, and the emotion in it, rang clear. She was sure this wasn't an invitation he made often. If ever.

Her heart jumped and she hated herself for it.

She nodded and hurried towards the stairs, only managing to hold back the silent tears until she reached the door of her own bedroom. Then they came.

She took her time removing the make-up, brushing out her hair, brushing her teeth. The everyday rituals calmed her, soothed her, until the tears finally stopped. Then she stepped out of the bathroom and rummaged through the closet.

Wendy had not had the foresight to pack any other sexy lingerie. The only sleep clothes she had were not designed for seduction. Instead, she pulled on a thin, silk kimono, which barely reached her thighs, and turned back to the door, pausing for a moment with her hand on the knob.

The adrenalin and the alcohol no longer zinged through her veins. What happened now could not be blamed on anything else but her desire for this man. Not because he was conveniently here, or because he was a hot man who knew how to make a woman feel as if she was as beautiful as Scarlett Johansson, but because he was Dominic Kelly and she'd had a thing for him from the first moment she'd lain eyes on him.

She swallowed and pushed open the door.

He lay on his back, his head cushioned on his arms as he waited for her, and he smiled as she stepped into the room. She smiled too. He was still buck-naked and the sight of him took her breath away.

He held out a hand to her and she moved towards him, climbing onto the bed. But she didn't lie down. She knelt at the foot of the bed and looked at him.

"Come here," he instructed.

She shook her head.

He sat up on his elbows. "What's wrong?"

"What if I want more than you're willing to give?" Her voice came out a whisper.

His expression remained neutral, which scared her more than if she'd seen a flare of panic in his eyes. At least then she would have known if she was about to screw everything up or not.

"What is it you want?"

Oh help. She needed a little of her family's legendary bravery. Just one smidgeon of her sister's tenacity or her father's fearlessness. "I want this to be more than just one night." She swallowed. "I don't want to go back to the ways things were before. I want to do this again."

The beginnings of a smile began to curve his mouth. "That's not more than I'm willing to give."

"I want to share your bed for the next five weeks. Exclusively." She'd heard the rumors that he wasn't averse to sharing, but she was. "When it gets awkward or stops being fun, then we end it."

The half-smile turned into a full-blown grin. "Anything else?"

She shook her head. For the moment, that was all she could think of. Her and Dominic naked and horizontal. As often as possible. Maybe not even horizontal.

"I think I can live with that." He reached for her, pulling her into his arms, and she went to him, ready and willing for his kiss.

Chapter Nine

Dom woke with the dawn and lay for a long moment staring across his neighbors' rooftop to the wide blue ocean. Another amazing Californian day stretched before them.

Nina still slept beside him, curled up on her side, facing away from him. He couldn't remember when last he'd woken with a woman in his bed. And he never slept the night through in *her* bed.

He rose, careful not to wake her, though he needn't have bothered. Over these past ten days he'd learned enough about Nina to know she slept like the dead. Even so, he moved to the windows and pulled the curtains shut so the sun wouldn't wake her.

He pulled on a pair of boxers, then headed downstairs, moving stiffly and slowly. There would be no morning run on the beach today. He'd given his hip as much abuse as it could take last night. He grinned as he reached the bottom of the stairs. The abuse had been worth it.

He baulked in the doorway to the kitchen. "I didn't hear you come in."

Juliet sat on a stool, swinging her legs as she peeled grapes at the counter. He hated when she did that.

"You're ruining perfectly good grapes," he said, stepping past her and heading for the coffee machine. "Why don't you eat them whole?"

She shrugged. "The skin absorbs all the pesticides."

"I buy organic from the farmer's market. You know that."

She popped a peeled grape into her mouth. "The guest bed wasn't slept in last night. Does that mean the actress has given up and gone home?"

She'd checked? He frowned. "No." He pulled two mugs from the cupboard above the coffee machine and didn't look at his sister.

"So you finally saw sense and decided to get her out of your system?"

"No." Sensible definitely wasn't what he'd been. Crazed would have been a better description. And Nina was very far from being out of his system.

He made green tea for himself, and an espresso for Nina, black and unsweetened, just the way she liked it. When he turned back, Juliet was watching him with narrowed eyes. He didn't like the look of speculation in them.

"Don't start getting ideas about me doing something stupid like settling down, either," he warned. "Just because I didn't show her the door straight after sex doesn't mean this is turning into a long-term commitment. It just means I'm not a complete cad." He didn't fall for women. Ever. He simply wasn't made that way.

Women equaled drama and he already had enough drama in his life from his sisters, thank you very much.

By now you'd think his sisters would have realized that, but no, they continued to throw broad hints that he should settle down to marriage and kids. Sometimes women could be completely clueless.

He shrugged. "One night or one month, it doesn't matter. It's still just sex."

Juliet concentrated on peeling another grape, but he wasn't fooled. "Spit it out," he said with a sigh.

"Would it be so bad? I mean, to stick with one woman for more than a few weeks? To try having a relationship with someone?"

And there we go again. "I'll let you know if I ever find out."

He shoved her arm playfully. "What are you doing here, anyway?"

"I thought I'd take Sandy out for a walk this morning. Save you doing anything stupid to your hip like going for a run." She glanced down at his hip, as if she had x-ray vision that could see through his boxers to the bone beneath. "How did your hip hold up to the strain last night anyway?"

"That is none of your damned business."

She grinned cheekily. "I'm your physio. I need to know these things."

"Then maybe I need to find myself a physio I'm not related to. Weren't you going to take Sandy for a walk?"

"Yeah, yeah." She hopped down off the kitchen stool. "I know. I've outstayed my welcome and you want to get back to bed. I'll let the others know to call first before they pop round for the next few weeks, shall I?"

"That would be nice."

Juliet let herself out the back door, whistling for Sandy, who was no doubt investigating the yard for signs of overnight predators. Dom latched the door shut behind them.

"Who was that?" Nina stumbled into the kitchen, rubbing her eyes. She'd put on the silk kimono, but it gaped in front, enough to give him a glimpse of the swell of her pale breasts.

"Jules. She's taken Sandy out for a run."

"Does that mean I get a day off for good behavior?" Nina perched on the stool Juliet had just vacated. Dom handed her a coffee mug. "Thanks. I feel positively decadent for having had a lie-in."

He laughed. "It's the same time I have to force you out of bed every day. The only difference is that the clocks changed at midnight for Daylight Savings. I can't imagine how you cope when you're working on a movie and have early calls."

"It's different for work. I don't love mornings any more than normal, but I love the work I do. I love arriving on a film set in the mornings, that electric buzz."

"You're working with me," he pointed out.

She set down her mug and crossed to him, wrapping her arms around his waist. Her eyes sparkled as she looked up at him. "This doesn't feel like work. This feels like play."

He kissed her forehead, and then, because that wasn't nearly enough, he kissed her lips, lingering over her cherry lip-gloss taste. Nina gave back as hungrily as she took, her hands roving over his bare skin, and just like that he was hard and aching to be inside her again.

But there would be no sweeping her off her feet and carrying her upstairs. Not until he'd had a little more recovery time and at least two anti-inflammatories.

The most he could do was sweep her up onto the kitchen counter. He spread her legs, smiled as he noticed she was naked beneath the kimono, and positioned himself between her thighs.

She was just as beautiful in person as she was on the magazine covers. Her skin was a little less flawless and more real, and her curves a little thicker than the retouched photographs suggested, but he liked her even more for it.

He stroked his fingers down her face, and her eyes fluttered closed. "You've never been more beautiful that you are right now," he said.

Her eyes flew open. "I'm not even wearing any make-up."

"Exactly."

She shook her head, just a small movement against his palm. "I've lost count of how many people have suggested I get a little work done to correct some of my imperfections."

"I love your imperfections. No one person can have the perfect everything or be the perfect everything." He slid a hand up her smooth thigh. Real. Flesh and blood. And very human. "You've done everything I asked of you for ten days and haven't asked for time off. Today you get to do whatever you want. Lunch out with your girlfriends, shopping, a day at the spa…?"

Her wicked smile set his blood on slow boil. "There's only one thing I want to do today." She ran her palm down over his chest, all the way from his pecs down to the waistband of his boxers. "You." Her hand moved lower, rubbing over his hardening erection. "I want to spend the day in bed with you."

There were worse things than being a sex object, right?

He grinned. "Who needs a bed?"

Forget recovery time. He untied the sash of her kimono and it fell open to reveal her perfect breasts, big and round, soft enough that he could tell they were the real thing. He cupped them, gently squeezing, rolling a dark nipple between his thumbs, and her eyes glazed over. She arched her back and moaned, pushing aside the bowl of half-eaten grape skins Juliet had left behind so she could lie back on the counter.

She opened herself up to him, wanton, inviting, and he bent over her, taking one taut aureole in his mouth, sucking hard. Nina whimpered.

His hand slid down over her cool, smooth skin to the juncture of her thighs. His thumb circled her clit as he dipped a finger into her. She bucked against him, already wet for him.

Gradually his finger moved faster and faster inside her, then he slid in another and another, stretching her, preparing her.

Her stomach muscles quivered as she responded to his touch, her skin flushed with desire.

She pushed up into his hand and he stroked and kneaded until she begged for more. With his free hand he pushed down his boxers and pressed his pulsing length against her heated core.

She struggled to her elbows, biting her lip. "Not without a condom." Her voice was ragged and breathless.

As if he'd forget. He reached behind her to the ceramic pot where he kept his car keys, breath mints…all the basic necessities. He pulled a foil packet out of the bowl and tore it open.

"You keep condoms in your kitchen?"

He shrugged. You never knew when you might need one.

He rolled it on and poised himself at her entrance. Her eyes

134

darkened, the dilated pupils turning them black and wild. Then he sank himself into her, grunting his relief as he buried himself hilt-deep into her warm, wet embrace.

She moved with him, her moans growing louder, driving him on. God! He loved that she was so responsive, so uninhibited. He loved that she held nothing back and abandoned herself to the pleasure. It took everything in him to hold back his release until she came, her body rippling around him, her cry fierce and fervent. Then he let himself go, with the same abandon, exploding inside her as the orgasm slammed through him.

Yeah, he could do five more weeks of this.

The next week of Nina's training was a lot less painful than her first. Her muscles grew accustomed to the strain, daily growing stronger, and it was a whole lot easier concentrating on whatever activities Dom set her without the constant push-pull of tension between them.

Which was just as well since, far from easing up on her now they were sleeping together, he seemed to have upped her training to a whole new level. The only benefit was that there was a whole lot more touching than before. She could forgive him being a hard taskmaster when he made up for it by stealing kisses at every opportunity.

In public, he was always discreet, maddeningly so, since Chrissie's Big Plan was becoming more attractive with each passing day. Maybe it would be good for her career to be photographed with a strapping, tough stunt man. But Dom kept a clear distance between them whenever anyone else was around. Because he didn't want his friends getting any ideas that this was more than it was? Or because he didn't want Nina getting the same idea?

She brushed away the hurt and focused on her training.

In addition to their early-morning runs, Dom now made her do endless push-ups and sit-ups too, and there was weight training every second day. Not the familiar circuit her personal trainer made her do; Dom's idea of weight training was closer to torture than exercise. But when he took her out for home-made gelato afterwards, at least she didn't feel guilty at the indulgence.

Monday was spent at the firing range, mercifully closed to the public so she could improve her marksmanship away from scrutiny. She learned to handle and assemble a variety of both decommissioned prop weapons as well as real ones, firing with blanks and live ammunition.

In their martial arts sessions she graduated to hand-to-hand combat, and at the race track Evan taught her better cornering skills and how to do donuts. Dom definitely got the benefit of *that* adrenalin rush afterwards.

The only aspect of her training she hadn't mastered was horse-riding. She still looked like a rank amateur and could barely walk for the bruises afterwards.

Blisters, bruises, pulled muscles, muscle cramps. She had them all. And each and every one felt like a trophy.

But even better than the adventure and adrenalin rush of her days was the thrill of her nights. They rarely left the house, enjoying sundowners in the oasis of Dom's yard, cooking together, eating together, enjoying long baths in his whirlpool tub, early nights in bed exploring one another...

She didn't sleep in the guest bedroom all week.

If she hadn't had a clue before what had been wrong between her and Paul, she knew now. Chemistry. If she'd had just a third of the chemistry with Paul that she had with Dom, she might have been tempted to say "yes" to him.

As it was, she found herself saying "yes" to Dominic rather a lot. Usually in short, breathy gasps or very loud screams. She wasn't normally a screamer, but with Dom she didn't seem able to hold anything back. He brought out a wild side in her she didn't even know she had. And she loved it.

By the following Saturday she was excited to get back on the trapeze, definitely her favorite part of her training so far. Now that she'd mastered the basics of midair somersaults and catches, Gianna moved her to the big rig, the one with proper safety nets.

"Concentrate," she chided, pushing Dom's hands off her hips when he was supposed to be securing her safety harness. Instead, she took advantage of his distraction with the harness to slide her own hands beneath his t-shirt. Dom *didn't* push her hands away. It felt like a victory of sorts.

"What's keeping you?" Gianna called down from the platform above their heads. With a grin, Dom slapped Nina's butt as she started up the ladder.

She climbed to the platform above, where Gianna waited for her. Today Gianna planned to introduce her to the lyra to improve her balance. The lyra was a circular metal hoop suspended in midair and used for various balancing and spinning aerial maneuvers, a combination of gymnastics, ballet, and athleticism.

Nina had played so many klutzy characters over the years that it was almost a surprise to learn she could be graceful. Maybe it was the freedom of being in midair, without the force of gravity holding her feet to the ground. Or maybe it was Dom watching her from below, making her feel like she could do anything, be anyone.

This feeling was why she'd turned her life around when she'd hit rock bottom. This was why she'd chosen to be an actress. For more years than she could remember, she'd wanted to be someone else. To be the woman she saw now in Dom's eyes when he looked at her.

It was usually a sensation she only experienced in front of the cameras.

But she had to tread carefully. She was dangerously close to letting Dom get too close. It was hard to keep her lack of inhibition in the bedroom from spilling over into their daily lives, and she couldn't afford to let her mask slip any further than it already had or he would realize that she was a fake, that she wasn't brave or strong or sassy, or any of the other things he admired in her. Or that the only time she took risks was in front of the cameras, where every move was scripted and choreographed.

Dom might like the Nina who didn't wear make-up and who wore glasses, but if he knew the scared, insecure woman beneath the sexy outer shell she'd worked so hard to create, he wouldn't want her anymore.

"Will we see you at the pub tonight?" Gianna asked when their training session was over.

Nina shrugged and looked at Dom. Other than for her training, they hadn't left the house all week. The novelty still hadn't worn off.

"It's a country-music band playing tonight," Gianna added.

Now that was different. "Please can we go?" She turned big, round eyes on him and Dom laughed.

"I never figured you for a country girl."

"Through and through."

This time Dom drove them to the pub. And this time Nina wore sensible, practical jeans. If the cropped tank top she wore was a little less sensible, flashing a whole lot of skin at her increasingly toned stomach, Dom didn't complain. In fact, the look in his eyes promised fun when they got home.

As they entered the pub, he placed a protective hand on her lower back and she was glad for the reassuring touch. Olivia wasn't on duty tonight, but still she had to face Jacob. She'd used him shamelessly to make Dom jealous, led him on then dropped him without a word, and she blushed when she saw him in the group that awaited them.

But Jacob didn't seem to hold a grudge. He kissed her cheek. "You're still here, then?"

"Yeah, I'm stubborn like that. When I want something, I don't give up until I get it."

Dom leaned in, his trademark crooked grin reaching his eyes. "I don't think he was talking about your training."

She leaned closer too and dropped her voice. "Neither was I."

Jacob raised an eyebrow as he looked between them. "You're a lucky bastard," he said to Dom, then turned his attention to the redhead serving the beers tonight.

Dom was careful not to touch her in public. As much as her head reasoned this was a good thing, her body wasn't happy. This was what 'no strings' meant, didn't it? She had no claim on him.

She had to keep it casual. So what would a 'casual' woman do? A casual woman would have fun, wouldn't she? She'd dance to the music and drink a beer and sway her hips, and she'd laugh and joke, and she wouldn't give a damn whether Dom treated her the same as he treated every other woman he'd ever been with. It had to be enough that tonight it wasn't any other woman at his side. Tonight it was *her* he had chosen. Even if no one else knew it.

The band took to the stage and began to play covers of popular country songs, lively tunes about summer parties, blue jeans, tailgates, and beers. Nina danced to the beat, singing along with the lyrics. At least this part of her 'keep it casual' role wasn't an act.

Vicki and her husband Ben joined the dancers in the open space before the band. Nina's feet itched to join them, and at last Dom held out his hand to her, "Care to dance?"

Hell, yes! Especially as it meant getting up close and personal with him. He placed his hand on her hip and they swayed to the music.

He swung her away and back again, catching her around her waist in a move that wouldn't have been out of place on *Dancing with the Stars*. She should have figured he'd be a great dancer, too. When it came to using his body, there wasn't anything Dom couldn't do – and do it better than anyone else.

He spun her around again and this time he pulled her tight against him.

"We could be seen," she whispered in warning. Though her heart picked up its pace a little at the thought.

His hands slid down her lower back, cupping the curve of her butt and pulling her in tight against him. As if she needed the reminder that there was one thing he was even more of a champion at than dancing.

Liquid heat soaked between her legs, starting a throb that escalated through her body.

Since the TV show had made her famous she'd become a recluse, avoiding leaving the privacy of her quiet condo complex, where her neighbors were often equally well known and equally camera-shy. She only left home for work or the kind of events where privacy was guaranteed and security details laid on – and those were never the kinds of events where country music was played.

Wendy ran her errands, paid her bills, did her shopping, and even read her emails so she didn't have to face the often hostile and very personal comments strangers felt entitled to make from behind the safety of their computers.

She hadn't even realized how trapped she'd felt in that lonely existence until she'd moved in with Dom. In these couple of weeks she'd been out in the wide world more than she had in years. If she ignored the occasional autograph-hunter or person wanting their photo taken with her, she almost felt like a normal human being again.

So normal she'd even begun to imagine doing things she'd once only dreamed about. Taking risks, rebelling against the diets and the expectations and the lengthy list of things she could no longer do in public. Fantasies that definitely weren't vanilla, and which she had never spoken aloud to anyone. Fantasies that this new *casual* persona wasn't afraid to indulge in.

Fantasies like make out in a public place.

PDAs were frowned on in her world. Unless you were Miley Cyrus. How she envied Miley her freedom to do whatever she wanted and screw the consequences.

The most demonstrative Paul had ever been was to hold her hand as they hurried from car to restaurant or car to party. And even then she'd wondered if that was more for the sake of the cameras than as an indication that he was into her.

Yet here she was in a public bar, Dom's arms around her, his body pressed against hers.

For so long she'd believed she would never get his attention, and yet here she was, in his arms. Fantasies could come true.

His hand slid beneath the hem of her shirt to stroke incendiary circles on the bare skin at her waist.

"Get a room," Jacob teased, his arms wrapped around a girl who looked as if she still needed to be carded to get into a place like this.

"Good idea," Nina said. "Perhaps we should go home."

Dom shook his head, a grin curving his wicked mouth. He pressed his lips close to her ear. "I have a much better idea."

He took her hand and led her away from the noise and the music, away from the bar that was now packed with people, to the quiet, dim-lit corridor leading to the restrooms. There he paused, turning to face her. "Want to pick up where we left off last time we were here?"

The beat still thumped through the soles of their feet, though the music was muted here. She glanced around, her heart thumping even more wildly than the music. Here – where anyone could see them?

"I can't wait until we get home," he whispered, nibbling small kisses down her neck.

He most certainly wasn't doing this for the benefit of any cameras. He was completely into her and didn't care who knew. Even his friends. There couldn't be any aphrodisiac stronger than that dizzying revelation.

Close by a toilet flushed and a faucet began to run.

With another of those wicked grins she loved so much, Dom pulled her down the corridor and pushed open a door further along. A walk-in supply closet.

He shoved her inside and followed, leaving the door ajar so a sliver of light turned the pitch blackness of the tiny room to murky shadow. Then he pulled her into his arms, his mouth unerringly finding hers in the dark. She opened up for him, kissing him back as she'd never have dared to do in the crowded bar room.

Outside in the corridor a door creaked open and there were footsteps and voices, a girlish giggle followed by a man's deeper rumble.

"Sounds like we're not the only ones with this idea," Nina whispered.

Her hands were already on his waistband, fumbling for the zipper of his jeans. Her heart raced, and she felt light-headed with the thrill, the adrenalin surge almost familiar now.

He hastily shoved away her hands, loosening his jeans and pushing them down over his hips. He was commando beneath the jeans. She sucked in a breath as he reached for her. Out in the corridor there were more voices, two women now, a little loud, more than a little drunk. The sound of her zipper seemed amplified in the tiny space and she caught her lower lip in her teeth.

Dom didn't pause. He pushed her jeans down, peeling them off her, baring her skin to the cool air. So much for sensible jeans, she should have worn a sensible, easy-access short skirt.

Then he lifted her off her feet, onto a pile of empty plastic packing crates she hadn't even known was there, and spread her legs. His fingers followed the line of her lacy thong, brushing over her clit, and she had to bite her lip to hold back the whimper that threatened to escape.

Then his hands were gone, deserting her. She slid her own hand between her legs and pulled on the lace, rubbing it over her swollen clit. Not that she needed any more stimulation than the heat of his body so close to hers or the scent of his skin in the dark.

She heard the rip of a foil packet, followed by the rubbery snap and roll of latex as he sheathed himself. His hands found their way back to her hips, angling her against the crates, and his erection pressed against her stomach.

"We could get caught," he whispered in her ear, leaning in close.

And she was as good as naked from the waist down. She shuddered. As if she needed the reminder. Nude pictures leaked on the net were not going to help her win the role of Sonia.

Yet the risk of what they were doing only made her hotter and wetter. These were the fantasies she'd played in her mind as she'd lain awake beside Paul, frustrated, unfulfilled.

Dom slid his erection between her legs, stroking over her core, teasing her, driving her wild. His hand stroked down over her stomach, over the swell of her mound, the feathery touch of his fingers over her clit drawing an involuntary moan from her. He fingered aside the scrap of lace. Then he was right there, his erection poised at her entrance.

As he thrust into her she bit her lip so hard to hold back the sound that she tasted blood. She was so wet for him that all it took was a shift of his hips and he was buried deep. His erection stretched her, massaged her. He drove deeper and deeper, his pace insistent and relentless. She braced her heels against the crates and opened herself up to him.

"I'm going to come," he warned, his voice low and tense. She nodded, though she knew he couldn't see. He hammered into her and her head rolled back against the wall as white-hot ecstasy slammed through her.

The pleasure was so intense she scarcely registered when he came inside her. His body shuddered, then stilled, and his head dropped to her shoulder. He placed a tender kiss on her neck before he pulled away.

So much for her elusive orgasm. There hadn't even been any foreplay.

Chapter Ten

F...

Dom bit back a flood of swear words as he turned away from Nina to dispose of the condom. His eyes had grown accustomed to the dark, but he didn't need to see to know that the freaking condom had torn.

He didn't want to worry Nina right now. Later, or in the morning, maybe, when she was no longer under the influence of either lust or alcohol.

Maybe never. She didn't need to know, did she?

Oh hell...

He groped for the pile of paper towels beside the work sink and handed her a few, grateful the darkness hid his panic. He cleaned himself up, tossed the paper towels in the open trashcan beneath the sink and zipped up his jeans. When he turned back she was still righting her clothing, pulling herself back together.

"We shouldn't go back out there together," she said. "I'll go out first. You can follow in a few minutes."

His chest tightened. He knew the score. He'd done this more times than he could count. In fact, he'd already banged at least one waitress in this very supply closet. That time, he'd had nothing to hide. They'd kept the lights on.

And that time he'd been more than happy to give her a head

144

start.

But this time was different. This wasn't some casual hook-up. This was Nina. He wanted to wrap his arms around her and hold her, enjoy a moment's privacy before returning to a room of too-loud, too-drunk people.

He wanted to walk out there with her and be damned if anyone knew they were together.

She flicked her hair, then pushed the door wider and peeked out into the corridor. Without a backward glance, she stepped out and disappeared from sight.

He shut the door behind her again. This time he reached for the light switch and harsh fluorescent light flooded the tiny window-less room. He washed his hands at the sink, relieved there was no mirror because he couldn't face his own reflection right now.

Maybe this hadn't been such a great idea.

The waitress had walked out of here all too happy for the world to know who she'd been with and what had put that smile on her face.

But Nina had done what *he* usually did. Taken her pleasure, barely said thank you, and walked away. And he'd thought she wasn't the casual-sex kind.

He ran his hands through his hair. He was getting too old for this shit. As his sisters often asked, when was he going to start growing up?

Perhaps he needed to start thinking with his brain and not his body. Perhaps it was time to start thinking about settling down and finding a woman to cuddle afterwards. A woman he didn't have to worry about condoms with.

And thinking of condoms...

He splashed water on his face.

Not once in all these years had he experienced a condom fail. He'd heard that, statistically, there was a chance. But he'd had the luck of the Irish on his side. Until now.

He looked down at his hands where they gripped the steel

edge of the sink, holding on as if afraid they might start shaking if he let go.

He had to tell her.

It was just the once. One teeny, tiny oops that would probably mean nothing in the big scheme of things, but still he had to tell her. With his history, she'd probably insist on getting tested, and he wouldn't blame her.

He was definitely getting too old for this.

When he figured he'd given her a more than generous lead, he switched off the light, opened the door and made his way down the darkened corridor. In the archway to the main room of the pub he paused, leaning against the cool brick wall of the arch for a moment to watch the room.

Nina was back in the circle of his friends. Jacob hovered protectively at her side as she signed the bare chest of a flush-faced young man. She handed back the sharpie to his grinning mates, smiling and joking with them, calm and in control, and looking nothing like a woman who'd just been thoroughly screwed in the back room of a bar.

She shook her head when the young men held up their phones, no doubt asking for pictures. His body stilled, primed and ready to leap in and intercede, but there was no need. Jacob and Evan stepped forward on either side, flanking her, and the youths backed away. Even Vicki stood at attention. He loved his friends, trusted them with his life, trusted them to look after Nina, but he couldn't stop the jealousy from surging. Looking after Nina was *his* job.

Not that she looked as if she needed any taking care of. She swayed to the music and laughed at something Vicki said. Not once did she look his way.

The one thing he hadn't figured Nina for was cold. Yet it was as if she'd flicked a switch and become another person.

Who the hell was she anyway? She was like half a dozen women rolled into one. One moment she was fearless and determined, the next vulnerable and insecure, the next a fun and flirty seductress.

He should have been pleased. He'd always said it would take more than one woman to keep him satisfied.

But he wasn't satisfied.

Dom rubbed his face. Something had changed for him these past couple of weeks she'd been living in his house. He didn't know what it was, but he didn't think he could go back now to the way things were before.

He wanted more than sex. He wanted to get to know her. The real her, not the person she pretended to be for her public.

Jacob leaned in to hear Nina better. Evan handed her another beer. They'd fallen under her spell and he could hardly blame his friends for being entranced. After all, she'd entranced him, the man with the heart of stone.

But for Nina it seemed he was nothing more than a plaything, a sex object. A fun way to pass the time of her training before she took the next role and moved on. He'd thought she was different. How had he got her so wrong? Was his sixth sense for women failing him?

Neither Nina nor any of his friends noticed him. No one appeared to think that anything was amiss. And why would they?

The stunning A-list movie star and the damaged stunt man in the twilight of his career. Why would anyone think this relationship was going anywhere?

He was deluding himself thinking he could hold onto her. He needed to take a leaf from her book and keep this casual.

A brunette in a shorter-than-short denim skirt pushed past him, coming from the direction of the restrooms. He pushed himself away from the wall and crossed the room to his friends. Jacob glanced his way, so he held his head high, kept his stride firm, and bugger the constant ache in his hip.

He still had his pride.

As he joined their circle, Nina glanced at him, and it wasn't the smoldering, unguarded Nina he'd woken beside these last weeks. The lust-crazed woman of minutes before was nowhere to be seen and he was demoted back to being her trainer, her buddy, like the BFF confidante in one of her rom-coms.

"One woman not enough for you?" Jacob asked, leaning in close and keeping his voice low. He inclined his head towards the brunette in the short denim skirt.

Dom's jaw tightened. He couldn't do this anymore. He needed to get out of here. He needed to get Nina out of here.

"We should be going," he said to her. "You have another long day of training ahead tomorrow."

She turned her dark, sultry eyes on him, pouting. "And I thought you knew how to play hard as well as work hard."

Evan laughed. "When did you turn into such a wet blanket, Dom? You're usually the hardest partier among us."

"Tomorrow Nina starts a crash course in Krav Maga with Vicki."

"Ah. Ouch."

"What's Krav Maga?" Nina asked.

"It's an Israeli self-defense system that's only one step removed from street fighting." Jacob explained. "And Vicki is merciless. I still have bruises from the last time we choreographed a fight scene together."

"Don't scare her," Vicki called across the circle. "That's my job."

"Too late. I'm already scared." Nina laughed. "But shouldn't Vicki also be getting an early night, then?"

Dom frowned. "Vicki's a lot more used to alcohol than you are. It's above my pay grade to be cleaning you up if you get sick."

He cocked his head toward the door and Nina sighed dramatically. "I won't be sick. I'm never sick. But I'll be a good girl and go home to get a good night's sleep."

They said their goodbyes, then he escorted her back to the car, careful to keep his hands to himself. He was in enough trouble without touching her.

He held the car door open as she hopped in, then he circled around to the driver's door, scowling at the group of smokers on the sidewalk who very clearly ogled Nina. He slammed the door shut and started the engine. He didn't need to look to know that, tipsy as she was, she was fully aware of their audience. It had been evident in the added swing in her hips. His hands fisted.

"What's going on with you tonight?" she asked, as they finally turned into the road behind his house. "You're not usually this grumpy after sex."

He didn't look at her. "Maybe I'm not used to being treated as if I don't exist after sex."

"Poor dear, is your ego bruised? Your other women might not be so discreet, but you must realize I have to be."

She didn't have to sound so off-hand talking about his other women. Couldn't she sound as if she cared? She was an actress, after all. The least she could do was pretend.

He sighed, letting go his tension. He'd liked that she didn't play games, so what had changed? She was right. His ego had been bruised and he needed to let it go.

He parked in his garage and pressed the remote to shut the door behind them. When the door sealed shut he turned to her. "We have to talk about what happened."

"We had a quickie. It was fun. What more is there to talk about?"

He pressed his lips together. He suspected she wasn't going to be so flippant a moment from now. "The condom broke."

Her eyes widened as she stared at him, very rapidly sobering up. "Are you on the pill?" he asked.

She shook her head.

Damn.

"I won't be offended if you want to take a test," he said.

She nodded. "I guess I should ask Wendy to pick up some contraceptives for me. And maybe the morning-after pill. It wouldn't be the first time she's had to fake something to get a prescription for me." She bit her lip, as if realizing she'd revealed more than she should.

"What else has she had to fake?" he asked, trying to sound nonchalant.

149

Nina shrugged, opened her car door and hopped out. "Nothing serious, but I can hardly leave the house with a big red nose and coughing and spluttering all over the place, so she gets my flu meds for me when I'm sick." She grinned. "And condoms, tampons, prune juice…all the products I can't be seen shopping for." She hopped out the car and hung on the door a moment. "Let's not worry about this. If anything happens, then we'll deal with it. What are the chances, anyway?"

She didn't really want an answer to that, did she? Clearly not, since she strode towards the house, head high, as if she didn't have a care in the world. He followed more slowly, and she was already in the shower when he'd locked up and headed upstairs.

When Nina woke Sunday morning, head thumping, Dom had already left the bed. He'd drawn the curtains shut and she was grateful. She hadn't really had that much to drink, had she? She tried to remember, but the evening was a blur. The only thing she remembered clearly was sex in the supply closet. And Dom's bombshell afterward.

What were the chances of her getting pregnant? With the constant adrenalin rushes and physical battering her body was experiencing at the moment, it had to be about a million to one.

She found Dom in the kitchen cooking up a massive breakfast. In nothing but baggy track pants. Eye candy for breakfast. Yum. And no calories.

She perched on a kitchen stool, her chin cupped in her hands, and enjoyed the view of his to-die-for eight pack. Even better than his abs were his arms. She'd always loved a man with strong shoulders and arms. There was a feeling that those arms could hold her safe and keep the world away. Which was stupid, because it was nothing more than an illusion. Nothing could keep the bad shit away.

The man knew his way around the kitchen, too. The food his sisters provided didn't go to waste.

Dom slid a plate in front of her, and then an espresso, but it was only as he started to dish fried eggs and sizzling sausages onto the plate that she truly woke up.

"I can't!" she protested, trying ineffectually to hold her hands over the plate.

"You will." He captured both her hands in one of his big ones and held them still while he added syrupy flapjacks to her plate. "You should look in the mirror sometime. You're expending a lot of calories every day. If you don't eat more you're going to be too gaunt to play Sonia."

"Never. The camera adds at least ten pounds."

He frowned. "You're a beautiful woman with a beautiful body. Why are you so hard on yourself?"

She bit her lip. This wasn't something she usually needed to explain. "I wasn't always one of the pretty girls. Halfway through high school I got the chance to change schools and I used the fresh start to re-invent myself. It felt so good, being the girl every guy in school wanted to date. Suddenly all the popular girls wanted to be my friend. I got used to guys whistling at me or men turning in the street to look at me. Aside from the fact that it was sometimes a little creepy, I liked it. I felt beautiful."

His crooked grin appeared. "I can just imagine. That short cheerleading skirt, the tight, low-cut top…" His hand wandered up the inside of her thigh towards the edge of her sleep shorts and she slapped it away.

"I'm being serious! That feeling didn't last long after I arrived here in LA. It was confusing because I didn't think there was anything wrong with me, but suddenly everyone was telling me I wasn't good enough. The other actresses were thinner than me, more perfect than me. I went to auditions and never got a callback. Over and over again, I was told I needed to pluck my eyebrows and whiten my teeth and lose 20 pounds. So I did, but it's not like waving a magic wand. Curves are in my genes and I'm still bigger than most other actresses. I have to work hard

151

to stay thin enough to keep working. Diets, fitness trainers, and weekly sessions at the spa. Do you have any idea how exhausting it is trying to be pretty in this town? Do you have any idea how hard it is to feel pretty when you're up for the same roles as Anna Kendrick or Emma Stone?"

He turned the stool she sat on so she faced him. "You're not bigger than most actresses. You're bigger than most anorexics. And unbelievably, there is a difference." His hand slid up her thigh again, and this time she didn't push it away. "And as far as I'm concerned, you're also far prettier than either of those actresses." His fingers brushed over the apex between her thighs. "And definitely sexier."

His kiss almost had her a believer. There was no doubting what women saw in him when his kiss could make any women feel like a goddess.

He broke the kiss and stepped away, flashing her a quick grin. "In comparison with most women – even here in LA where people's body images are skewed – you have a really terrific figure." He winked. "Take it from an expert in women's bodies."

Okay, so that last comment deflated a little of the heady rush, but she was pretty sure she was still glowing as she ate up everything he'd dished on her plate. He thought she had a terrific figure? Not just good, not even great, but terrific?

She lifted a bite of flapjack to her mouth. And closed her eyes to savor the taste. When last had she tasted a flapjack? It made a wonderful change from her usual bran and fresh fruit.

Dom laughed, a throaty, seductive sound. "That's how you looked on the beach at Point Dume. As if you were about to have an orgasm from eating a burger."

"That was my first burger in over a year. It almost was as good as an orgasm." At that time she hadn't had an orgasm in over a year either. She'd lost count how many she'd had in this past week. She licked a drop of syrup from the corner of her mouth.

If only she could retain Dom as her personal trainer, maybe she could indulge like this more often.

Who was she kidding? He'd soon grow bored. Dom liked to stay active and on the move. There was no way he'd sit around waiting for her through the long hours she was on set. Dom needed new challenges like other people needed air to breathe.

If only she could keep him around as her boyfriend…

She shook her head so vehemently she nearly choked on the next piece of flapjack. Dom needed new challenges there, too. There was no way he'd stick with just one woman.

She thrust the half-full plate away, unable to eat another mouthful. The food suddenly tasted like charcoal in her mouth.

She moved to stack the dishwasher and start cleaning the kitchen. "So what are our plans for today? After Vicki has beaten me black and blue, that is?"

"Nothing special. You don't have any friends you want to meet up with?"

She shook her head and didn't look at him. She didn't have friends. Her friends from before she was famous resented the attention she attracted and didn't want to know her anymore. The people she'd met since… "No one I'd ring up on a Sunday morning and say 'let's hang out together'."

"So what do you like to do in your spare time, then? Go out for a movie? Or I know a great pizzeria…"

"No more food! And movies aren't an option unless it's a premiere or a private cinema. Besides, I don't feel up to going out in public today."

Fame was fun. It was a high unlike any other. But it was a double-edged sword. She could only face the outside world if she felt good about herself. And if she had the energy. The constant interruptions and being nice to everyone she met, the strain of filtering everything she said and did to ensure it fitted with her public image, required a level of mental stamina she didn't possess today. She sighed. "But don't let me hold you back if you want to go out. You must be bored stiff doing nothing but supervising my training and going to your local pub once a week."

He took her hand. "I'm not bored. You're very entertaining to have around."

She raised a skeptical eyebrow.

Dom grinned. "I'm always wondering which personality you'll be wearing today."

"Are you suggesting I have a split personality?" She reached out to smack him playfully and he caught her hand, kissing her wrist.

"Multiple personality disorder might be more accurate. It's one of the things I love about you."

Her heart did a complete backward flip in her chest. He hadn't really used the L word, had he? Because if he had, then this had to end. Now. And she wasn't ready for it to end yet.

But he didn't mean it. He'd said the word 'love' as flippantly as he'd said 'flapjack' or 'movies'.

His lips had moved from her wrist to the palm of her hand when they heard the tentative knock at the door.

Nina wrenched her hand away and sat straighter. She was still dressed in her rumpled sleep shorts and shirt. She hadn't even brushed her hair.

"Only me," Juliet's voice called through the kitchen door, and with a sigh Dom rose to unlock it. Nina scraped her fingers through her tangled hair and pricked her cheeks to sting color to them.

Juliet bounced into the room. "I'm so glad I caught you home. I wanted to check on my baby bro. And also to remind you that we're having a barbecue at the folks' place this afternoon and thought you might like to join us. For a change," she added, with a pointed look at him. "We haven't seen you in a while."

Dom shrugged and looked away.

"Don't stay home on my account," Nina said. "Go have fun with your family. I'll be quite happy to spend the afternoon curled up with a book."

And after Vicki was through with her, that might be all she was able to do.

"You're invited too, of course." Juliet sounded offhand, but tension prickled through Nina. She'd heard that tone often enough. Was this a set-up? Was she going to be paraded before all their friends and family, like a giraffe in the zoo, the celebrity attraction? No thanks.

"It'll just be family," Dom said, his voice quiet. He was doing that reading-her-mind thing again. How did he do that when she'd been so careful to keep her expression neutral?

"Maybe she thinks we're not good enough for her?" Juliet said, and the bite in her tone was now unmistakable.

"Jules…" Dom's voice was heavy with warning.

"I'm sorry," Juliet said. She even sounded sorry. But the look in her eyes was anything but.

Nina hadn't seen that look in years. Not since she'd been a plump teenager in glasses and braces who'd been forced to make friends in a new town. She'd turned that look around. She'd reinvented herself, lost the glasses and the braces and a ton of weight. When the boys started swarming around her, like the proverbial flies, those same girls had practically begged her to try out for their precious cheerleading squad.

She'd turned it around then, and she'd turn it around now.

Nina's chin rose in defiance, but her smile was sweet. "I'd love to come, and I'd love to meet your family. Now if you'll excuse me, I have an appointment to take a beating." Holding her back straight and her head high, she exited the room.

Dom turned to his sister, eyes flashing. "What's got into you, Jules? When did you turn into such a bitch?"

She had the decency to look ashamed. "I'm sorry. I don't know what gets into me. She's just so…uppity. As if she doesn't trust anyone."

"She doesn't. It's a defense mechanism and most famous people are like that. It's nothing personal."

He scrubbed his face. He needed to remember that too. No matter how intimate he and Nina got, no matter how many nights they slept in the same bed, it still felt like she wasn't really there. As if there was a chasm between them. Like last night, when she'd left him in the supply closet and gone to party with his friends as if nothing had happened. The sting was still sharp.

What did he need to do to break through that wall, to earn Nina's trust?

"Christian isn't like that," Jules said. "He doesn't disappear whenever we come to visit."

"Christian's different. He loves the attention. Nina does too, but she's been isolated by it." He sighed. "She's been a celebrity long enough to have been burned by people using her, but not long enough yet to learn to separate the people who only want to know her for what she does from the people who want to know her for who she is."

Some celebrities never learned. They either became so distrusting they closed themselves off from everyone, or they became like Paul de Angelo – so sucked into their own hype that they believed themselves better than everyone else.

Paul. Just the name in his head made his fists clench. He was one of those who had used Nina and hurt her. He hadn't cared to get to know Nina, had he? He'd wanted her only for what she could do for his image.

"Just give her a chance to get to know you, okay? Without being a bitch."

Juliet leaned on the counter and helped herself to one of the sausages Nina had left untouched. "You like her. This is getting serious, isn't it?"

Dom scowled. "Of course I like her. She's a hard worker, very committed to everything she does, and she's a nice person on top of that. But don't make it more than what it is." He turned away to feed the last of the leftover sausages to Sandy. "I need to get Nina to the dojo for her Krav Maga lesson with Vicki. You can show yourself out."

Chapter Eleven

Dominic's parents lived in a sprawling, modern single-storey ranch house in the Valley. Out back was a big yard with a swimming pool and camp chairs set in the shade of a wide-spreading elm. At first glance, the yard seemed full of people, most of them congregated around an oversized barbecue grill. It reminded Nina of her own childhood home. Different trees, different pool, but the same comfortable homeliness and happy voices.

She squashed the memory. It didn't help to dwell on things that were gone.

There were kids splashing in the pool, at least four that Nina could count. Eric spotted her and grinned, and she waved back. She wished she could join them. Entertaining the kids would be infinitely easier than dealing with Dom's phalanx of sisters. Sisters who didn't seem to like her much. She'd almost forgotten how it felt not to be liked. These days most people pretended to be her best friends, even if they didn't know her.

"Just be yourself," Dom said, "and they'll love you."

She'd much rather channel the fearless Sonia than be herself. Sonia wouldn't care what anyone thought of her.

She hung back as Dom hugged his sisters, then wrapped his arms around his mother and lifted her off the ground. She squealed.

"You must be Nina." Dom's father reached around them to

extend a hand to her. The resemblance between father and son was overwhelming; the same laughing green eyes, the same rugged good looks. If this was Dom in another thirty years, he was still going to be fighting off adoring women.

"Hello," Nina responded, shaking the outstretched hand.

"No need to be so formal with us," his mother said, engulfing Nina in a hug. For a second, Nina froze, awkward. She couldn't remember when last she'd hugged anyone – even her sister. In her world, people didn't hug. They air-kissed or cheek-pressed for the cameras.

Dom's mother's eyes crinkled as she grinned, and now Nina knew where he'd inherited his smile. "After all, you're the first girl Dom's ever brought home."

"Nina's my boss, Mom," he warned. "She's hired me to train her."

"If you say so." With a wink at Nina, she turned away, and a little of the knot in Nina's stomach unraveled. She liked Dom's parents. They seemed like warm, genuine people.

Then Dom introduced her to the family she hadn't yet met: Moira, his eldest sister, and Laura, with a baby on her hip. "My third," she said proudly once Nina had done the obligatory cooing over the dribbling child.

Then Laura's husband, who worked with his wife and Dom's father in the family construction business.

"Would you like a beer?" Juliet asked, once the introductions were done. She held out a bottle misted with icy droplets to Nina. "Or would you prefer wine?"

The lack of barb in Juliet's voice almost made Nina do a double-take. "Just water, thanks." Nina glanced at Dom. "I'm in training."

And on a diet, though that hardly needed to be said. She'd been on a diet since 2005.

"Nina very rarely drinks alcohol," Dom said.

"That must be a novel experience for you." Moira tangled her arm in her brother's. "Aren't most of the women you 'date' usually drunk when you meet them?"

"Low blow, Sis." But he laughed, not denying it.

They sat beneath the shade of the large tree making conversation as they watched the children play in the pool. Dom's mother and sisters plied her with so many questions it would have felt like an interrogation if they hadn't been delivered with such friendly curiosity. Nina had done enough interviews to know how to play this. She answered them as if she were on a talk show, regaling them with fun anecdotes from her film shoots, drawing laughter, watching their eyes grow big as she mentioned some of the major names she'd worked with and met.

"Dom never tells us fun stories like this," Laura said, bouncing her baby on her knee. "And we've missed having Christian around to entertain us."

This was why she avoided hanging out with non-celebrities. Easy for Dom to tell her to be "herself". Being herself was exhausting when she was the performing seal, having to be "on" all the time.

"Where is Christian, anyway?" Kathy asked. "We've hardly seen him since he got married."

Dom shrugged. "Working on this new project of his." He turned to Nina. "You're not the only one reinventing yourself at the moment."

Then the barbecue food was set out on a table on the patio and Nina helped to lay out the crockery and cutlery. The mouthwatering display of foods was enough to make her stomach groan. She couldn't touch at least half the foods on display, not without gaining at least five extra pounds, but the temptation was harder than usual.

"This looks amazing," Nina commented to Dom's mother. "Now I can see where Dom gets his cooking skills."

Juliet coughed and both Dom and his father looked away, stifling grins.

"Mom's a terrible cook. We don't allow her anywhere near the kitchen," Laura explained.

"I'm sorry." Nina stuttered as unaccustomed heat flooded her

159

face. So much for making them like her.

"Don't be." Dom's mother patted her arm. "It's because I can screw up even a boiled egg that my children have all emerged such excellent cooks." She leaned close and stage-whispered. "It was all part of my diabolical master plan."

Dom laughed and placed a reassuring hand on Nina's waist. "I'll show you the hole in the kitchen floor from what we call the Exploding Turkey Incident."

His touch steadied her. It was that night at the *Vanity Fair* party all over again, and Dom was her lifeline, her anchor in treacherous waters.

Then she caught Moira's raised eyebrow and slight smile, her gaze on Dom's hand at Nina's waist, and she flinched away from his touch.

She did not need Dom's family getting any ideas that this was going anywhere. It meant nothing. Meeting his family meant nothing. The way that meeting his friends had meant nothing. The way the intimacy they shared when they were alone meant nothing.

She swallowed the lump in her throat and kept her smile bright. Sonia wouldn't get a lump in her throat over things she couldn't change either.

"Here, Dom, have another kebab." Laura placed a skewer of roasted lamb and peppers on his plate, beside all the other offerings piled on it.

He frowned, trying to duck his plate away. "I'm a grown man, for heaven's sake. I can get my own food if I'm hungry."

When no one was paying them any attention she whispered in his ear: "Now I get it."

"Get what?"

"Your need to jump in to help every damsel in distress you meet. You're surrounded by women who dote on you and baby you, so with every other woman you need to be The Man."

His frown cleared and he laughed. "I *am* The Man. And I'll prove it to you later."

160

His hand snuck to her ass and she giggled. "Oh goodie."

After lunch, Nina helped clear away the empty plates.

"The coffee mugs are in there," Juliet said, pointing to a cupboard as she started making a pot of coffee. "You'll need to start learning where everything is."

Nina stopped in her tracks. "What do you mean?"

"This is a 'help yourself' kind of household, so next time you'll be expected to look after yourself."

Next time? There wouldn't be a next time.

Blinking against the sudden rush of emotions assaulting her, Nina fetched the mugs, set them down beside Juliet and leaned against the counter.

The hole in the laminate kitchen floor was unmistakable.

"Thanksgiving 2005," Juliet explained with a laugh. "The last time Mom attempted cooking a turkey."

An electric shock shot through Nina. She remembered that year's Thanksgiving only too well. But while Dom and his family had been laughing over a spoiled turkey dinner, she'd stood beside her father's empty casket. They still hadn't found his body.

And then her mother had left too.

"What's wrong?" Juliet asked, grabbing her arm. "You look like you're about to pass out."

Nina shook her head. "I'm okay." The dizzying feeling passed, the prickle of tears subsided. "It's nothing."

She tried to move away, but Juliet still held her arm. "I'm sorry I've been such a bitch. I'm a little over-protective of my little brother. It's something I need to work on, I know. Even though he's a grown man, I still remember when he was a kid and he wanted to be Superman and he tried to fly off the roof. I still don't want to see him hurt."

He wasn't the one likely to get hurt this time. It was more likely to be the other way around. Because that's what happened every time Nina let someone into her heart. They left and she got hurt.

She couldn't go through that again. Never again would she open

161

her heart to someone. She hadn't wanted to marry Paul, but she'd been safe with him. There was no risk of losing her heart to him.

But Dominic Kelly was a risk. If he weren't, then she wouldn't be the blubbering mess she was right now. Grief she'd kept at bay for years crept in through the crack he'd opened in the wall she'd built around herself.

Grief intermingled with loneliness and with fear. Fear of losing him the way she'd lost everyone else she'd ever loved. She needed to get real and quickly. Before the inevitable hurt turned into full-on heartbreak.

She needed to remember that at any moment a big wave could roll in off the sea and sweep everything away. Things like that happened all the time.

As long as she remembered that, the crack wouldn't get any wider.

She shook her head, swallowed the lump in her throat, and smiled at Juliet. "I understand. I won't hurt him."

"Friends, then?"

She nodded. Though that was hardly likely either. In a few weeks her training would be over and they'd never see each other again.

Returning to the yard, they were confronted with screams and tears. One of Laura's little children had been hurt in a boisterous game and blood streamed from her knee.

"It was an accident!" wailed Eric's sister, an older child on the cusp of teenagehood.

"Take Liam," Laura said, thrusting her baby at Nina as she and Juliet ran to attend to the drama.

Given no choice, Nina took the baby, holding him awkwardly in the crook of an arm. What was one supposed to do with a baby? She bounced him on her hip and resisted the urge to swear as sticky fingers covered in soggy cookie crumbs twisted in her hair.

And her sister wanted one of these things so badly she'd practically taken out a second mortgage?

She looked at the baby's downy head. So soft, smelling of warm, sweet baby smell. Her hands started to shake as a long-suppressed memory grasped hold of her.

She sighed in audible relief as Moira arrived and took the baby from her.

"You don't have much experience with babies, do you?" Moira asked, grinning.

Nina shuddered. "No, and I don't plan to either."

"You don't want to have a family of your own?" Moira's eyes widened, her voice hushed as if Nina had spoken some kind of sacrilege.

Nina shrugged and looked away. "Babies don't exactly fit in very well with my chosen career."

"You'll feel different when you're older." The words were spoken with that sort of smug authority that mothers got.

Nina shook her head. The long hours she worked on set weren't conducive to raising children. And why bother having them at all if you were just going to pay someone else to raise them?

"But family is everything," Moira persisted.

To the Kelly clan, family obviously was everything. They were a big, noisy family, who lived in each other's pockets. But the Alexanders had never been like that. Service to others always came before family. After Dad died and first mom then Jess had gone off to save the world, it had just been her and Gran left in that empty, echoing house in Cedar Falls. Much as she loved her grandmother, family for her was nothing like the one she was in right now.

Nina shivered. "Not wondering how I'm going to pay my bills every month is much more important to me."

Moira laughed, but it sounded strained. "Surely you're rich enough you don't need to worry about paying bills?"

It hadn't always been that way, but that was exactly how Nina planned to keep it. She had a condo she owned outright and no one was ever taking it from her.

She plastered on a smile. "Besides, I love being famous. Living inside a goldfish bowl comes with a lot of perks and opens all sorts of doors. I can get tickets to any show, invitations to any party, reservations at any restaurant. And now that I can afford to buy stuff, people keep offering it to me for free! It's a great life, but it's not fair on partners or children and I wouldn't want to put an innocent child through that."

"You could make it work if you wanted to. Other people have."

Nina shook her head. She'd met a few of the grown-up children of celebrities and they were even more screwed up than their parents.

"But what if you fall in love with a man who wants a family?" Moira asked and something clicked in Nina's head. Moira wasn't defending the virtues of familyhood. She was projecting a future for Dom. With Nina. And children.

She suppressed the manic laugh that bubbled up inside her. So not going to happen. Even if Dom were a different kind of man, she wasn't about to become a different kind of woman.

And the moment they got out of here she was calling Wendy. The sooner she could get her hands on the morning-after pill, the better.

She'd made uncomfortable requests of her PA before. None was as excruciating as asking Wendy for contraceptives and a pregnancy test kit. As always, her PA remained professional. Nina was the one who was mortified.

"It should be effective up to three days after unprotected sex, but the longer you wait, the less effective it is," Wendy said. "How long has it been?"

Nina's face flamed. "Not that long," she mumbled, hiding the brown-paper packet beneath the breakfast table before Dom's housekeeper could spot it.

"You have the Easter Red Cross benefit in a few weeks. They want to know if you're bringing a date. For the seating arrangements."

Nina was sure that was a glint in Wendy's eye as she asked, but her PA got extra credit for not glancing towards the French doors, where Dom had disappeared into the house.

"I don't think so." Nina's cheeks couldn't get any hotter. She'd forgotten all about the fundraiser. She'd need a new dress. Preferably one that wouldn't reveal the yellowing bruises from the damage Vicki had inflicted on her yesterday. Dom had taken her at her word when she'd said she wanted to toughen up. Yesterday's session hadn't been stage fighting, it had been for real.

"You can be my date." Again. One of the many perks of being a celebrity assistant was the entrée into the hottest events in town. Wendy got more of those than most.

Wendy poured herself a glass of fresh-squeezed orange juice from the jug on the table. "I had lunch with the Celebrity Assistants Association on the weekend." Her voice was a study in casual. "One of the assistants has a connection at the studio. Rumor has it Jenn Law was offered the role of Sonia, but she turned it down. It's too similar to her role in *Hunger Games* and she doesn't want to be typecast."

"Any speculation on who else they're looking at?" Nina's stomach clenched with anxiety. If they'd already offered the role to someone else, then all this training was in vain. There would be no point in continuing.

She didn't know which was worse: losing the role or stopping training.

"There are a few names on the shortlist."

Nina's heart thudded to the bottom of her ruby-red ballet flats. The carefully guarded look on Wendy's face said everything her words didn't. Whoever was on the producers' shortlist, she wasn't.

"Which names?" she managed to ask.

"Gracie Carr's the current front runner." Wendy arranged her face in a cheery smile. "But she hasn't signed a contract, so it's not over yet. We just need to up your game."

"I can't do any more than I already am."

Wendy's voice dropped so low even Nina barely caught the

165

words. "But nobody knows what you're doing. We need to leak pictures of you in training."

Nina rubbed her temple. Dom wouldn't like it. But Wendy was right. There were no second prizes in this contest, and she was in it to win. She wasn't about to lose the role of a lifetime to save Dom's feelings. "Not someone from the press. They can't be trusted. We need a photographer we can trust to take the pictures we want. Someone with connections to the right kind of magazines, who'll do exactly what we say."

"Chrissie has a guy. He'll be discreet. Dominic will never know."

It didn't surprise her that her PA and her publicist had already planned this out between them. After all, all their careers depended on Nina staying on the A-list as much as hers did. The responsibility weighed her shoulders down and she sighed. "Okay, call him. Today Dom's starting me boxing. That should make for some interesting pictures. I'll text you the address. Tell him to bring a long lens. Dom mustn't know."

But it wouldn't be long before he'd find out. And too soon this idyll would be over.

Her PA had left by the time Dom returned outside, his gym bag slung over his shoulder, his t-shirt pulling up to reveal his tanned, lean abs. Nina allowed herself a satisfied smile. She'd just have to make the most of every uninterrupted minute she had left with him.

"Ready to go?" he asked.

"Give me a moment." She hurried inside, clutching the brown paper bag. Locking herself in the bathroom, she swallowed the morning-after pill then pulled out a pregnancy test kit. Wendy had brought three. Nina fumbled open the first box.

The first rose-pink line took forever to appear. Long, heart-stopping moments as the second hand on her wristwatch ticked around. One line. The hands on her watch ticked over to five minutes.

If there was going to be a second line it would have appeared by now, surely.

Dom banged on the door. "We're going to be late," he called.

She carefully wrapped the remaining test kits back in the brown-paper bag and stashed them inside her toiletry bag. Then she threw away the used test and washed her hands.

When she emerged from the bathroom, it was with a bounce in her step. "Okay, I'm good to go." Everything was going to be okay. Anything was possible.

Another two weeks flew past. Now and then Nina caught a glint of light she was sure was the lens of a camera, but Dom didn't seem to notice and she kept her mouth shut. But the knowledge that every day together could be their last hung over her like the Sword of Damocles.

Not that she had time to dwell on her fears. Dom kept her working until long after dark each day, without a day off. In addition to boxing and Krav Maga, he'd started her doing actual stunts, everyday bread-and-butter work for stunt people, but the kinds of things most actors never attempted. The kind of things that would give film insurers heebie-jeebies if they suspected their prize actors were even attempting them.

She mastered climbing walls and sword fighting, abseiled and learned how to do low falls – step-outs and headers and back falls. Dom taught her to ride a motorcycle and how to roll across the hood of a slow-moving car, making it look as if she'd been hit.

They had their first argument when he refused to let her try a full-body burn, but she took part in a SWAT team tactical training exercise, a building entry and clearance which ended in a choreographed gun fight, complete with live ammunition and squibs exploding all around.

Using what she'd learned on the trapeze and the lyra, she did simple wirework and one of the biggest thrills was being shot off an air ram into an airbag, as if she'd been thrown by an explosion. This was a world away from the sweet rom-com roles she'd played before and it was *fun*. She wanted the role of Sonia more than ever because the thought of spending the next two years of her life being paid to do this almost every day was the biggest carrot ever dangled before her. It would make the dull work of press junkets and premieres much more palatable.

By far the most fascinating aspect of stunt work, she discovered, was the planning that went into it. She listened carefully as Dom and his team plotted out every step, scrutinized the risks, discussed the safety measures. There wasn't a single element of any stunt that was left to chance. She learned to look at stunt people in a whole new light. Like true warriors, they weren't daredevils or adrenalin junkies. They took their work seriously.

She looked at Dom differently, too. He wasn't the badass she'd once believed him to be. He was a professional, devoted to a job he loved, and doing it to the best of his abilities. She understood that better than anyone.

"When am I going to see you do a real stunt?" she asked, as they lay in bed one night. Her fingers trailed idly over his chest. "Vicki tells me your specialty is high falls and that you're in very big demand."

"I'm not accepting any stunt jobs right now. I'm training you."

Her hand stilled. "Wendy showed me the invoice you sent her. You've charged your friends' regular daily fees and for the hard costs of the protective gear and the materials you're using to train me, but you're not charging much for your own time."

Dom shrugged, a slight move that dislodged her head from where it had lain against his shoulder. She leaned up on her elbow to look at him. "You'd be earning a great deal more taking on proper paying stunt work. Don't you need the money?"

"I'm good, thanks."

She frowned and sat up, brushing the hair out of her eyes. This bungalow might not be large, but the trendy neighborhood wasn't exactly cheap. Nor was the brand-new Jeep parked in his garage. And from what she'd seen of his family home, his parents were comfortable but not wealthy, so it wasn't as if they were bank-rolling him. How was he able to maintain this lifestyle without working?

Cold fear gripped her stomach. She wasn't a stranger to friends and lovers trying to worm their way into her life in hopes of an easy ride to riches. She hadn't thought Dom was one of them.

He sighed and rose to sit beside her, the sheet falling away to bare his torso. She looked quickly away, but he caught her chin and forced her to look back at him.

"I don't need you for your money, Nina. I'm a self-made man and I have everything I need and want right here."

"All this from doing stunts?" she waved a hand around at the room, wanting hard to believe him but still not able to suppress the mistrust that seemed to have grown and grown inside her since the day her safe 16-year-old life had been blown apart.

"The more dangerous the stunt, the higher the adjustment fee I earn, and I've done quite a few big stunts in my time. So, yes, all this comes courtesy of me throwing myself off things or into things. I get great residuals, too, and a lot of the cash in my bank account comes courtesy of Christian."

She raised an eyebrow. How did his friend, her former co-star Christian Taylor, fit into this?

"I get a percentage of the gross on a few of his movies."

Wow. That would add up to some serious small change. A ghost of a smile curved her lips. "So you don't need me for my money?"

"Nope." He pulled her down beside him, tumbling her into his arms. "But I do need something else from you and I'm not getting it with all this talk."

His mouth pressed down on hers, driving her fears and her insecurities back into that dark place inside her, where she tried to keep them contained. She wrapped her arms around his neck and allowed herself to let go, giving in to his touch. *This*, at least, she trusted.

Chapter Twelve

Nina lay on the lounger in the enclosed part of Dominic's yard, where the sun seemed to bake down the hottest. Though her book lay open in her lap, she hadn't absorbed much. Her eyes kept drifting closed.

Paul's house in the Hollywood Hills had an infinity pool and a view that went on forever, the kind of security that guaranteed privacy, and servants on hand to cater to every whim. Yet she'd never felt as comfortable or as safe there as she did here in this tiny, sunny yard.

Since Dom had given her a day off to recover from the grueling week he'd put her through, she could have gone home to her condo. She could be soaking in the hot tub right now, or lazing beside the communal pool. But Dom hadn't suggested she leave and neither had she.

She couldn't remember when last she'd had a day of doing absolutely nothing. Today she could simply be herself for a few hours. Whoever that was.

She hadn't even bothered with make-up.

Not that there seemed much point anymore. According to her agent, the producers had offered the role in *Revelations* to Gracie Carr. The news wasn't out yet, but with the intense public interest in the movies, how much longer would it be?

The clock was ticking. Like a time-bomb.

She should tell Dom, before he heard the news from someone else. She should end her training and move home. Though Dom's bungalow felt more like home now than her sterile apartment ever had.

She should, but she wouldn't. Maybe tomorrow. Today, she was too tired to think about it.

Her eyes drifted closed again and she soaked in the rich fragrance of the flowers that filled the raised beds around her. A wind chime sang softly and beyond, the sound now so ingrained in her psyche it no longer sounded threatening but rather lulling, was the constant song of the sea.

The yard gate squeaked open and she twisted around, then smiled and waved. "Over here."

"Good morning," Wendy greeted her, setting down a brown-paper shopping bag and a dress bag on the empty chair beside Nina. "I've brought your dress for the fundraiser."

Nina shaded her eyes against the bright light. She needed her sunglasses. She was going to give herself wrinkles. "Did you get the face cream I asked for?"

Wendy nodded and rooted in the shopping bag. But it wasn't face cream she pulled out. She removed a popular weekly tabloid. "It's on page five."

Nina took the magazine, flicked it open. No wonder it had taken so long for the pictures to surface. Not just one single shot, but an entire double-page spread.

She'd rather have had one grainy long-lens photo published a couple of weeks ago when she still had a fighting chance at the role.

"Hi, Wendy, you arrived at a good time. Would you like coffee?" Dom entered the yard carrying a tray of cups and a French press. Rich coffee aroma filled the air.

Nina hurriedly closed the magazine, but of course Dom noticed. "What is it?" he asked.

Better to get this over with, right?

171

She held out the magazine and he set down the tray to take it from her. She tried not to flinch as he looked at the pictures. Pictures of her in the boxing ring, looking suitably kickass. Another of the two of them on his bike, her arms wrapped intimately around him, her cheek resting on his shoulder. Another of the two of them walking through the farmers' market, holding hands and laughing. That had been careless. Careless but wonderful.

The largest picture in the spread had been taken the day he'd introduced her to the air ram. She wore a body harness, primed and ready to be catapulted into the waiting mats, and Dom stood behind her, his hands on her hips. But the camera wasn't focused on her. It was focused on Dom. Shirtless.

She imagined a lot of women drooling over that picture. *She* wanted to drool over it.

She should get Wendy to ask the magazine for a high-res, blown-up version to keep the memories alive when her training was over. Her chest tightened and tears pricked at her eyes. She must really be tired. She seemed on the verge of tears a lot these days.

"Chrissie's work again?" Dom asked.

Wendy shook her head. "The article cites a 'resident of Venice Beach' who's seen you around. That must have tipped the magazine off that Nina's still in town, and they've probably had someone following you for a few days."

She lied well. Nina owed her a raise. She was immensely grateful she hadn't had to lie outright to Dom herself.

"I'm sorry," she said, begging Dom to look at her.

He shrugged. "What do you need to feel sorry for? It was inevitable." He finally looked up from the pages. "Nice pictures, though why anyone would be interested that you wore red pumps to the market beats me."

"You won't believe the intense public interest in everything she does," Wendy said, moving the dress bag to sit on the chair next to Nina. "The one time she went to the supermarket, a celebrity gossip site posted a complete list of everything she bought. You should have seen the heated debate in the comments section on whether the tomatoes were local or imported."

"You're not mad?" Nina asked, needing an answer, her stomach still squeezed tight.

Dom passed the magazine back. "I don't like being manipulated. When Chrissie leaked the pictures, it felt exploitative. But this..." he waved at the paper. "This couldn't be helped."

Far from feeling relief, the tense knot in her stomach tightened. Did it count as manipulation if he didn't know about it?

Dom shrugged. "It'll be an inconvenience going out if people are watching for you and crowding you for autographs everywhere we go, but you're the one who said you didn't want to stop living your life because of your fame. So we carry on your training until something changes."

'Something changes' being a euphemism for when the producers announced they'd filled the main role in *Revelations*. The announcement could only be days away. With pre-production already in full swing, they had to have someone contracted and in training for the role soon. This magazine exclusive was Nina's last hope, and even that might be too late. Tears burned her eyes again and this time she couldn't blink them back.

Thanks to a scandal involving everyone's favorite clean-cut boy-band lead singer and a male prostitute, the media frenzy Dom expected never materialized. There were a few more cameras wherever they went, a few more autograph-hunters, but the residents of Venice Beach took it in their stride that a celebrity was living among them and left them alone.

"It wasn't us who leaked the news," his neighbor said, bringing over a bottle of wine, which they shared on the deck as the sun set over the ocean.

Nina shrugged and looked away. "It was bound to happen, I guess."

Dom frowned as he watched her. Perhaps he'd overworked

her. She tired so easily these days and seemed preoccupied and withdrawn. He noticed the effort it cost her to keep up her perky persona in public.

Something was troubling her, he was sure.

According to his sources, pre-production on *Revelations* was progressing at a rapid pace. He hadn't heard yet if the role of Sonia had been offered to anyone. Surely she would tell him if she'd heard?

"Not everyone can keep up your pace," Juliet commented, popping in the next morning to take Sandy out for a run.

He shook his head. If anyone could keep up with him, it was Nina.

Nearly five weeks now she'd been living with him and not once had she complained about any task he'd set her. She'd fitted into his life and into his home as if she belonged there. Now that the press knew she was in town and training, she could have returned home to her condo. But she hadn't, and he wasn't going to be the first to suggest it.

Even so, a distance had sprung up between them. In bed Nina was as playful and uninhibited as before, but outside the bedroom it was as though she was holding something back. He was too afraid to ask what it was. If it meant the end of their relationship, then he didn't want to know.

Only in the quiet moments while Nina slept, before the pain-killers kicked in and enabled him to sleep too, did he admit to mixed feelings about her getting the role. As much as he wanted her to succeed, if Nina won the role of Sonia she would be gone out of his life without a backward glance.

And he'd have surgery and a long recuperation period ahead. He wouldn't be able to return to stunt work for many months. If ever. And he'd be alone. His future gaped empty before him.

Dom found Nina in the guest bedroom trying on a pair of jeans. "The zipper goes all the way to the top!" she announced, face aglow with excitement.

He leaned against the doorframe. "Isn't that what they're supposed to do?"

"Not this pair! I'm going to have to send my stylist shopping for a kickass new wardrobe to go with this kickass new body." She ran her hands down over her hips and grinned back at him over her shoulder. "I should have hired you a long time ago."

He crossed to her, wrapped his arms around her, and nuzzled her neck. She tilted her head back against his shoulder to give him better access. "Mmm... there are a lot of things I should have done a long time ago."

He tasted the beat of her pulse against his tongue. "Like?" he managed to murmur.

"This." She turned in his arms, pressed her lips to his.

It was tempting to let the kiss go on forever. Even more tempting to tumble her onto the bed and get between her legs. But then the chances were pretty good at least half the morning would be gone before he came up for air.

With a groan, he pulled out of the kiss. "Put on your swim suit. We're going to the beach."

"Why do I need a swim suit to go running?"

"We're not going running. Juliet's taken Sandy out for us instead." He swallowed as she unzipped the jeans and began to peel them off. "There's a south swell this morning and I'm taking you to San Onofre State Beach."

"Another day off?" She smiled and the light was back in her eyes. "Would it be terribly un-Sonia-like of me to ask if this means I can get to lie on the beach and read?"

"If you want, though that seems a terrible waste of a trip to the beach."

"It's my idea of heaven."

The jeans came off and he had to turn away. The bed was rapidly becoming a much more attractive option than the beach, but it wasn't every day the surf conditions were this ideal. And there was one final task he wanted Nina to accomplish before he'd consider her training complete.

He had the car loaded with his longboard, cooler box, and other paraphernalia by the time Nina emerged from the house dressed in a flannel check shirt open over a white tank top, cut-off denim shorts that made her tanned legs appear to go on for miles, and flip flops. She chucked her big beach bag into the car seat behind them and hopped in beside him.

The drive to San Clemente took over an hour. With the sun shining, the windows down, and rock music blaring, it felt like a holiday. Especially with all the impatient commuters headed in the opposite direction.

On a weekend, the beach would be packed, but it was just another weekday. A handful of tourists, a couple of moms with their kids, and the die-hard surfers, black seal-like figures in the water, were the only occupants of the beach. Nevertheless, Nina pulled on a big beach hat and sunglasses to conceal her identity.

Dom chose an unoccupied part of the beach, well back from the water, and spread out a vast beach blanket and shade cover.

"Will you rub lotion into my back?" Nina asked.

He took the lotion bottle she held out, his breath catching as she stripped off her t-shirt and shorts, and stretched out on the blanket in a bikini that left little to his imagination. He'd explored every inch of her body these last few weeks, knew how to make her moan and how to make her scream, yet he still couldn't get enough of her.

Maybe this settling down-with-one-woman thing wasn't as bad as he'd always believed it to be. But wasn't it just bloody typical that he finally found a woman who could do 'no complications' even better than he could and he wanted to try for something more with her?

He knelt beside her and poured the lotion onto his hands. Then he began the slow slide of his hands over her body.

Nina was definitely thinner and more angular than when she'd started training, her muscles more defined. With her Mediterranean coloring her skin tanned easily, but the tan looked more natural now than before. As much as he missed the softer, more feminine roundness of her curves, he had to admit he liked this new Nina, too. Now she had the kickass body to match her kickass temperament.

He stroked the lotion into her skin, a long glide of his hands over her back. Up and over her shoulders, brushing the edges of her breasts. Nina closed her eyes and moaned. Exactly the response he'd hoped to elicit, but now he wanted to moan, too.

"You don't want to be making sounds like that here where everyone can see us," he suggested, his voice a low growl. "Unless you want me to do something very, very bad to you in a public place."

"Okay, I'll be a good girl," she promised, burying her head in her arms. But he noticed she had to bite her lip as his hands slid over the curve of her buttocks, down the sensitive skin of her thighs.

His temperature must have shot up by at least ten degrees, and it had nothing to do with the baking spring sunshine. Public sex has always been his biggest turn-on, the risk of getting caught heightening the experience, and he suspected Nina felt the same. But this beach was *too* public. Even for him.

He glanced around. No one on the beach looked their way. He rolled her over and poured more lotion on his hands, then started on her stomach, stroking circles over her smooth skin, inching toward her breasts.

Nina moaned again and he leaned down to catch the sound with his mouth, pinning her to the blanket, his hands splayed on either side of her breasts. She opened up in response, their tongues tangled, and he lost himself in her taste, in her soft, wet wildness.

She ran her hands up his chest and he shivered against her touch.

"I think you need to stop now," she whimpered. "Or I am going to do something very, very bad to *you* in a public place."

"Yes, please do stop," a voice intruded.

They shot apart.

Christian Taylor stood over them, hands on hips, feet planted wide. Beside him stood his new bride, a half-smile curving her mouth.

"You texted you were coming down here today, so we thought we'd join you."

Dom rolled away from Nina, scowling. "That wasn't an invitation."

"No, but just as well we're here. It looks like you two need supervision if you're not going to end up in the tabloids for all the wrong reasons."

"Are there any right reasons to be in the tabloids?" Dom rose and wiped off his hands, then helped his friend spread out another beach blanket beside theirs.

Christian shrugged. "Are we going to stand here talking all day, or are we going to hit the surf?"

Dom glanced at Nina and she nodded.

"Enjoy your book." He stripped off his shirt, bent down to brush a kiss against her cheek, then picked up his longboard and headed for the water's edge.

"Could be good for your reputation to be seen with a lovely, wholesome girl like Nina," Christian said, catching him up. Which wasn't hard since he'd slowed to a walk. The anti-inflammatories no longer seemed to be enough to keep the constant ache at bay.

"It'll be a whole lot worse for her reputation to be seen with me," Dom muttered.

No one cared what a stunt man did when he wasn't in front of the camera. But the boyfriend of an A-list movie star...he'd certainly provided plenty of fodder for the tabloid gossips if they dug into his past.

He added a burst of speed and sprinted into the waves, gritting his teeth against the pain.

"Hi." Nina forced warmth into her voice as she greeted Teresa.

178

The willowy blonde stretched out on the blanket beside her with the lithe elegance of a cat. "It's good to see you again."

Nina had always felt inferior in the other woman's presence, but who wouldn't? Not only was Teresa as flawlessly perfect as most models could only be after hours of a stylist's attention and skilled airbrushing, but she was an aristocrat and heiress to boot.

Christian's harsher critics suggested he'd only snagged such a prize bride because of his newly revealed royal bloodline. Nina knew better. She'd had the privilege of watching from the sidelines as Christian changed from philandering heart throb to a man with eyes for only one woman. Any woman would find that seductive.

Nina shaded her eyes and looked out to sea, her heart pulling tight as she searched anxiously for Dominic, only breathing again when she spotted him paddling out into deeper water. She watched as he stood on the board and surfed back in on the crest of a wave. He made it look effortless and graceful, while the beginners in the shallows fumbled and fell.

He knew what he was doing. He was a stunt man, for heaven's sake. He could take care of himself. But as irrational as her fear was, it wouldn't let go its tight hold on her stomach.

She forced her gaze away, instead pulling her copy of *An Astronaut's Guide to Life on Earth* out of her bag, pleased to notice that Teresa had also brought out a romance novel, so she wouldn't be expected to make conversation.

But her attention refused to stay on the page. At last, Dom strode out of the water, his board beneath his arm, water sluicing down his bare chest, his hair wet, and his board shorts plastered to his thighs. He was the most heart-stoppingly gorgeous man she'd ever seen.

She drank in the sight of him, trying to burn the memory into her brain. She would have to tell him soon that Gracie Carr had been offered the role in *Revelations*.

Dom planted the board in the sand and flopped down beside her on the blanket, splattering her with droplets. She squealed and he laughed, leaning in to kiss her. His lips were hot and wet, and tangy from the sea. She opened her mouth to him, and she could almost taste the adrenalin still pumping through him.

But when he pulled away, his adrenalin rush ebbing, she noticed the pinched look around his mouth, as if he were in pain. He rubbed his hip. She wasn't sure he was even conscious of the movement, but he'd been doing it increasingly of late. "What's wrong?"

"Nothing." He flashed a smile, a little too bright, a little too offhand. "I just need a rest before I go back out there again."

Christian didn't need a rest. He sat astride his board far out, a dark speck against the glare of water, waiting for the next big wave to roll in.

Her eyes narrowed as she turned back to Dom. She wanted to push, to force him to open up to her and be honest, but she didn't have that right, did she? She'd agreed to "casual" and casual lovers didn't pry.

Teresa seemed to have no such qualms. She leaned forward to look past Nina at Dom. "Is that still the injury from Paris bothering you?"

He shrugged, not looking at Nina.

A wave of anger, concern, and fear engulfed her. "You're injured?" she demanded.

He didn't answer.

"Should you even be training me?"

At that he looked up, but his face was a mask, shutting her out. "Training you hasn't been that difficult. A lot of other people have done the grunt work."

She held his gaze for a long moment, but he gave away nothing more. He'd taken her running almost every day. He'd taught her *jiu jitsu* and ridden horses and done things in bed that most ordinary men would find difficult. Surely he couldn't do all that if he were injured?

But something nagged at her memory.

Dom looked away. "You want to use my board?" he asked Teresa.

Teresa rose.

"You surf?" Nina asked, unable to hide her surprise. The always-elegant blonde had never struck her as the athletic sort.

Teresa smiled, not a half-smile this time but a brilliant, wide smile. "Dom taught me when we were in the Caribbean filming the rest of *The Pirate's Revenge*. He's an excellent teacher, isn't he?"

Envy stirred. Nina hadn't been involved in that leg of the shoot. For the first time since she'd started training with him, she felt like an outsider. There was so much she didn't know about him, so many parts of his life she was excluded from.

A painful reminder that even though she'd met his friends and his family, and achieved a far greater intimacy with him than she ever had with Paul, she was nothing more than just another woman passing through the revolving door of his life. The blasted tears welled again and she had to blink them back.

"Of course the waves in Los Pajaros aren't ideal for surfing, but it was a safe place to learn." Teresa hefted the surfboard and sent them a backward wave as she headed down the beach to join her husband in the water.

"This is a good beginner beach," Dom said, stretching out beside Nina.

Though he didn't look at her, she shuddered. "No way are you teaching me to surf!"

"Why not? Until you've conquered the last of your fears, you won't be ready to play Sonia."

She wouldn't be playing Sonia. And that wouldn't change, even if she stopped being afraid. This would be a good time to tell him. But she couldn't bring herself to do it. She still hadn't quite come to terms with it herself.

Besides, she'd contracted him for one more week of training. Even if it was pointless, she wasn't ready for it to end yet.

"I got through the water obstacle in that commando course," she said instead.

"You got through it. But you were a mess when you came out

181

the other side. That's facing your fears, but not conquering them."

"What do you know about fear? You're not afraid of anything." She bit her lip. She hadn't meant for the words to spill out so full of emotion. What had gotten into her?

He caught her face and looked her in the eyes. "There are a lot of things I'm afraid of. Heights is one of them. But I've been conquering that fear since I was a kid. I refused to let my fear beat me. I've studied it and learned to control it. But here you sit on the beach on a glorious day and you won't even get your feet wet in the water. That's letting your fear control you."

With his thumb he wiped away the lone tear that leaked down her cheek.

"Come with me into the water. I'll keep you safe."

She knew he would. But that wasn't enough. He couldn't stop the memories from rising up and choking her. She looked out at the ocean. "I can't." She tried to make light of it. "I'm from Iowa, remember. Not a lot of sea there."

Dom frowned. "You told Jacob you grew up in Louisiana."

She swallowed down the emotions that welled. They seemed unusually raw today, too close to the surface. "We moved away when I was 16."

"When your father died."

Did he really have to go into this *now*?

Try not to let the emotions show. She nodded.

"You're in your mid-twenties now. Were you living there when Katrina hit?"

"Yes." Damn. She hadn't been able to hide the harsh abruptness of her tone. She definitely had his attention now.

"And you evacuated to Iowa?"

Slowly she shook her head. "We didn't evacuate."

His eyes widened as he took in the words. "You were there? You stayed through it all?"

She nodded. "My parents both worked in emergency services. They couldn't leave and they didn't want to leave. And my mother didn't want me and Jess travelling out of state with strangers. She didn't want to split up the family." The irony. "So we stayed. It wasn't supposed to be so bad. My mother took us to work with her. At least the hospital had generators in the basement. It should have been a safe place."

"But it wasn't."

"There aren't words to describe what it was like, and I didn't even have it so bad. So many people had it a lot worse."

He said nothing, just waited. Would it be rude to say "*I don't want to talk about it anymore*"? Probably. And it would throw up that wall between them again. She was growing tired of that damned wall.

"The basement flooded and the generators failed. It was stinking hot and there was so little food and drinking water. And the smell…" she choked, as the familiar foul smell overwhelmed her, the memory so tangible she could have been back there.

Four days of that water everywhere. Water that smelled of death. She coughed on the taste in her mouth. "I need a drink."

She rose and moved to the cooler box set in the shade. She dug her hands into the ice, tempted to rub a handful of ice chips across the back of her neck. Instead, she took out two bottles of water and returned to the beach blanket. Dom hadn't moved.

"You never told me," he said, taking the icy bottle she held out to him.

She shrugged. "It didn't come up."

"There's more, isn't there?"

She no longer cared if it was rude. "I don't want to talk about it."

"Talking is good for you. You can't keep it bottled up inside."

Wanna bet? She'd got through the last ten years by bottling it up, by hiding it behind the wall she'd built around her heart to keep the rest of the world out. "Do you talk like this with all the women you sleep with?" she joked.

"No, this is a first. But I'm up for the challenge if you are."

She couldn't remember when last she'd spoken about those

days to anyone. Perhaps never. Her family didn't talk about things like this. Alexanders didn't need counseling. They gave it to other people. Alexanders were strong and brave and fearless.

Everything she wasn't.

"Tell me about it." He didn't sound morbidly curious, like most of the people she'd met. He sounded concerned.

And he was probably right. She needed to talk about it.

"Sitting around doing nothing was even worse. My sister is very much like my parents. She volunteered to work on the wards. I…" Nina swallowed a mouthful of cold water as she fought for control. "I'm not a hero. I'm not good with sickness and suffering. I spent most of my time in the maternity ward, helping with the babies. Until…with the power out, even the babies were vulnerable. One died."

A baby whose mother had a difficult birth. A baby Nina had cuddled and helped to feed. She shook her head. Some memories were better suppressed.

"We lived in Mandeville, in a regular suburb with nice houses and friendly neighbors. I hear it's like that again. I read somewhere it's one of the Top 100 places to live in the country now. But when we finally managed to get home, there was nothing left for us. The storm surge had done so much damage the house couldn't be saved. We were homeless. After a couple of weeks living in a shelter, we moved to live with my Gran in Iowa."

"How did your father die?"

She shrugged and stared out to sea. "We're not really sure. They never found his body. He probably drowned and was washed out to sea." She pressed the cold bottle to her temple. "He was part of a search and rescue team. Though he worked on the frontline, we weren't worried for him. My father was Superman. Danger never fazed him. But he always put other people's wellbeing over his own safety. It's a family trait." She pressed her mouth into a tight line. A trait that had somehow skipped over her and she was glad. Her family might think her selfish for the way she lived her life, but she was okay with that.

"When we couldn't reach him for days, I was afraid. I had this terrible sense of foreboding. My mother told me I was being foolish. He was just busy and communications were down."

But she hadn't been foolish. She'd been right.

She breathed out a heavy sigh, releasing tension she hadn't realized she'd been carrying with her. "Katrina polarized everything for my family." At last she dragged her gaze away from the waves and looked at him. "When my mother finally accepted he was gone, she decided that losing everything, the house, all our possessions, even the dog…" Nina hiccuped. "She decided it was a sign that she needed to help other people who'd been through what we'd been through. When the insurance money paid out, Mom didn't buy a new home. She left me and Jess with Gran, joined the Red Cross and that's where she's been ever since: travelling from one disaster zone to another. Jess only stayed at home as long as it took her to graduate. Then she left, too. She and her husband work for FEMA these days. Also saving the world and being heroic."

"And you haven't felt part of a family since."

She met his gaze. "It doesn't matter. I'm okay on my own."

At least she had been until she'd met Dom. Until he'd reminded her how it felt to be part of something bigger than just herself, to be part of a family and a circle of friends rather than an entourage of pseudo-friends she paid to do her bidding. She bit her lip. "You know how lucky you are?" she asked softly.

He nodded, but she didn't think he truly realized what he had.

"Now I know where you get your strength and your fearlessness from," he said, the beginnings of a grin lifting his mouth. "You're obviously your father's daughter."

"I'm not fearless! And I'm not strong. My sister Jessie's the strong one. I'm the odd one out in the family."

He arched an eyebrow. "These last few weeks, I've watched you tackle things that most ordinary people wouldn't even imagine doing. And you've tackled them with dedication, commitment, and passion. I'm sure your father would have been proud of you."

She couldn't speak.

He stroked her face, his cool fingers brushing a tendril of hair away from her over-heated face. "I'm proud of you."

She turned into his hand, closing her eyes as wave after wave of emotion channeled through her. For once, she didn't stop the emotions, didn't chase them back into the dark, unexplored part of herself. She let the tears roll.

The tears would have frightened off a lesser man. She should have known Dom wouldn't bat an eye. He had four sisters, after all.

"Feeling better yet?" he asked her at last, when the tears finally stopped rolling. He handed her a towel to mop up her face, though she didn't think it would be enough to fix her ravaged make-up. Oh hell – what if a camera saw her now?

But she nodded and handed the towel back, then took a long drink of water from her bottle.

He rose and held out a hand to her. "So you're ready to give the water a try now?"

She shook her head in alarm. "No way. You are not getting me in there."

"Want to bet?" With a smirk he scooped her up off the ground. She shrieked and flailed against his chest, but he held her fast, until he'd walked clear into the breakers. Then he dropped her slowly to her feet, keeping his arms firmly around her.

The water came to her hip height and it was a lot colder than she'd expected. A wave washed in around them, heading for the sandy beach, then pulled back, sucking at them as it went and rocking her against Dom. She clung to him.

"Not so bad, is it?" he asked.

Not so bad. Goosebumps rose on her arms, but not for any of the usual reasons. The water didn't smell like death, and it hadn't swept her off her feet. "Don't let go," she warned.

"I won't." He grinned at her and then he dropped his mouth to hers and kissed her. She delighted in the salty taste of his tongue, in the solid bunched muscle of his arms beneath her clinging fingers, in the rasp of his unshaved cheek over her sensitive skin. She barely noticed the push and pull of the waves around them now. She was too busy making new memories to erase the old ones.

The four of them shared a picnic lunch together. An entire morning had passed by without a single fan hassling them for a photograph or a signature. With the weight of the past magically lifted off her shoulders, Nina was almost able to forget that the role of Sonia Fairchild was now someone else's. She was even almost able to forget that her time with Dom was nearly at an end.

She reveled in the feel of the sun on her skin. What did it matter if she turned pink tomorrow? It wasn't as if she had a role to keep herself flawless for. She smiled when Teresa insisted on taking a picture of her and Dom together, laughed when he and Christian started clowning around, and when Dom again suggested he teach her how to surf…she said yes.

It was late afternoon and her skin had begun to tingle with the mix of water droplets and sun when she finally waded in out of the sea and collapsed, exhausted but happy, on the beach blanket. The men were still out there, engaged in a friendly competition, and Teresa was now buried in her book. Nina had barely glanced at hers all day.

She lay back on the blanket, closing her eyes and letting the sated feeling take over her body. The buzz of her phone in her bag interrupted the welcome moment of rest.

She dug in her bag. Five missed calls. Oops.

With an apologetic grimace to Teresa, she took the call.

"Why haven't you been answering your phone?" Dane demanded.

"My bad. I'm at the beach." Though from the sounds of surf and wind, he could hardly have missed that.

"I thought you were in training 24/7?" But he didn't sound reproving, and she let out a relieved breath. "Whatever it is you're doing, you need to cancel it."

She had to hold her hand over her other ear to hear. "Why?"

"Because Gracie Carr just turned down the role of Sonia. The silly girl's gone and got herself knocked up and she wants to keep it. They need to re-cast in a hurry. You really owe Chrissie big time. The casting director saw that spread of you in the magazine, so you're back in with a shot. Can you do a callback with the director tomorrow morning?"

The air sucked out of her lungs and for a moment she felt faint. She glanced down at her fingernails. She hadn't had a manicure since before Oscar night. Her skin would be an unsightly shade of pink tomorrow. And her dark roots were growing out.

"Tomorrow afternoon?" she asked, hoping fervently she wasn't pushing her luck. Her stylist would have to pull out all the stops to get her ready for the cameras.

"I'll let you know when and where."

She hung up the phone and took a steadying breath. Her heart hammered against her ribs as she stashed the phone inside her bag. *Yes!!*

She looked for Dom. He and Christian stood at the water's edge, talking. The tips of their surfboards dug into the sand. She rose on unsteady legs and at the movement Dom turned to look at her.

Clear across the distance of the beach, his gaze met hers. He raised an eyebrow and she could no longer contain her smile. She waved and shouted. "I got it! I got the callback!"

Chapter Thirteen

Nina opened her eyes and wished she hadn't. Though she hadn't moved a muscle, her stomach lurched. She was glad she slept on the side of the bed closest to the bathroom door because she only just made it to the toilet in time. Not that there was a lot in her stomach to throw up, but it kept coming anyway, until her whole body shook.

Great. Just great.

She hadn't been sick like this before an audition in years. Did the nerves really have to kick back in now, when she had a callback in…she glanced through the open door at the wall clock in Dom's room…only seven hours?

She often suffered a paralyzing attack of nerves the first morning of a new shoot, but never this bad. Usually she couldn't sleep a wink the night before a new shoot either, but with Dom's arms cradling her, she'd slept like a baby last night. So why now?

Maybe it wasn't nerves. Maybe it was last night's seafood dinner. It had tasted all right at the time… She had to bend down over the toilet bowl again as another wave of nausea hit.

Okay, better not to think about seafood.

Better to figure out how she was going to pull herself together enough to give a blinding performance in the callback.

She peered back into the murky bedroom. Dom's side of the

bed was empty. He must have gone for his usual morning run and let her sleep in. Again. He'd been doing that a lot lately. Because he was growing tired of having her in his space and wanted time away from her? Or because her training was nearly done and he didn't need to work her so hard?

All going well, she wouldn't need any more training after today. All going well, she'd be more concerned with negotiating her fee and the size of her trailer for the role of Sonia. Though in all honesty, she'd *pay* the producers to give her the role.

No more training.

No more trapeze, no more Evan or Gianna or Vicki, or the half dozen other amazing friends she'd made on this journey.

No more Dom.

This time when she bent over the toilet bowl, there was nothing left in her stomach. But the dry retching made her cold and shivery.

This had to stop. Now.

Downstairs a door banged and she heard Sandy's playful bark. She couldn't let Dom see her like this.

She opened the door of the closet beneath the basin and her eyes widened. It took her a moment to regroup before she started searching amongst the medicines for something to combat nausea. She found it at the back of the packed cupboard, managed to pull herself to standing, swallow two tablets and splash her face with water, before Dom appeared in the door.

"I got us fresh croissants from the bakery," he said. "Are you okay?"

"Just a bad case of nerves. Are you running some sort of Canadian online pharmacy from your bathroom?"

"What?" His brow furrowed.

She pointed to the open closet door. "You have more painkillers and anti-inflammatories than a drugstore. And steroid injections."

"Occupational hazard." Dom shut the closet door and turned away. "I'll make a pot of coffee to go with the croissants."

Nina brushed her teeth and hair and dressed in a summery

blouse and jeans. Her stylist would provide more Sonia-appropriate clothing for the audition, but for now the jeans were a trophy. They were the cast-off jeans she hadn't been able to fit into the first morning she'd woken in Dom's house. It seemed a lifetime ago.

Dom had laid out a spread on the kitchen counter, but she couldn't face eating. She sipped the coffee, too strung-out to make conversation, and Dom seemed to understand. Before her previous Sonia audition, Paul hadn't stopped talking, giving her tips and advice until she'd been in a hurry to get away to the safety of her stylist's care.

"Do you want me to pick you up after the callback?" he asked at last, pulling her out of her abstraction. "Perhaps I could take you out for dinner somewhere to celebrate?"

She shook her head.

His face was a mask, but she didn't need to see his expression to know what he was thinking. And she was flattered. No, flattered wasn't the right word. She was pleased. Hopefully this meant he wasn't quite done with her yet.

She rose from the stool and moved around the counter to stand between his knees. "I don't want you to pick me up afterwards because I want you to come with me. I *need* you there with me."

He wrapped an arm around her waist and pulled her in close against his body. She lost herself in his warmth and strength. She needed him there with her because she couldn't do this without him. Even now, his touch drove away her fears, as it had done in the pounding surf yesterday.

She buried her head in his shoulder so he wouldn't see her tears. What was wrong with her? It was unlike her to get so emotional, so tearful, no matter how keyed-up she was for a callback.

"That'll be your car," Dom said, pushing her gently away. She hadn't even heard a car, but a moment later the doorbell rang. It wasn't Wendy, though.

"I wasn't sure what to bring you," Juliet said, handing a big bunch of flowers to Nina. "They're for good luck. Break a leg and all that stuff. I really hope you get the role."

"Are you also going to ask me to put in a good word for them to make Dom the stunt coordinator if I get the job?" Nina teased back. Though she was only half joking. All of Dom's friends had asked it at some point.

Juliet shot Dom an arch look and shook her head. "No, I don't want Dom to get the job."

Dom scowled back and Nina looked between them. But she couldn't guess what had caused the sudden tension in the air. Dom was his usual taciturn self, giving little away, and for once his sister seemed to have decided to keep her mouth shut.

The kitchen was so quiet that this time the purr of an engine followed by a car door slam was unmistakable.

"That's my ride," she said, eager to get away from the atmosphere between the siblings.

She hurried to her room to fetch her bag, not bothering to close the door behind her. And even though the voices in the kitchen were muted, she managed to catch Juliet's words. "You haven't told her, have you?"

Dom's response was drowned out by the chime of the doorbell.

Slinging the bag strap over her shoulder she hurried to greet Wendy at the door. Her stomach churned and she prayed she wouldn't be sick again.

What hadn't Dom told her? And did she really want to know? She didn't want complications, remember?

But she did want to know. And she did want complications. Which was a complication all its own.

"I'll pick you up at the spa later and take you to the callback," Dom said.

She nodded, unable to speak, and hurried after Wendy to the waiting car. Her assistant wasn't driving today. For such a big occasion she'd hired a sedan with darkened windows and a professional driver.

"You're very quiet today," Wendy said when they were nearly

at the luxury Beverly Hills spa where they'd arranged to meet Nina's stylist.

Nina shrugged. "I really want this role."

Wendy gave her a sideways look. "Usually you talk a lot when you're anxious. But I haven't seen you really anxious since you moved in with Dominic. He's good for you."

Moved in with. Wendy made it sound so natural, so planned. As if their living under the same roof was more than an expedient work arrangement.

But it wasn't just a convenient solution to a logistical problem anymore, was it? Somewhere along the way, it had changed into something more. Into something that most definitely wasn't 'casual.'

Yesterday had been everything but casual.

She wasn't sure how she felt about that yet. She'd figure it out once the callback was over.

They passed through the high-security gates to the spa and wound up the long drive. The car stopped beneath a portico, which looked more like something an exclusive hotel would boast rather than a day spa, and the driver got out to open the door for her.

Nina stepped out, then bent back down to look at Wendy. "Could you do me a favor? I'd like you to find out for me what an arthroplasty is."

Wendy nodded. "Do you need it before the callback?"

Nina shook her head. "No hurry. After will be fine."

"Wow!" Dom wolf-whistled as Nina stepped out of the day spa, flanked by her entourage. Her hair was back to the luscious long brunette waves he preferred. And she was dressed for the part. Blue jeans that looked as if they'd been painted on her, a plain black t-shirt, leather jacket slung over her shoulder. And a pair of Doc Marten boots that looked as if they'd been artfully worn in.

Admittedly, the fake lashes were back, but those he could live with.

"Lara Croft move over, Sonia Fairchild is here," he said, bending down to kiss her cheek. He'd much rather have kissed that luscious pink mouth, but he didn't want to mess her make-up.

Nina grinned, mischief sparkling in her eyes. She might have been groomed and polished these last few hours, the rough edges of his training buffed out of her, but she was still the same Nina he'd spent the last five weeks with. Determined, spunky, indomitable.

Fearless. Incredible.

He'd never met a woman he admired as much. Wanted as much. Loved as much.

His chest squeezed so tight it hurt.

He'd thought himself incapable of loving any woman this way, had said it would take a very rare woman to make him want to give up all the others. Nina was that woman.

"I have a gift for you," he said, holding out the package. He wished he'd thought to giftwrap it, but it was too late now. She took the t-shirt out of the clear plastic wrapping, shook it out, and laughed.

Printed across the chest of the shirt were the words "I do my own stunts" and a simple graphic of a rider being thrown from a horse.

"Best gift ever." She rose to the tips of her toes to kiss him. Not a kiss on the cheek, but a full-on, open-mouthed kiss.

Behind her, Dane gave a discreet cough and Dom broke the kiss. He looked up, caught Chrissie's eye. She looked like a proud mother hen.

"You don't want to be late," Dane said. "Have you taken your beta blockers?"

Nina shook her head. "I don't need them today. I've got Dom." The smile she sent him was enough to knock him off his feet.

"Your chariot awaits, my lady," he said, waving towards his Wrangler parked in the car park.

For a moment, Nina appeared crestfallen. "No motorcycle today?"

"You don't want to muss up that gorgeous hair with a helmet," he pointed out.

She shrugged. "But it sure would be a kickass way to arrive at the callback."

His chest squeezed tight again, but not in a pleasant way this time. She wasn't disappointed because she wasn't going to ride the short distance to the casting director's office with her arms wrapped intimately around him, but because she wanted to make an impression with her arrival.

Once again, her career took center stage. She'd always been honest that her career was the most important thing in her life. And he'd understood.

There was a time he'd agreed.

Only it didn't seem enough anymore. Nor for him, at any rate. Not with his own career at an end. And not after everything they'd shared yesterday.

"Thank you for coming today." The casting assistant who greeted them at the door looked straight past Nina at Dom as she spoke. "I'm Veronique. And you are?"

"Dominic." He didn't venture anything further.

She smiled coyly at him. "Is there anything I can get you?"

"Green tea would be great, if you have any, and Evian for Nina."

"Of course." She blushed as she finally remembered which one of them was the star.

The assistant led them to a plush waiting room, which looked like it belonged in the pages of an interior design magazine. There were already half a dozen people in the room, who all turned at Nina's entrance, wreathed in smiles.

The casting director, a voluptuous woman who reminded Dom of Sophia Loren, conducted the introductions. "The director is already in the studio. I'll take you through to him shortly," she said to Nina. "Of course, you know Jordan."

She waved a heavily ringed hand towards the reed-thin actress behind her.

"Of course." Nina inclined her head politely, her voice smooth, but Dom wasn't fooled. Her smile was tight, as if she wanted to throw something.

Oh-oh. He'd been unusually candid about his fling with Jordan back on Oscar night, hadn't he?

"I'm up for the role of Sonia's sister," Jordan gushed. "Wouldn't it be awesome if we played sisters again?"

"Awesome." Nina's voice was dry.

"If you don't mind, Jordan, will you wait here while I take Nina through to the studio?" the casting director asked. "We'll call you when we're ready for you."

"No problem," Jordan cooed, her gaze rolling over Dom. "I'll be right here."

Nina's eyes narrowed, but she followed the casting director out the room without a word. He watched her stride away and frowned. That wasn't her usual walk. It took a moment for him to place the movement, then he grinned. Nina had managed to exactly nail Vicki's stance and pace.

The flock of assistants and producers trailed after them, leaving Dom alone with Jordan.

He took a seat in the only armchair in the room. Not that it deterred Jordan any. She ignored the two spacious sofas and moved to sit on the arm of his chair, her thigh brushing his in a completely unambiguous way. He shifted away.

"We have at least half an hour to kill," she said, stroking her dark-red fingernails down his bare arm. "I wonder what we could do to fill the time?"

He removed her hand from his arm. "I'm not interested."

Her eyes grew big and round. It was the same pleading look he'd seen Nina do a dozen times, but on Jordan it wasn't endearing. It felt manipulative.

She pouted. "You used to be a lot more adventurous."

"I'm with Nina now."

"So? You know I don't mind sharing."

"I do."

Jordan looked to where Nina had disappeared down the corridor. "She really owes Gracie Carr big time."

"What do you mean?"

"You didn't know Gracie was signed for the role?"

He shook his head slowly. Had Nina known? Of course she had. It explained her strange behavior recently. "So why does Nina owe Gracie?"

"Gracie's pregnant and she decided to keep the baby rather than the role." Jordan leaned in, her hair brushing his shoulder. She wrinkled her nose. "Babies make you fat. If it was me, I'd have had an abortion."

He had no doubt she would. For Jordan, the only person who mattered was Jordan.

She slid off the chair's arm and into his lap. "Nina doesn't have to know."

He shoved her off. The thought of anyone touching him but Nina made his skin crawl. The thought of anyone touching Nina… made him want to commit murder.

With a glare, Jordan picked herself up off the floor and flounced across the room to the sofa. "Your loss."

Great. Time to kill with no entertainment but a pouty actress in a snit. An actress whose assets had never included her conversational ability.

Dom reached for the battered novel resting on top of a pile of glossy beauty magazines. He hadn't read a novel in years, but it was more appealing than flicking through page after page of cosmetic ads, and definitely more appealing than watching Jordan scowl at him for the next half hour.

He was several pages into *Revelations* and already eagerly turning the pages when the casting assistant finally brought his tea. He barely noticed when Jordan was called away.

When Nina returned to the room, again surrounded by the flock of attendants, he set down the book and stood. She ignored the flattery and effusive farewells and looked for him, their gazes catching and holding. She smiled and he grinned back.

He was pleased the callback had gone as well for her as it had for him.

He'd discovered two things in the time she'd been gone. The first, and perhaps the most surprising, was that he really wanted to finish reading this book. The second was that he wanted to keep Nina in his life. He wasn't yet ready to use words like *forever* and *marriage*, but he didn't want what they had to end, and he planned to tell her. Maybe not today, when she was still hyped from the callback, but soon.

The director, Tarquin, turned to follow the direction of Nina's gaze and his mouth dropped open. "Dom! How the hell are you, mate?" He crossed the room to pump Dom's hand. "Long time, no see."

"You know each other?" Nina asked, arching one perfect eyebrow in Dom's direction.

"We worked together on a movie I shot in England a few years ago," he explained.

"That was fun, wasn't it?" Tarquin grinned. "If you aren't busy, we should get together for a drink and catch up. How about tomorrow night? We can pick up some chicks and make a night of it."

Now both of Nina's eyebrows had lifted. At least the movement made it obvious she didn't use botox.

"I'm up for the drink, but I'm over the picking-up-chicks bit." Dom didn't look at Tarquin but at Nina as he spoke. "And we have plans for tomorrow night."

Tarquin glanced between them. "So you're the guy who's been training Nina? Everyone's very impressed with the effort she's put in. Is she any good?"

Dom smothered his grin. "Very. Give her the role and see for yourself."

Tarquin smiled at Nina. "Maybe I will." Then he turned back to Dom. "Hey, how come we aren't talking to you about working on this movie?"

"I'm not going to be doing stunt work for a while." Even without looking at her, Dom could feel Nina's gaze burning into him.

Another thing he needed to come clean with her about.

If he was going to offer himself up to her, she needed to know what she was getting. He wasn't getting any younger, and he was damaged. He prayed fervently she'd still want him when she knew. It was a risk he had to take. Do or die. That was the war cry he and Christian had used as kids, the motto he'd lived his life by.

It was a risk he had to take. But as with any risk, he'd have to prepare her for it. He wasn't some angsty teenager blurting out his feelings.

"Pity. You change your mind, you let me know – okay?" Tarquin said.

It was a while before Nina was able to extricate herself from the cluster of film producers and casting people, but at last they were in his car and alone. As they passed through the gates, Nina sagged back against her seat, depleted.

No longer channeling Sonia, she suddenly seemed fragile and vulnerable. Like the woman he'd walked on the beach at Point Dume with all those weeks ago.

"So it went well?" he asked.

She nodded, but she bit her lip, which wasn't a good sign. "I can't go anywhere with you tomorrow night. I have a fundraiser I have to attend."

"The annual Easter fundraiser for the Red Cross."

She turned in her seat to look at him properly, eyes widening. "You know about it?"

"Christian and I go every year. I suspect I'm going to be very much a third wheel now that he has a wife. I was sorta hoping you'd go with me."

Her face lit up. "It'll be very public. And there'll be cameras. If you go with me, you won't be able to stay anonymous anymore."

"You had me at public. Do you think there'll be a handy supply closet?"

She laughed and he was relieved. It made her look less tired and drawn. He'd definitely worked her too hard, but five weeks was hardly enough time to teach someone everything he'd learned in a lifetime.

"So do you want to go somewhere to celebrate the successful callback?"

She leaned her head against the headrest and smiled. "No. Just take me home."

He didn't ask which home. He headed the car for Venice Beach.

Chapter Fourteen

"You need to get up and dressed. We're leaving in an hour. And if I know anything about women you'll need at least an hour and a half to get ready."

Nina buried her face in the pillow. Dom knew way too much about women.

"I can't get up," she moaned. "I ache everywhere. And I mean *everywhere*."

While they waited for news from the callback there seemed little point in continuing her training. But she'd needed a distraction from the waiting, so Dom had challenged her to do the commando course again. She'd done it in less than half the time and the water obstacle hadn't fazed her. But she'd still had to push her body to its limits.

"Not quite everywhere," Dom said. The bed dipped as he moved to lie behind her, his hand on her hip.

Little did he know! With him in such close proximity, and smelling freshly showered and all masculine eau-de-cologny, even places that had very regular exercise lately were beginning to ache.

She rolled to face him. "If you wanted me to get up, joining me on the bed is a really bad idea." She stroked a hand down his bicep. "Perhaps we should ditch the fundraiser and stay here in bed?"

Not that she meant it. She was expected and her absence would become gossip fodder.

Dom grinned and shook his head. "And I was worried *I* might be the one getting distracted." His hand slid beneath the soft silk of her kimono to stroke her breasts. They felt even more ultra-sensitive than usual, the nipples peaking with the barest brush of his knuckles. Her breasts seemed fuller these days too. It must be that time of month.

It was hard to do a mental calculation, though, with Dom's hands on her, stroking her into a frenzy. She couldn't remember when last she'd had a period. She had to be overdue. No doubt it was all the extra exercise lately that had thrown her body clock for a loop.

Dom pushed aside the fabric of the kimono and sucked a nipple into his mouth. She arched against him, murmuring incoherently.

A door slammed downstairs and she heard voices. She couldn't rein in her groan. Just when things were getting good. "Damn! I think we need to change the locks."

"You said your stylist already had a booking today so I called in reinforcements." Dom nuzzled her neck, but she rolled away. She could hardly lie here making out with Dom while his sisters waited downstairs.

"I'm going to take a shower."

"Would you like me to scrub your back?"

Yes. "No."

Nina forced herself up and off the bed and headed to the bathroom. She showered and dressed, then made her way downstairs. The little house had never seemed so full of people.

Eric and Dom sat side by side on the sofa, engrossed in a game on the Wii. Dom was already dressed in an evening suit and Nina's pulse kicked up at the sight of him. Eric's younger sister sprawled in the armchair, one leg looped over the arm, equally engrossed in her book.

Three of Dom's sisters sat at the rarely used dining table, where Kathy had once again spread out her make-up kit. All three looked up as Nina entered.

"Look at you!" Juliet whistled. "You look stunning! That's a gorgeous dress."

Nina blushed. "Thank you."

She twirled for them, showing off the dress – a tightly fitted black bodice with a champagne-colored tulle skirt. The skirt had so many layers it would take an angle grinder to rip it to shreds. And even if she should have an unfortunate incident with an angle grinder, she wasn't wearing her granny pants tonight. With any luck, she wouldn't need to wear those granny pants for another few years.

While Kathy styled her hair and made up her face, the sisters chatted around her. Nina didn't take part in the conversation, just let it flow over her. Their conversation was very different from the chatter that usually surrounded her when she sat in the make-up chair. Usually she was surrounded by posturing people trying to impress with how cool they were, swapping beauty tips and fashion tips, and brand-name dropping. Instead, Dom's sisters chatted about normal stuff like their kids' progress in school, work worries, and their plans for a barbecue on the upcoming Easter weekend, complete with a chocolate-egg hunt for the kids.

When Kathy was done, she held up a mirror and Nina had to agree she'd done as good a job as her stylist would have. Maybe better, because instead of her usual smoky make-up, Kathy had gone for a fresh, nude look.

"What do I owe you?" Nina asked awkwardly.

Kathy shook her head. "Nothing. I don't charge for…" Then she glanced towards her brother and didn't finish what she'd been about to say. She shrugged. "What else was I going to do on a Thursday night?"

A clammy chill skated over Nina's skin. Kathy had been going to say, "I don't charge for family." And she hadn't meant that she'd done it as a favor for Dom. She'd done it as a favor for Nina. She'd included Nina in the family circle.

Sweet as that was, Nina's jaw clenched. How the hell had this gone so far, so quickly? Why did they all think she and Dom were so serious? This wasn't serious. This was still just sex. Really great sex, perhaps with a little friendship thrown in, but nothing more.

It couldn't be anything more.

But it was. And she still didn't know how she felt about that.

"Let's have coffee before you go." Moira rose and headed to the kitchen. "I'll put the machine on. Who wants?"

There was a chorus of *yes, pleases* and one request for green tea from Dom.

Nina trailed Moira into the kitchen, fetched the coffee mugs and the cream from the refrigerator.

"Espresso, right?" Moira asked, turning back to the coffee machine. She poured a double espresso. No cream, no sugar. Just the way Nina drank it.

Nina took the cup with narrowed eyes. Then she set it back down, as the urgent compulsion to gag overwhelmed her. "What is that smell?"

Moira sniffed. "The only thing I smell is the espresso."

Espresso. That was it. Except so much more pungent and bitter than usual. Nina clapped her hand to her mouth. "Please excuse me."

Dom found Nina on her knees beside the toilet bowl in the guest bathroom. She looked pale beneath the make-up.

"You okay?" he asked, kneeling beside her and stroking back the hair from her face.

She nodded weakly and sat back. "I think it's all out now."

She looked shaken, but with a visible effort she pulled herself together. He helped her up off the cold, tiled floor.

"I'm sorry. It must be something I ate. Let me take something for the nausea, brush my teeth and re-do my lipstick, then we can leave."

He wrapped an arm around her. "Are you sure? We can stay

home if you'd prefer."

She shook her head. "I'll be fine. And I have to go. I'm expected." She smiled, already looking perkier. "Besides, we wouldn't want to waste all Kathy's hard work."

He searched her face. She looked better, her color almost back to normal, her eyes bright. He nodded. "I'll call the driver to check he's close by."

He shut the door, leaving her alone for a moment, and called the number of the driver Wendy had given him.

When Nina emerged from the guest room she carried her small clutch bag. He took her hand and they headed outside to the waiting limousine, his sisters trailing behind. He held the door and Nina slid inside.

As he was about to slide in after her, Moira laid a hand on his arm. "How far along is she?" she asked in a low voice.

"What do you mean?"

Her cheeks reddened. "I'm sorry. I just assumed... her tiredness, the nausea, the way she keeps running to the bathroom."

She stepped back and he closed the door. As the limo pulled away, awkwardly navigating the narrow street, Nina looked back to where he knew his sisters would be standing, waving them off.

He didn't look back. He was still too stunned.

Moira thought Nina was *pregnant*?

They'd only ever had unprotected sex that one time. How long ago had that been? Three weeks?

It could be. He remembered how his sisters had been when they were pregnant. Tired, sick, bright-eyed, swinging from joy to tears in a moment.

His chest closed until he couldn't breathe. He was going to be a father?

Unless she'd been pregnant before she moved in with him...

Could it be Paul de Angelo's child?

Did Nina even know?

He thought of all the things he'd pushed her to do these last few weeks. Could any of her training exercises have hurt the baby?

Why hadn't she told him?

Even with the window closed between the driver and their compartment, this wasn't the time or place to ask. But it killed him to sit still as the limousine edged up Rodeo Drive towards the iconic Beverly Wilshire Hotel.

Somewhere about the time the car pulled up before the red carpet, and the door opened to the bright lights, camera flashes and shouts, his protective instincts kicked in. Whether or not the baby was his, it didn't matter right now. All that mattered was that Nina stayed safe until they could talk.

Dom didn't let go of her the entire evening. If his fingers weren't entwined through hers, then he had his hand on her lower back or on her hip, protective, possessive. She rather liked the whole Neanderthal 'this girl is mine' thing, though she knew he was probably only warding off other potential interest rather than staking his claim.

He also seemed fidgety tonight. She tried not to let it get to her, but it required effort. She'd known this day would come, even if his sisters seemed oblivious.

He was getting restless.

Still, at least he wasn't on the prowl for another woman, the way it had been the handful of times they'd both appeared at events like these in the past. It was infinitely better to be here with Dominic, even a Dominic on edge, than watching him flirt with some other woman from across the ballroom.

He was very quiet tonight, too. He wasn't a big talker at the best of times, but tonight he seemed preoccupied, as if he was just going through the motions. He let her take the lead as they chatted to the other guests, made small talk and admired dresses and jewels. They posed for the obligatory cameras, then they were seated at a banquet table with Christian and Teresa and a group of Christian's colleagues from the movie he was currently producing.

Chrissie would be so pleased. Nina had been given Dom's 'plus one' seat. If that didn't confirm the rumors, nothing else would.

Wendy sat across the room, not looking at all put out that Nina had abandoned her since a hunky young Red Cross doctor had been given the vacant seat beside her.

They ate a sumptuous meal and shared a few bottles of champagne, though Nina ate little of the rich food and stuck to sparkling water. With her stomach already in a fragile condition, she didn't want to tempt fate. The queues for the bathrooms were diabolical. She'd never make it in time if another wave of nausea hit.

Through the speeches and the fund-raising pitch, Dom held her hand, tracing idle circles against her palm, lulling her into a trance. Her thoughts drifted and she missed most of the video showing what work tonight's funds would be used for.

Earlier this evening, when he'd held her hair back as she'd been sick, for one moment she'd seen her future flash before her eyes.

As much as it terrified her to think of herself as part of a family, as much as she didn't want all the complications and emotions that came with being part of a family, it had felt incredibly good not to be alone on that bathroom floor.

She'd felt as if she stood at a crossroads. One way lay the safe path, the one without complications, a smooth path to stardom and security.

On the other side lay a path fraught with complications. But at least it wouldn't be a lonely path to travel. She would have someone to hold her hand when times were tough. Someone to take care of her when she was sick, and not because she paid them to do it.

A relationship didn't have to affect her career, did it? Dom was just as dedicated to his career. He would understand that work had to come first.

Maybe they could even work together.

He withdrew his fingers from hers to reach for his champagne glass and her chest contracted, so painfully tight she could hardly breathe.

Because without his soothing touch to calm her, the little fantasy shattered. What had she overheard Juliet say before the callback? *You haven't told her...*

She'd pushed it out of her mind, needing to focus on the callback. What was Dom keeping from her? It had to be something important or Juliet wouldn't have mentioned it.

Something he hadn't trusted her enough to tell her. Or cared enough to tell her.

Even after everything she'd shared with him, he still wasn't ready to let her into his life. What hope did she have of keeping hold of a man like Dominic Kelly when so many others had failed?

She blinked back the sting in her eyes. The end had been inevitable from the start. And it would be better to end it soon, before she trusted him with anything more of herself.

"Earth to Dom," Christian said, when the speeches and video were done. Nina blinked as both she and Dom turned to look at him.

"That was the second time I called your name." Christian grinned cheerfully. "You two not getting enough sleep or something?"

"Or something," Dom replied.

"We're going to dance. You coming to join us?"

Dom shook his head and Nina's heart sank. She'd have loved to dance with Dom again, properly this time. One last time. She sipped at her water, saying nothing.

She probably should be mingling. But she couldn't scrape the will power together to leave Dom's side. Not with time running against them and every moment bringing them closer to the end.

She leaned closer. "If I get the role in *Revelations*, I want to make it a condition of my contract that they hire you as the stunt coordinator."

Dom shook his head. He didn't quite look at her and his expression was unreadable, shutting her out. "I already told you, I'm taking a break for a few months."

"You can take a break after the movie. It's only 15 weeks of principal photography, and Tarquin really likes you."

"I'm sure they've contracted someone else for the job already."

"They haven't. I asked."

A deep furrow appeared in Dom's brow. "I don't want to work on it. Just drop it."

She held her back straight and her chin high, but the tears were back, pushing against her eyelids. What had just happened here?

Did Dom not want to work with her? Was he that eager to end this arrangement and move on?

She needed to get out of here, needed to get alone, somewhere she could breathe again. Was it too soon to suggest they leave the party?

Her muscles had begun to seize up again after the morning's ordeal. And her heart was beginning to seize up too.

Torn with indecision, she smiled and watched the dancers on the dance floor, grateful for the diversion when one of the chief fundraisers stopped beside her chair.

"It's such a pleasure to see you again," he said, bending to kiss her cheek.

"Hi, Tony." She smiled up at him, waving him to the empty seat beside her.

"Tony used to work with my mom," she explained to Dom.

The older man wrinkled his nose. "Back in the good old days before I got stuck behind a desk begging people for money."

She laughed. "But you're so good at it."

"*You* make me look good."

"Oh?" Dom asked, leaning forward.

"Nina is one of our most generous benefactors. She has single-handedly paid for the rebuilding of more storm-damaged houses than anyone else I know."

"Those were supposed to be anonymous donations," she chided. "Which reminds me, I'd better cut you a check now or everyone will think I'm just here for the free food."

Tony laughed. "It's hardly free. It's hugely over-priced, and I'd far prefer a burger from In-N-Out. But I won't complain since more than half the extravagant fee everyone's paid to be here tonight goes to a good cause." He patted her knee in a fatherly gesture. "You're looking radiant tonight."

"I don't feel radiant. To be honest, I haven't been feeling well. I've been feeling nauseous and tired lately."

Dom's hand squeezed hers painfully tight and she frowned at him before turning back to Tony. "It's probably just stress. I'm waiting for news about a big role."

Tony nodded slowly. "Well, I need to get back to schmoozing money out of all these rich people. Don't be a stranger, okay?"

He kissed her cheek in farewell and when he'd gone, weaving away through the crowd, Nina turned to Dom. "Ow! What the hell was that for?"

"You don't know?" he asked. His eyes were sharp, no longer preoccupied.

"Know what?"

"We need to talk."

She nodded. "But not here. It's too public."

The urge to throw up was back again. Was this it: the moment when he said it was over between them?

"I need the toilet before we leave," she said, rising unsteadily from her chair. "Could you please arrange the car? I'll meet you in the lobby."

The ladies' room was too full of chattering women touching up their make-up for her to find the moment's peace she needed there. At least the wave of nausea passed. She couldn't be sick with so many witnesses. Her reflection in the mirror appeared more calm and composed than she felt, if a little pale. No one would guess the turmoil churning beneath the surface.

"I've been looking everywhere for you," Wendy elbowed her way to Nina's side. "I've been hoping to get a moment alone with you."

They were hardly alone, but Nina nodded for her to continue.

"I got that information you wanted. A whole file of printouts

I'll bring to you tomorrow. Quick version is that an arthroplasty is basically hip replacement surgery, usually to repair a tear in the hip cartilage. Is your Gran okay?"

Nina's chest pulled even tighter. "Gran's fine," she managed. "Thanks for finding out."

Dom had injured his hip in Paris. The pain pills and steroid injections.

"Dom and I are leaving now. We'll talk tomorrow, okay?"

"Having an early night?" Wendy winked and grinned at her. "I wonder if the dishy doctor would also like an 'early night'?"

Nina attempted a laugh and turned away. The spacious ladies' room suddenly seemed stifling and airless, and way too full of people.

She paused in the hall outside.

Now she understood why he didn't want to work on *Revelations*.

The arthroplasty had been scheduled for weeks ago and he'd put it off. For her? Maybe not for her, since he'd barely known her when he'd agreed to train her.

Hip replacement surgery couldn't be good for a stunt man. It was as good as a career- killer, wasn't it?

But the pain wasn't good, either. All those times she'd caught his grimace as he moved, the times his smile had seemed over-bright and too casual.

He should have told her. He should have been honest with her.

But he hadn't. Even when she'd given him the perfect opening not twenty minutes ago.

So much for that vision of a rosy future for the two of them together. It had never been an option, had it? Because if she'd meant anything to him at all, he would have told her.

He wouldn't have lied.

He wouldn't have cut her out.

She leaned back against the wall and closed her eyes. Once again, she'd been a fool. And she thought Jess was the hopeless romantic?

How many times did she have to go through this? Making

friends, dating guys, only to find out that none of it had been real, that they were only using her.

As it had been with Paul de Angelo, and the boyfriend before him, and pretty much every other person she'd known since she'd left hurricane-wrecked Louisiana and started a new life as a new person in Iowa.

People thought the pretty girls, the popular girls, had it all. They had no idea.

That plump girl with glasses and braces and her nose forever stuck in a book might have been happier than Nina Alexander, Oscar nominee and *Vogue* cover girl.

She rubbed her eyes and didn't give a damn if it turned her into a panda. If only she could undo these last ten years. Go back to the way things were when Dad was still alive, when they'd still been a family. When she'd known what was what and who was who.

But it was too late. The past could not be undone. She'd made her choices and she would stick with them.

Mechanically, she pushed herself away from the wall and began to walk. Down the hall, across the ballroom. People stopped her to say a few words here or there, but no one looked at her strangely, so hopefully her panda look wasn't too bad.

Without Dom's hand at her waist the walk was an ordeal. This was how it had been that night after the Academy Awards, before she'd had Dom's steadying presence at her side.

She lifted her chin and smiled for all she was worth. She was strong. She'd survived a hurricane and its aftermath, losing her home, and the break-up of her family. She could survive one stupid walk across a ballroom without losing it.

"Nina!" She turned to the raised voice, the British accent drawing her attention.

"Hello, Tarquin. I didn't realize you were here tonight."

"Yeah, I just arrived. I was in a casting meeting until late, then I wanted to be the one to make the call offering the role of Sonia, so I missed half the party."

No. Not now. She couldn't take this now. Dealing with Dom's rejection was hard enough. Two at once was unbearable.

Her smile slipped.

"No! I said that all wrong. I meant I wanted to phone *your* agent personally. We've offered you the role. Hadn't you heard?"

She shook her head. "I didn't bring my phone with me tonight." Then she blinked. "I got the role? I'm Sonia?"

Tarquin swung an arm around her shoulder. "I've already made some notes I'd like to discuss with you. Let's meet as soon as your contract's signed. My assistant will call your assistant."

"Of course." She nodded numbly. She had the role. The one that would take her career to a whole new level. No more rom-com princesses. No more fairy tales. She could show the world, and her family, that she was better than that.

She should have felt joy. Instead she only felt relief.

At least she would have something to keep her busy and occupy her thoughts as she got over Dom.

Because tonight it would end. If he didn't do it, she would. She had to.

A tear leaked out of her eye before she could blink it back. Great. Now she probably had mascara tracks to add to the panda eyes. "Thank you."

"Please don't cry," he begged, patting her arm awkwardly.

She managed a wan smile. "I'm sorry. I have to go. Dom's waiting for me. I'll see you soon."

"Sure." Tarquin grinned. "And don't forget to thank him too. Dom's opinion carries a lot of weight in this town. He's the reason the producers finally agreed to take the chance on you."

Chapter Fifteen

They didn't speak the entire drive home. Nina stared fixedly at the silhouette of the driver's head through the dark glass, and after a while Dom quit trying to snag her attention and stared out the window.

He'd been an ass. He hadn't handled this well. He'd been angry and scared and he'd shut her out, and now her walls had gone up again.

The drive took an excruciatingly long time. At last they turned into the street behind Dom's house. He gave her a hand to help her out the car, waved off the driver, then held the yard gate open for her.

The house was dark and unwelcoming. He'd forgotten to leave a single light on. Sandy waited at the door for them, eager to get out, tail wagging furiously. Nina knelt down to pet her, then Dom let the dog out into the yard, and Nina moved to sit on the sofa, her hands folded primly in her lap, seemingly unaware of the dog hairs now clinging to her voluminous skirt.

"You wanted to talk?" she said.

Now that the moment was here, he had no idea what to say. It had seemed so easy when he'd been angry and the words had buzzed around inside his head like a swarm of bees.

But how could he demand "am I the father?" when she clearly

had no idea she was pregnant? At this rate, the story would be halfway around town and in every gossip column imaginable before she woke up to the blindingly obvious.

While he'd already progressed to imagining himself pushing a girl with ponytails the same color as Nina's on a swing, she hadn't even contemplated the possibility.

Or she refused to acknowledge it.

He sat down on the coffee table across from her and reached for her hands. She pulled them away. He frowned.

"When last did you have your period?" he asked.

Her mouth opened and closed again, like a goldfish. "What does that have to do with anything?" she asked at last.

"Just answer me."

Looking confused, she closed her eyes and counted. Days. Weeks. Months. She frowned as she opened her eyes again. "I'm late, but that's not surprising considering the heavy exercise I've been doing lately."

He didn't say anything, just let the silence stretch as she filled in the blanks.

Nina shook her head again. "I'm not pregnant. I took the morning-after pill."

"And you were always careful with Paul?"

Indignation flashed in her dark eyes, turning them coal black. "Not that it's any of your business, but Paul and I weren't exactly… I mean, we had sex, but we weren't particularly…active." Her cheeks flushed a dark red. "We were always careful. And I did a test. After we had that condom fail. It was negative." She sounded smug at that last bit and his stomach clenched.

The image of the little girl shattered like a pane of breakaway glass in a stunt. On the plus side, if she wasn't pregnant with his child, then at least she wasn't pregnant with Paul's child either.

"And you did a second test in case the first was faulty?"

Chagrin replaced the indignation. "I'll gladly do it now. I still have the spares Wendy bought."

He raised an eyebrow and nodded towards the bathroom.

"*That* is what this is all about?" Her brow cleared. "You've been on edge all night because of my stupid period?"

She didn't have to sound relieved. Pregnancy was a pretty major, life-changing event. "I needed to know."

"You're not breaking up with me?" There was a catch in her voice. She still didn't sound or look any happier.

He swallowed. That was the other talk they needed to have. But before they could talk about his feelings, or where this relationship was headed, first they needed to get rid of the elephant in the room. He shook his head. "I'm not breaking up with you."

He followed her to the bathroom, watched as she dug a brown-paper bag out of a big cosmetic bag. Watched as she did the test. Watched as a pink line appeared.

"See!" She held the stick out to him, triumphant. "Only one line."

And he watched the horror grow in her face as another pink line appeared beside it. A very clear, very definite, second pink line.

Even he knew what that meant.

Nina threw the stick down. "It must be faulty." She ripped open the packaging of the last box, her fingers shaking so much he had to remove the stick from the packaging for her.

She did the test again. Not two pink lines this time. Just a smiley face in the little window.

Nina dropped down to sit on the edge of the bath. "I can't be pregnant. I *can't* be." She sank her head into her hands. "This isn't happening."

He sat beside her, rubbing gentle circles on her back. He understood the shock she was experiencing right now. He'd gone through the same thing earlier in the evening.

"It'll take time to adjust, but we can make this work," he said, at last, into the silence.

With her head still in her hands, she said, "This was just supposed to be a bit of fun. It was supposed to be 'no strings'." She hiccupped. "I don't want to stop acting. I love my job. And I

216

love being famous. I love the doors it opens for me, the access it gives me to experiences I would never have otherwise. And I like being admired, and I don't care if that's selfish."

"You wouldn't have to give up your career." He could give his up instead. It wasn't like he had a choice, anyway.

Nina finally looked up. "Tarquin offered me the role of Sonia as we were leaving tonight."

Oh.

His hand stilled on her back. That was different.

She could hardly take on such a physically active role while suffering through morning sickness. Fit and determined as she was, and even if she didn't start showing until principal photography was over, there was still the promotional campaign that would follow, and the sequels to be shot. Those would be almost impossible with a newborn baby in tow.

"I'm sorry," he said. "I know how much you wanted the role."

Her eyes blazed. "I didn't go through everything these last few weeks to throw it all away at the last moment. This role means too much to me."

He frowned, confused. "And what about the baby?"

She didn't say anything. The angry, irrational fire in her eyes frightened him. He'd never seen Nina like this before. It had to be the pregnancy hormones turning her so unreasonable. Not that he'd say it out loud. He'd learned that one the hard way when Moira was pregnant with Eric.

The little bathroom was so still he could hear the crash of breakers in the background.

"I don't want a baby." Her words were soft, but they fell into the silence like a jackhammer on concrete. She cleared her throat. "You've seen what my life is like. It doesn't belong to me anymore. My fame has taken on a life of its own. Can you imagine a child growing up with that? The constant scrutiny. Never being able to go out as a family and do family stuff without strangers interrupting and pushing their way into our family circle. People treating him

217

or her as if they're somehow less special than me because I'm the famous one. It wouldn't be healthy and it wouldn't be fair, and there's only so much I can do to protect my child from that."

"You wouldn't have to do it alone. I'd be there. *I'd* protect our child. Together we can make this work."

She shook her head. "Everywhere I go, I'm a walking target and everyone wants something from me. I get peopled out. When I come home, I want to be alone. I need to be alone. No visitors dropping by unannounced, and certainly no baby demanding what little is left of me."

He reeled back as if she'd slapped him. Who was this woman sitting next to him? Because the Nina he'd fallen in love with wasn't this selfish and uncaring. "And what about me? Is there any place for me in this life of yours?"

Slowly she shook her head.

He stared at her, unable to breathe. Then he paced away to the bathroom door and turned, leaning back against it, his arms crossed over his chest. "You're willing to give up everything to make a few movies? To win a few awards? Is that the only thing you care about: to be patted on the back at the world's most self-congratulatory spectacle by a self-obsessed, self-centered industry?"

She lifted her chin. "You've made a pretty damn good living out of this business, too."

"Yeah, but I can still see it for what it is. Making movies is a great job, but it's still just a job, not a religion. There's no point doing it if you don't have a life outside of work. People who love you. Hollywood is just a town full of tourists, not a dream."

He swallowed as his words echoed off the walls. Making movies had been as good as a religion to him, too. But all it had taken to show him the light were two little pink lines.

He didn't need to throw himself off of buildings to be happy. There were more important things in life. Home. Friends. Family.

The irrational fire still blazed in Nina's eyes. "You can mock all you like, but this *is* my dream. This is as close to the fairy tale that a twenty-first-century girl from Nowheresville can get. I don't care that it's not noble or heroic. I *like* being a Somebody."

"Then when Paul de Angelo handed you the glass slipper, why didn't you take it? You could be living the life of the princess in the castle right now. You didn't take it because you're not that person, Nina. You're not shallow and selfish." He hoped. In fact, he was staking his own future happiness on it. "Forget Sonia. Take a chance on me and the baby. Let's try to make a go of being a family."

"I am that selfish," she whispered. "You might be willing to give up everything to raise a child, but I'm not." She rose from the edge of the bath, pulling herself up to her full height. In the ridiculously high heels she still wore, that height made her imposing. "And you're only offering these things because your own movie career is over."

He uncrossed his arms. "What did you say?"

"You were supposed to have surgery weeks ago."

How the hell did she know about that? Which one of his sisters blabbed? He was going to kill them.

"Why didn't you tell me you were injured? You shouldn't even have taken on my training, should you?" She didn't wait for him to answer. "Why should I give up everything I've worked for this last decade for you? You haven't even been honest with me. You're no better than Paul was. It's all about what *you* want." She swallowed visibly, and her eyes shone with tears. "How can I even trust you?"

He didn't have any answers for her. If he was a woman, he wouldn't trust himself, either. He'd been a player all his life. But with Nina he felt like a better man. She made him want to be a better man.

Especially now when he could see that the selfishness was only a shield against hurt.

"I'm not Paul and I'm not your mother," he said, laying a hand on her arm. "I won't leave you when the going gets tough."

She shrugged away from his touch, crossing her arms protectively across her chest. "It doesn't matter. The only person I can rely on is me." She faced him, lifting her chin. "We said we'd end this when it got awkward or stopped being fun. It just became both. In case that wasn't clear enough: *I* am breaking up with *you*. You and I are over."

The sparks were no longer in her eyes. She was calm now. Too calm. He'd lost her.

"What about the baby?"

She blinked. He had a suspicion she was trying very hard *not* to think about the baby.

"I'll take care of it."

He flinched. He hoped she didn't mean what he thought that meant.

But he couldn't reason with her now. Not in the state she was in, and not without making this worse between them. He could only pray that when she'd had a chance to calm down, to absorb this news, she'd see reason.

"My offer is still on the table if you change your mind."

He let himself out the back door, whistling for Sandy. All he wanted right now was a run on the beach, to clear his thoughts and ease his frustrations. But even if he hadn't still been dressed in his penguin suit, he wouldn't have been able to run.

He may not have been convinced he needed surgery a month ago, but now he was. His hip locked up more than ever these days, and even medication was no longer able to keep the pain at bay. At a slow walk he headed along the familiar path toward the pub, Sandy bounding along beside him.

Whiskey wasn't going to fix either the pain in his hip or the pain in the region of his chest. But it would help numb it.

By the time he staggered home several hours later, Nina was gone. There wasn't even as much as an empty shampoo bottle left to show she had ever been there.

Chapter Sixteen

Nina had always thought of Wendy as a friend. Her only friend. But Wendy's stony silence the entire drive back to Nina's apartment block starkly reminded her they weren't friends. Wendy was her employee. An employee who would ditch her date if called upon, but she wouldn't do it willingly or happily.

"I'm sorry," she said for the second time.

"Mike only has a week in town before his next deployment."

"You can take the next week off," Nina offered.

Wendy shrugged, non-committal.

Only when they were in the secure basement parking beneath Nina's building did Wendy finally look at her. "What was wrong with this one?" she asked.

Why did she assume Nina was the one to break off the relationship? So it was true, but Wendy didn't know that. And okay, technically Nina had also called it off with Paul, and the guy she'd dated before that...

"He kept a lot of stuff from me," she said. Which was also true. Partly. And much easier than admitting the other reason they'd argued.

Wendy shrugged. "And you've shared everything about yourself with him?"

More than with any other person. Nina sighed. "Relationships are too complicated."

"Of course they're complicated. But my mother often quotes President Roosevelt: 'Nothing in the world is worth having or worth doing unless it means effort'. Yes, there's always the risk it won't last or you'll get hurt, but complicated is still better than never growing attached to anything, never loving anyone. I'd rather have one week with Dr. Mike than nothing at all. Hell, even one night would be nice."

"I'm sorry," Nina said it again. Maybe if she said it often enough, Wendy would believe her. She really did feel bad about wrecking her PA's evening. She couldn't be completely selfish if she felt bad, could she?

Many celebrities she'd met wouldn't have given their PA's time or personal life a second thought. In fact, they would have been offended if their PA even had a personal life.

She opened the car door and moved around to the trunk to fetch her bags.

"I'll get those," Wendy said, unclipping her seatbelt.

Nina shook her head. "I'll manage. You've done enough for me tonight. Go back to your dishy doctor. And text me if you decide to take the week off."

She watched the car headlights disappear up the ramp to the street and the solid gates close behind Wendy before she headed for the elevator, burdened by way more bags than she'd started at Dom's house with.

Her condo was dark and silent, and smelled musty and unlived in, even though the housekeeper still came in daily. She dropped her bags inside the door and looked around.

The blinds were open, revealing a view of city lights. Nowhere near the view of some Hollywood apartment blocks, and nothing like the view from the *Vanity Fair* party, but she liked it. Except tonight the twinkling cityscape beyond the windows only made the vast living room feel cold and empty. She shut the blinds and switched on a couple of lights.

It didn't help.

The apartment was cold and empty. Lifeless.

Though the designer had intended a comfortable, homely look, without a single personal item it just looked like one of those show houses in a magazine spread. Even film sets had more personality.

Nina wandered through to her bedroom, her sanctuary. She'd missed her spacious walk-in closet and the organized shoe racks.

But even the darkened bedroom seemed bare. The only personal item, the only thing that didn't look as if it belonged in a hotel suite, was the battered copy of the first *Revelations* book on the nightstand.

The last gift she'd received from her father before he died. The only thing she'd taken with her that dreadful Sunday when her world had blown apart. The only thing she still owned from the days before she'd re-invented herself that hadn't been thrown in a skip, too water- damaged to be of any use.

She'd had plenty of opportunities since then to amass a new stock of sentimental keepsakes. But she hadn't held onto anything.

Gifts from fans and crew and fellow cast members had been donated to charity or given to Wendy. Books she'd read and given away. Photographs she'd deleted from her phone without ever backing up.

She hadn't held on to anything that had any meaning.

Including people.

She sat on the edge of the bed and buried her face in her hands.

She should get out of the designer dress and remove her make-up, but she didn't have the energy to move. In the ringing silence, the inevitable could no longer be avoided. She had to acknowledge what she had been working very hard not to see.

She had a baby inside her. Right now.

A little life that in eight months' time she would have to give birth to.

Dom's baby.

And she had a decision to make.

Stretching out on the bed, she pulled the soft cashmere throw over her and buried her face in the soft-scented pillows. She squeezed her eyes shut, but that didn't stop them leaking dark smudges onto the pristine, white linen.

Jessie was going to kill her. Five years and an endless number of IVFs later, and Nina got pregnant with just one condom fail.

She could get rid of the baby and take the role of Sonia. But that went against everything she'd been raised to believe. As much as she didn't want this baby, terminating its life before it even began was unthinkable.

She could have the baby and give it to Jessie. She wouldn't have to re-arrange her life for a baby and she could make her sister's dream come true.

She stroked her stomach through the layers of crushed tulle. She'd be the glamorous out-of-town aunt, dropping by with gifts once in a blue moon, watching from the sidelines as Dom's child called someone else mother.

The smudge turned into a salty puddle. She hadn't expected that thought to hurt so much. But it did, tearing at her insides with sharp claws.

The one piece of Dominic that was hers to keep, the greatest gift she'd ever been given, and she would give it away as she had given away everything else in her life.

But there would still be a cost to pay. She would still have to give up the dream she'd chased for nearly a decade. The only thing that had kept her going through her darkest moments.

When she'd first come to LA as an 18-year-old with stars in her eyes, she'd lived in a crummy studio apartment with creaking pipes and a constant smell of damp. Even waitressing jobs had been hard to get in those days. She'd washed dishes and scrubbed floors to pay for her acting classes. And at night, when she'd had no money to go out and party as normal 18-year-olds were doing, she'd read and re-read the *Revelations* books. She'd sworn if they ever made the movie, she was going to be in it. Everything she'd done since then had been toward this one goal.

And now that the role was hers, she would have to walk away.

The puddle on the pillow grew as the sobs came. Big gulping sobs she couldn't stem, and a flood of tears along with them. Sobs that racked her aching body and tears that burned, but neither had anything on the sharp, stabbing pain in her heart.

If she gave up on her dream, what did she have left? No friends, a family more divided than together, and an apartment that was no homelier than a hotel suite. The only thing she had left was the carefully nurtured safety net in her bank account.

Nothing of value.

At last the gulps subsided into uneven hiccups.

There were no tissues within reach and every muscle in her body had gone on strike, so she used the sheets to clean her face. Her housekeeper was not going to be happy tomorrow.

And that was how she fell asleep, with the housekeeper's face in her thoughts. It was hardly surprising she slept badly and had disturbed dreams, dreams in which her sister chased her with a massive carving knife while an alien monster tried to claw itself out of her stomach. A dream in which Dom did not ride in to her rescue.

She had lost all control of her life. Dane signed the contract before she'd barely even figured out what she was having for breakfast, and Chrissie set a date with the studio publicists to make the big announcement. The producers immediately provided a driver to escort Nina to script meetings and wardrobe fittings, and sword practice with a stunt coordinator who very definitely wasn't Dom. This stunt coordinator treated her with kid gloves, as if she were a porcelain doll about to break, until she wanted to scream in frustration. Why had they bothered hiring her for the role if they were going to treat her like some pampered princess afraid to break a nail?

But at least this stunt coordinator didn't make her pulse giddy, as Dom did.

If her daylight hours were too busy to think, her nighttime hours were excruciating. She tossed and turned, unable to sleep, unable to make a decision. Those rare moments she slept, she woke reaching for Dom.

She'd been with him every hour of every day for weeks. She hadn't realized how much a part of her life he'd become. Without him near, she felt unable to breathe.

There was no Wendy either. She'd taken Nina at her word and put in for a week's leave. If her Instagram pictures were anything to go by, she and Dr. Mike were having a wonderful time. In her darkest moments, Nina hated her for her happiness.

On Easter Sunday she stayed curled up in bed with a book and tried very hard not to imagine Dom with his nieces and nephews, hunting out chocolate eggs in his parents' garden. Tried and failed.

She was so deeply lost in her imagination that she jumped when her cell phone rang. She reached for the phone, knocking it to the floor in her haste, and hit the answer button without even checking caller ID.

"You there?" Jess sounded breathless and giggly. Happy. Nina hadn't heard that sound in her sister's voice in a very long time.

She hated to bring her sister down, so she injected as much joy into her voice and gave the performance of her life. "Hi Jess."

"How's your hottie?"

It had become Jess's standard opening question, almost a joke between them. Nina swallowed the lump in her throat. She'd avoided her sister for several days. She hadn't been able to face telling Jess that news. Amongst other things. "We broke up."

"What?! When did that happen? And why the hell did you dump him? He was perfect for you!"

Nina pinched the bridge of her nose. "We broke up a few days ago. And why do you assume *I* broke up with him? He's the one with the reputation for loving-and-leaving."

"You know, Sugar, you've achieved some incredible things and

I'm really proud of you, but sometimes I think you're not very bright."

"Gee thanks. I love you too, Sis."

"I mean, everyone knows that when a man with a reputation like his finally falls, he falls hard. Dominic wasn't planning to let you go anytime soon. So it must have been you who left him. Though why you'd want to leave the best thing that's ever happened to you, I have no idea!"

"Why do you think he was so good for me?" Apart from the amazing sex, of course. Nina bit her lip to stem a fresh flood of emotion.

"You've been playing someone else for so long that whenever I call, I'm not sure who I'm going to get. But when you're with Dom you're just yourself."

Whoever that was. "What makes you think he wasn't going to leave me?" Nina asked. Her voice sounded thready and she cleared her throat.

"He introduced you to his friends and his family."

"He does that to everyone. He runs an open house and his friends and family drop in all the time."

"Sure, but you think most women he's bedded get taken to the family barbecue?"

His mother had said she was the first woman he'd ever brought home. Something stirred in Nina's stomach. Too soon to be the baby moving, and the nausea had abated these last few days. It felt just a little like hope.

Stupid, stupid stomach.

"Then why did he lie to me? He has a bad injury and he needs surgery. Hip replacement surgery that he should have had more than a month ago. Wendy researched it for me. If he doesn't have the surgery he could end up unable to walk, and the longer he delays the worse it will be. It's pretty much the end of his career. And he didn't tell me any of this. I had to figure it out for myself."

She blinked back the perpetual tears. Just thinking about how

227

bleak he must be feeling made her want to weep. But he hadn't shared any of those emotions with her.

"He's a guy. They don't talk about stuff like that."

"He had plenty of chances to tell me, but he didn't. He excluded me. You don't exclude people you love."

"Oh really? That is definitely a case of pots and kettles."

Nina pressed her lips together. What did Jess know anyway? She sniffed haughtily. "I don't know what you mean."

"You're so much like Mom. You don't let anyone close, and you bury your pain and grief in work. I'll just bet you've been keeping yourself really busy and pretending everything's just great and that you're happy to be alone again. But you shouldn't be alone, no one should be. You should be loved."

"I am loved. Just ask my fans."

"This isn't a joke. Don't you want to be loved for yourself? In those moments when you're at home and no one else can see?"

Nina reached for a tissue beside the bed. It was the second box she'd gone through in the last few days. "Of course I want to be loved. But there are no guarantees I won't be left alone again anyway."

Jess's voice was gentle, but it wasn't her 'therapist' voice. "No, there are no guarantees. Love can be rough around the edges, but it's still absolutely worth it." She paused a beat. "And not everyone runs away like Mom did."

Nina hiccupped and fought to get control. "I'm sorry for being such a downer. You sounded so happy when you called."

"I am." She could hear the grin back in Jess's voice. "I have big news. The last IVF took."

It was a moment before the words had any meaning. Nina gasped. "You're pregnant?"

"It's still very early days and we're not telling anyone, not even Lucas's family. Not until we're well into the second trimester and sure the baby's safe and going to make it."

"But you're telling me."

"Of course I'm telling you. You're my sister. Who else would I tell?"

A tear splashed down Nina's cheek. Thank heavens her sister didn't do Facetime.

Their relationship wasn't a two-way street. She still wasn't able to tell Jess her own news. She still wasn't even sure what she was going to do.

She felt as if she were on a runaway train headed straight for a cliff and she couldn't get off.

"I'm so happy for you, Jess. Really, really happy." And she meant it.

When she ended the call, Nina set aside her book and phone and climbed off the bed.

She'd missed having a full-length mirror all the weeks she'd spent at Dom's. It wasn't that she was vain and wanted to see her reflection – not with the love/hate relationship she had with her body – but this body was her brand. She couldn't afford to let herself go.

She faced the mirror. She still wore sleep shorts that revealed her long, tanned legs, more muscled and athletic than they'd ever been before in her life. She lifted her tank top and placed her hands over her toned, smooth belly.

How long would it be before she started to show? How long could she keep this baby a secret? Three or four months, as Jess planned to do? Long enough to get through 15 weeks of filming without someone realizing she was pregnant? She didn't trust those odds.

Especially with her breasts already so full and aching they were like a teenager's wet dream.

She'd only allowed herself to think ahead to the next few weeks. If she could just keep her pregnancy secret through the first few weeks of principal photography, a month at most, the movie would be too far underway for them to replace her.

Once she was through the all-important first month of filming she could break the news to the producers and ask them to cut her some slack with the riskier action shots. There were always ways to cheat angles and to use body doubles.

But by the end of filming, everyone would know, wouldn't they? It would be an impossible secret to keep on a film set with hundreds of people. Location film shoots, especially, were hotbeds of gossip, everyone living in one another's pockets for months on end.

And then when she gave the baby away, everyone would know that too.

She'd be known as the actress who gave away her baby. Chrissie would really have her job cut out putting a good spin on that.

And what were the chances Jess would even want her baby now, with her own on the way?

Which left only one last option.

Nina would have to keep the baby.

Could she keep her career too? It wasn't as if she'd be the first movie star to be a single, unwed mother. It would mean nannies and night nurses, and raising a child inside the goldfish bowl that was her life, and all those things she'd sworn she didn't want, but the thought didn't seem nearly as scary as it had a few days ago.

She could keep the baby.

Her hands stroked over the curve of her stomach. Though there was nothing yet to see or feel, her body felt different. There was a new life growing inside her.

And she was hungry.

With a bounce in her step, she headed for the kitchen. She only kept bread in the house for the housekeeper, but she was going to make herself the most giant-ass sandwich imaginable, with all the trimmings. She had a baby to feed.

She was halfway through lathering mayonnaise onto the bread when a blinding thought stopped her hand in midair.

If she kept the baby, Dom would want to be involved.

Whether they wanted it or not, their lives would be entangled forever.

The vision that followed rapidly on the heels of that thought was an instant appetite suppressant. What if Dom met someone else? Started a family with someone else? What if her son or daughter grew up with half siblings and a stepmother?

What if she had to sit on the sidelines, alone, and watch them be a happy family together?

The urge to throw up was back in force, but this time it wasn't morning sickness. Tossing the half-made sandwich in the bin, she headed back to bed.

Maybe she wasn't as ready for this as she'd thought.

Without Wendy, she had to make her own appointment with a doctor, selecting one of those exclusive Beverly Hills clinics masquerading as a spa, where the staff could be relied upon to be discreet. She even drove herself there.

The appointment took a lot less time than she thought it would.

Now that the decision was made, a weight had lifted off her shoulders. She smiled and laughed with her new trainers, made friends with her co-stars. The old Nina was back, the perky, outgoing Nina, and it was no longer an act. Only now the ditsiness was gone, replaced by a harder edge that no one could see, but she could feel.

She threw herself into work, into rehearsals and press interviews, and absolutely anything else that would take her mind off Dom and where he was and what he was doing.

The press conference to announce the final cast of *Revelations* was scheduled for the same day her training with Dom should have ended. It was impossible not to think of him.

She woke reaching out for him in the bed.

She showered, remembering the time they'd scrubbed beach sand off each other in the outdoor shower in his yard, though it had been so chilly they'd run straight indoors and got warm again in the best way possible.

She dressed in a pair of skinny black jeans, gray silky blouse, and heeled leather boots, remembering the borrowed jeans she'd left neatly folded in the closet in Dom's guest bedroom.

She ate breakfast alone in her kitchen and remembered the time he'd made her orgasm right there on his kitchen counter. Best breakfast ever.

Her stylist arrived to prepare her for the cameras, and as they made inconsequential small talk she remembered the fast-paced, overlapping conversation of Dom's sisters as Kathy readied her for the fundraiser.

The studio driver drove her to the Beverly Hills Hotel for the press conference and she had to close her eyes against the memories of the last time she'd been in a car with Dom, the last time she'd held his hand.

"We're here," the driver said.

She opened her eyes. Her chest felt tight again, so tight she could hardly breathe. Then the door opened and there was no more time to be sentimental or to wallow in self-pity for everything she'd lost. This was her moment. This was the first day of the rest of her life.

"God, I could use a drink," her co-star said as they were led to the private suite where refreshments had been laid out for them ahead of the press conference. "I hate these press junkets." He pulled a face. "Small price to pay for making a living at this job, though, isn't it?"

She nodded. There were far bigger prices to be paid. She glanced at her wristwatch. The press conference would be starting soon and she was almost out of time.

"Mineral water," she said to the hovering waitress, and her co-star pulled another face. Once she had her mineral water and he his bourbon, they toasted each other. She liked him already, though they had zero chemistry. Always a good thing since the key to having great sexual chemistry on-screen was having none off-screen.

"I didn't see Dominic here today," Tarquin said, putting an arm around her shoulders as he joined them.

She shook her head and steeled her nerve. A strong part of her wanted to run away, to play a part, and pretend nothing was wrong. But she'd already gone too far down this road to turn back. "There's something I need to discuss with you."

Tarquin nodded and she added: "Privately."

With a wry shrug to her co-star, Tarquin led her outside into the hotel gardens, where the photographers were setting up their lights.

They were still talking when the anxious publicist called them into the press conference. For the next hour, Nina bantered with her new colleagues and co-stars, made all the obligatory flattering sound bites required of her in the Q&A, then posed for photos in the garden.

The die had been cast. There was no going back now.

At last it was over. Barely pausing to say goodbye to her co-stars or the producers, she hurried to the residents-only car park. She caught the driver unawares, leaning up against the black Escalade smoking a cigarette. He stubbed it out hastily. "I'm sorry. They didn't tell me you were ready to leave."

"Please take me to Venice Beach." She gave him the address.

But Dom wasn't home.

Was she too late? What if he'd already gone to have the surgery?

"He's out," Eric said, sitting up on the sofa and shoving aside the Wii controller. "You guys had a fight or something? We missed you at the barbecue on Sunday."

He hadn't told his family they'd broken up? A spark of hope ignited in her stomach. "I've been busy."

"Yeah, Dom said you got the part in that *Revelations* movie. My girlfriend's really stoked. She wants to know if she can get your autograph."

"Do you have any idea where Dom is?"

Eric shrugged. "He only told me he needed space to think."

She hadn't asked the driver to wait. Where she needed to go

went above and beyond the job he'd been hired to do anyway. She found the keys for Dom's Jeep in the bowl on the kitchen counter. There were no longer condoms in the bowl.

As she headed north along the Pacific Coast Highway she hoped Eric stayed so absorbed in his game he didn't realize she'd stolen Dom's car. Her *Revelations* contract included a morality clause she was pretty sure covered grand theft auto.

Once through the worst of the afternoon traffic, she opened all the windows to hear the crash of the surf and smell the briny scent of the ocean. She threaded through Malibu, then out the other side, enjoying the dramatic ocean views and the wild flowers in bloom at the base of the rocky cliffs. Considering what she had to do, her heart felt unexpectedly buoyant.

She had to pay for parking, then put up with the gawkers in the car park who stared open-mouthed as she strode past, head high and shoulders back, feigning a confidence she didn't feel.

Now that the moment was here, terror began to replace the hope. She hadn't felt this scared since the day her father had stopped answering his phone.

What if Dom wanted nothing more to do with her?

She wouldn't blame him. She had done nothing to earn his trust or his heart. But she was going to ask for them anyway. After laying her own heart bare.

He'd rejected her enough times in the past. Perhaps that had just been practice for today. It would be so much easier to do what she always did: run away.

But she had to do this. She wasn't going to repeat her mother's mistakes. She had to face her fear and do it anyway. Because if she didn't say what she needed to say to Dom, she'd never forgive herself, and it would become the greatest "what if" of her life.

No matter what the outcome.

At the top of the steep metal staircase she paused to take off her heeled boots before she made her way down to the beach, cautiously picking her way across the rocks to reach the sand. She

234

should have stopped for sneakers along the way.

There were no sea lions to be heard today, and the beach wasn't as deserted as it had been that first night. The breakers were bigger, crashing in against the rocks and spraying her with cool, salty droplets. But the beach was quiet and wild, and she understood why this was the place Dom came to think.

Even if he wasn't here as she hoped, it would be worth it for the fresh breeze blowing in off the sea and the spectacular view of steep cliffs plunging into the Pacific. This place was as close to paradise as she'd yet found in LA.

But Dom was here. She found him halfway along the crescent of beach, staring out toward the sea, his eyes concealed by dark sunglasses. Her heart beat frantically against her ribs as she stopped before him.

He looked up, squinting into the sunlight, and a distinct furrow appeared between his eyes. For a long moment he said nothing. She shifted awkwardly from one foot to the other.

"The press conference went well?"

So he knew about that. She nodded, biting her lip.

"You made your decision, then." His tone was flat, emotionless, but she knew it was there, bubbling beneath his calm control.

She knelt down in the white sand and pushed her own sunglasses up on her head. He needed to read her expression. He needed to know she was sincere, that this wasn't another act.

"I screwed up, and I'm sorry."

"Yeah, you did."

What did she expect – that he'd make this easy for her?

She dragged in a deep breath. "I told Tarquin I'd take the job on three conditions, and he agreed."

He shrugged as if he didn't care.

"The first condition was that I wouldn't work with Jordan."

She couldn't think of anything worse than spending ten hour days sharing a make-up trailer with Jordan. Four years on the same sitcom had been more than enough for one lifetime. Still…

235

for a moment she'd been tempted to use her Oscar-loser status to ask Tarquin to rewrite the script, so instead of rescuing Jordan's character in the woods she could leave her to the wolves, where she belonged.

Dom cleared his throat. "If you're trying to avoid women I've slept with, you've set yourself one hell of a task." He said it without humor, but the spark in her stomach flared.

"My second condition was that I would only do the movie if you worked on it too."

He finally looked at her. His eyes were hard, his expression closed, scaring her more than his indifference had. There was a very real chance he wouldn't forgive her, that she'd lost him forever.

"That's one condition that won't be met. I've rescheduled the arthroplasty for tomorrow. I won't be able to do another stunt for months."

"Tarquin wants to offer you the job of second unit director. You won't be in front of the camera, you'll be behind it, directing the stunts."

At last she saw a crack of emotion, a flicker of interest. Then he shook his head. "Even if they offer me the moon, I still won't take it. I don't want to be anywhere near you." His voice came out harsh and she flinched.

It was nothing less than she'd expected. Nothing less than she deserved. But she wasn't giving up yet, and she wasn't above begging. "I need you. Please take the job. For me."

"Why should I help you? I don't even know who you are." The bitterness in his voice cut into her. "The Nina I knew had a heart. She wouldn't even contemplate…"

"Do you want to know what my third condition was?"

"Not really."

"I told Tarquin I want Vicki as my body double."

Dom looked away. "She's over-qualified for the job, since you'll be doing most of your own stunts."

She reached out for his hands. "There are some stunts I won't

236

be able to do. Please take the job. If you won't do it for me, then do it for our baby."

He looked at her. Properly. In the eyes. Then he blinked. "You didn't get rid of it?"

"Of course not! Though I did think about giving the baby up." Her voice cracked. "But I couldn't face that either. Even if you still hate me and never want to see me again, this baby is the one piece of you I get to keep." *Especially* then. "And I've learned there are a few things in my life I really want to hold on to. That's why I can't do this job without you. I need your help to keep our baby safe while I work on this movie."

His expression still gave nothing away. Did she have a chance? Could he forgive her for running out on him, for rejecting him, for even contemplating giving away his child? For signing up to play the most intense role of her career with his baby growing inside her?

What if he didn't want her, or their baby, after all?

Her voice came out small. "I'm hoping your offer still stands."

Tears she hadn't even known were there gathered on her lashes. She'd thought she was all cried out.

Dom brushed them away with his fingertips and her heart leapt. "My offer still stands."

She turned her face into his hand and closed her eyes against the onslaught of relief and joy. "I need you, Dom. And not just for the baby's sake, because if I have to I'll do that on my own. I need you for *me*. I want you in my life. For as long as you'll have me."

He pulled her close, tumbling her into his lap. "That could be a very long time. I've been thinking about giving this settling-down thing a try."

"We probably won't be able to go to so many parties or have much of a social life once the baby arrives," she warned.

"I was getting bored of all the partying anyway."

She leaned into him, her head on his shoulder and looked out at the breakers beating against the beach. They no longer scared her.

Nothing scared her. Not with Dom's strong arms holding her tight.

"You're not the only one who screwed up. I'm sorry too." His soft voice vibrated against her cheek. "I'm sorry I didn't tell you about the surgery, and I'm sorry I didn't tell you I love you. Because I do."

She wrapped her arms around him, clinging tightly to him. "I love you, too."

His lips caressed her jawline. Then his mouth was on hers and he kissed her through her tears, tears she couldn't stem – happy tears that no longer stung.

He licked the salt from her lips and pulled away. "Does Tarquin know?"

She nodded. "I nearly didn't tell him. I gather it's normal not to announce a pregnancy to the world until the first trimester's over, and he could have replaced me. Probably should have replaced me. But he didn't. I had a long talk with my doctor. She's confident we can make this work. *I'm* confident I can make this work. But the second unit director is the one in charge of filming the stunts. He's the person who'll have the final call on how those scenes get shot. I want that person to be you and Tarquin agreed."

Dom stroked a finger down her cheek. "And have his producers agreed, too?"

She bit her lip. "We haven't told them. Tarquin's sworn to keep our secret until principal photography is well under way. I'd like to keep this between you and me until then." She smiled. Her first real smile in nearly a week. "And my sister."

"And my sisters?"

She pretended to debate her answer. "Okay. Maybe even your parents. And your nieces and nephews. But that's it!" They might as well take out an ad in the *New York Times*.

He slid his hand beneath her blouse, beneath the waistband of her jeans, to rest his splayed fingers over her stomach. "Before I'll consider Tarquin's job offer, I have one condition of my own."

"Oh?" Her breath caught as anxiety bloomed afresh.

He laughed softly and bent his head to kiss the last of her tears away. "You're going to have to start trusting me."

This time she didn't hesitate and she didn't lie. She'd trusted him to teach her to surf. She could trust him with her heart. "I learned something else these last few days," she said, smiling up at him. "That thing I thought was a crack in the walls around my heart – it wasn't a crack. It was a bridge."

He tumbled her onto her back on the sand, his arms on either side of her head, holding himself off her.

"Was that your condition?" she asked.

He shook his head. "My condition is that if it's a boy I want to name him Nicholas."

Her father's name.

She didn't give a damn where they were or who could see. She wrapped her arms around his neck, pulled him down on top of her, and kissed him.

Now she knew that what she wanted wasn't more than he was willing to give, she was never going to let him go. And she never made promises she didn't keep.

Epilogue

A hot August sun blazed down as they hiked through the scrub to the top of Point Dume. After 17 long weeks of filming across three states, including re-shoots and pick-ups, she'd earned a rest. But instead of giving her a day off to enjoy their first day home, Dom had brought her hiking.

One advantage of trying to keep up with a boyfriend like Dominic Kelly was that she didn't have to worry about her weight any more. She had to be the fittest pregnant woman in the country.

Nina paused for a sip from her water bottle, though it was more an excuse to catch her breath. She lifted her sun hat to enjoy the refreshing ocean breeze gusting around them and placed her hand on her swollen belly, feeling the sudden flutter of movement she was learning was the baby kicking rather than indigestion. She had no doubt Nick was going to be as active as his father.

"Hurry up," Dom called from further up the path.

She groaned. "Where's the fire?" But she started walking again, her hand still on the side of her stomach.

"The tide's coming in." Dom grinned back at her. "We probably shouldn't have stopped for that quickie on the way here."

She glanced around, but thankfully the elderly couple they'd passed on the way up had moved well out of earshot.

The late afternoon sun slanted down across the sky when they reached the highest point at the very edge of the cliff. The barks of the sea lions drifted up from the rookery below and a blue heron swept past on an updraft. Nina sighed as she took in the panoramic view. The spectacular scenery was well worth the trek up.

"Do you remember the first time I brought you here?" Dom asked.

She held back the hair that whipped across her face and nodded.

"You asked me then how I would propose."

He stepped aside. She looked down past where he'd stood to the wide sweep of pristine white beach, where a team of people appeared to be raking giant-sized letters into the white sand. It took her a moment to make sense of the etched words. *Marry me?*

No wonder he'd been in a hurry. The incoming waves already licked at the edges of the letters. Soon they would be washed away.

Dom knelt down before her on the dirt path. "Does this proposal meet with your approval?"

No audience, no champagne, and no fancy designer clothes. Just a windswept hilltop, the wide-open sea, and sturdy shoes. This proposal beat the last one hands-down.

"Yes, yes it does."

She smiled. There was also none of that sickening sensation she'd felt in her stomach when Paul proposed. Only joy, so bright, bursting out of her. She'd never been as happy as she was in this moment.

Dom held out his hands to her and she took them, but he didn't get up. "If you don't want to live close to the sea, we can find a house inland."

"But you love seeing the sea first thing when you wake up every morning."

"I love waking up and seeing you first thing even more. If that means a house in the hills, then so be it."

God, she loved this man more every day. "You know, I think the sea is growing on me. I rather like the idea of living close to the beach. Somewhere more homely than those soulless mansions in the hills. Perhaps a cute little craftsman cottage in a quiet little walk street, with trendy boutique shops and an alehouse close by. I don't suppose you know anyone with a place like that?"

He rose and pulled her close, wrapping her in his arms and tucking her head beneath his chin. She closed her eyes and breathed him in, that wild scent that made her feel as if anything was possible. And it was. They'd proved it a thousand times over since that first night he'd brought her here.

"I have just the place in mind. Even comes with a fully stocked kitchen."

"Oh no!" She pulled away. "I love your family, but tomorrow we're changing all the locks."

She'd spent the entire flight home yesterday imagining them alone together in that whirlpool tub in Dom's master bathroom. Instead, they'd walked into a house full of people. The last visitors had only left after midnight.

Dom grinned. "By the time we get home, the locksmith should be done." He reached into his pocket and pulled out a key, tied to a gold ribbon. And also attached to the ribbon was the most beautiful diamond ring she'd ever seen. Half the size of the one Paul had offered her, the white diamond nestled in a cradle of gold petals.

"It's beautiful," she whispered, her eyes misting.

Dom arched an eyebrow at her, waiting.

She hadn't answered him, she realized. Not the important question, anyway. "Yes, I'll marry you, Dominic Kelly."